Dear Friends,

I can call us friends now, right? :) I have such deeply warm feelings toward all the booksellers, librarians, reviewers and readers who so kindly supported my first book, *Seoulmates*. You all took a chance on me and my debut, and I am eternally grateful.

I can't believe it, but a year later, I get to once again open up my heart and my pages to you all with a new book, *The Name Drop*. It's a YA contemporary romance novel that starts with a case of mistaken identity, moves on to a seemingly harmless idea to trade places for the summer, and ends with two people falling in love... and all the drama and growth that happens along the way.

When I sold my first novel, writing was still a hobby, and I was knee-deep in a career crisis. I'd worked in "corporate America" for many years and carried a lot of trauma from that experience as a woman, a person of color, and oftentimes the only one who looked like me sitting at the table. And though my identity was deeply entrenched in my career, my title, my accomplishments, I was incredibly unhappy and unfulfilled. Writing gave me an unexpected outlet. And publishing gave me a way to reinvent myself.

One of the main messages in *The Name Drop* is the danger of putting so much pressure on young people these days to make decisions that form their entire futures. Throughout my adult life, I've pivoted and changed my path multiple times. But every instance, these choices were met with doubt and not a lot of support. I was often seen as flighty or unable to commit. As a society, we don't give a lot of leeway to those who want to switch courses of study, careers, locations...to want different things, to start anew. I hope we can come to a place where change is more accepted, however.

Because the ability to change brought me here...writing books, offering them for you to read, hoping my stories reach people in the places they need and want them the most.

I'm a writer now. And I'm happy and fulfilled. And none of this would have been possible without you all. So thank you, thank you, thank you.

I hope you'll enjoy *The Name Drop*. It's for each and all of you.

Best,

Susan

Books by Susan Lee
available from Inkyard Press

Seoulmates
The Name Drop

THE NAME DROP

SUSAN LEE

ISBN-13: 978-1-335-45798-1

The Name Drop

For questions and comments about the quality of this book, please contact us at
CustomerService@Harlequin.com.

Inkyard Press
22 Adelaide St. West, 41st Floor
Toronto, Ontario M5H 4E3, Canada
www.InkyardPress.com

Printed in U.S.A.

Recycling programs
for this product may
not exist in your area.

To all those who, in whatever your situation,
maybe even by your own voice, have been told that you can't...
I've been there.

But, I believe in you.

You are beautiful. Now, run. —KNJ

keep walking

jessica

"Dad, I'm fine. I don't need you to walk me inside. You'll get a ticket if you leave your car in the drop-off zone," I say. I hope it's just enough to convince him to let me go. Sometimes money is the only language my very cheap father understands.

His eyes close for a brief moment as he weighs the options: walk his only daughter into the airport to make sure she starts off okay on her very first solo trip. Or, risk getting a ticket and possibly towed. I can practically see his mind working as he calculates how far it would set back his monthly emergency fund.

He grabs my hand and squeezes gently. "Jessica, it's not too late to change your plans for the summer," he says, back in broken record mode.

"Dad, please, not this again. I know you're not thrilled with me going, but you eventually agreed. Do we need to rehash this? You've worked at Haneul for over ten years. If you can survive that, surely I'll survive one summer internship." I smile, hoping it'll appease his concerns.

He looks like he's about to keep arguing but thankfully my mother steps in and gives me a hug. "Remember to say thank you to everyone who works on the airplane. And to insa with a bow to everyone who works at the company. And to give a small smile to everyone who works at the bus and subway stops."

"Umma, I get it...show respect. I know, I know. You've hammered this into my head my entire life. Have I ever disappointed you?" The knot in my stomach tightens. *My choice in college notwithstanding*, I think to myself.

"We just worry, Jessica. But we're also very, very proud." I spot the tears welling up in her eyes immediately and I am not having it. Nope. I will not cry.

I turn my attention to my father. His back is ramrod straight, lips held in a tight line not betraying any emotion. This could go one of two ways. Either he changes his mind... again...and drags me back in the car and home to Cerritos where I work at my part-time job saving up money for tuition. The safe path. Or he lets me go and challenge myself in an ultracompetitive internship program in New York City. Which just so happens to be for the same company he works for, and oh yeah, hates.

His brows are stitched together. He swallows, and I track the movement in his neck. The weight of his internal war presses heavy in my heart. I hold my breath.

"Jessica, don't spend money frivolously like on eating out and shopping." He pauses, clears his throat before continuing. "And stay out of trouble. Don't bring needless attention to yourself. Don't walk anywhere alone. And only buy toilet paper on sale. Better yet, roll some up from the office bathroom and take it home with you, but make sure no one notices."

I breathe a sigh of relief. It's his best effort to let me go and I'll take it. Plus, it's not bad advice about stockpiling some office TP.

"I'll be fine. I promise," I say.

"But most of all, don't let this internship change you," he says. He doesn't meet my eyes.

Thing is, I absolutely intend to be changed by this experience. It's my first chance to do something big on my own and I'm going to make the most of it. I open my mouth to tell my dad this very thing, but the words get stuck behind all the emotion in my throat.

Better yet, I'll just show him.

"I'm going to make you both very proud," I say. "Love you." I push the last words out but can't avoid the crack that betrays everything I'm feeling—anticipation, determination...fear.

I quickly grab the handle of my suitcase and turn toward the airport entrance.

Don't look back, I tell myself. *Keep walking.*

And I do.

elijah

"Mom, I'm fine. Don't get out of the car." I lean through the window to give my mom a reassuring smile. Our family driver in the States meets my eyes in the rearview mirror and gives me a small nod. He'll help me avoid a big emotional goodbye. If there's anything my mom hates, it's a scene. She's the queen of decorum.

"Honey, are you sure you don't want me to go with you to New York? I could always, I don't know, make a shopping trip out of it. Maybe your sister will fly out to meet us? We can spend some time getting lost at The Met, then catch a hot new show, and have brunch the next day at Balthazar. I'd hate for you to miss Balthazar your first time in the city. There's so much I want to introduce you to in New York."

I watch as my mom makes an alternate plan for my summer right before my eyes. Not gonna lie, her suggestions sound a lot better than what my dad has in store for me. Spending nine-to-five days in a glass prison with a bunch of stuffy corporate types in some made-up "executive training" role for kids of VIPs is not my idea of a good time.

But I've spent months trying to come up with excuses to get out of it. And my dad has hit his wit's end with me. If I survive the summer, maybe he'll get off my back about all the other ways I've disappointed him and fallen short of the family name when I come home to Korea.

"Mom, Grandpa would be disappointed if you cut your visit with him short. Plus, I need to do this on my own. Isn't that what you and Dad expect from me? To start showing that I can be responsible and figure my shit out?"

She lets out a deep sigh. "Elijah," she warns.

"I know Mom, watch my language. I'll try." I flash her a smile and her eyes immediately warm.

"Go and do your best, Elijah. But," she pauses and looks into the distance at something I can't see, a future she's not even sure of yet, "have fun and…be happy."

I want to tell her I don't know what that looks like, what that takes. I want to tell her the irony is that there's no room in our life of luxury for the ultimate luxury of being happy. I want to remind her who my father is, as if she isn't constantly reminded of the man she's married to.

Instead, I cock my head and say, "Oh, I plan to have a lot of fun, Mom, don't you worry."

"If you need anything, anything at all, just let someone on staff know who you are. They'll take care of you," she says.

"Mom, we agreed that I'm going to be incognito this summer. I'll do what Dad wants of me, but I don't want anyone bending over backward because of who I am, because of who he is."

Her entire face collapses with worry.

"I'll be okay. Trust me. I'm scrappier than you think," I say, trying to convince her. I wink at her and she laughs. I knew that would get her.

"I love you, Son," she says to me.

My heart starts to race. It's go time. I'm heading into the shark-infested waters of my dad's company without anyone there as a safety net.

"Love you too, Mom," I say, my voice sounding small in my own ears, betraying my nerves, my hesitation…my dread.

I quickly back away from the window, tap the car twice to let the driver know that I'm leaving, throw my backpack over my shoulder, and head into the airport. I walk toward a future I'm uncertain about, one I don't even think I want.

Keep walking, I tell myself.

And I do.

chapter one

———

jessica

A warm afternoon in June…

It takes three deep breaths for me to convince myself it's not my time to die.

Why did I think it was a good idea to fly alone to New York City again? Outside with my parents, all I wanted was to get away. But now, inside on my own? I'm sweating bullets.

"Are you okay?" The irritated woman at the airline counter is clearly not into my inopportune potential panic attack, not with the line behind me snaking back and forth with impatient passengers waiting to take my spot.

I remember what I researched via the University of Google, reminding myself again how statistically unlikely it would be for my particular plane to crash and burn while I'm on it, before answering the question. I release one more deep breath and nod.

"Name," the woman—Julie from Tampa, FL, according to her name tag—asks.

"Jessica Lee," I answer. I pull out my driver's license and hand it over to her.

Julie From Tampa looks down at my ID and back up at me. I stand mesmerized at how only her eyeballs move and the sheer disdain with which they laser themselves into me.

"Oh, sorry. My Korean name, the one on my license, is Yoo-Jin Lee." I swallow the lump lodged in my throat. "I've been meaning to change it officially on my license and everything when I turned eighteen, but I haven't gotten around to it yet. It gets confusing. I'm usually much more organized than this. So much so that people find it annoying. But officially changing one's name feels kinda monumental, ya know? Anyways, I'm flying to New York City…for an internship. It's my first. I just graduated. I'm going to junior college in the fall. It's the smart financial decision for me right now."

Her eyeballs make their move again, rolling up to look directly at me, and then continuing upward toward her forehead, making her lashes flutter, screaming without words that she well and truly could not care less.

Right. Busy airport, irritated airline worker, not exactly the best place for me to break out into my nervous habit of oversharing. I force an awkward smile.

"Just the facts, Jessica," my mom always says when I get sidetracked. "You sound smarter if you just speak the facts."

This is a huge moment and I'm not going to ruin it by causing a ruckus at the airport. It's my first time flying alone.

My first time living without my parents. I've saved up enough money from my after-school job to supplement the pennies I'll make from the internship and hopefully survive a summer in New York City.

If I can make it there, I can make it anywhere. At least, that's what I hear.

And, best of all, there will be no overprotective father looking over my shoulder. It'll be good for us both. I need to grow and make my own decisions, good and bad. And he needs to learn to let me go, his only child, his baby girl.

The conversation we had minutes ago was nothing compared to how angry Dad was when I announced I was taking a job at his place of employment, Haneul Corporation, Korea's second largest technology company. My grouchy, overworked, underpaid father, is some kind of finance guy in their Los Angeles branch. You'd be hard pressed to find someone who hates their job more.

Dad may not have wanted this for me, but I don't think he gets how much I want it for myself, how much I need it, actually. Dad works in numbers, but he doesn't understand the messed-up math of college financials. Our family is too poor to afford any of the schools I got into. But according to the system, on paper, we're too "rich" to get financial aid. And the few scholarships I was eligible for needed referrals, recommendations...connections. Middle-class people like us don't have connections. So I didn't even apply.

It's better my dad believes I was too slow in getting applications done, too late to get support, too unimpressive to be granted help. Otherwise, he'd blame himself, and what else could he have done to put us in a different position in life?

This is just how it is. The rich get all the opportunities and the rest of us have to figure out other ways.

This internship is my other way.

I picked Haneul not only because working for a Korean company is important to me, but I'm way more likely to get a recommendation from a Korean person-of-note. That is, as long as I am able to stand out and impress them. But I'm up for it. The competition for the internship was fierce. Rumor has it that there were thousands of applicants. But I'm proud to say that I am now one of ten new interns to be selected for the program. Step one, done.

Activate internal happy dance.

I look around, taking in the massive production that is LAX. I wonder how many people fly through this airport every day. It's packed full of travelers unfazed by the thought of flying. That's a good sign. I, too, can be unfazed, I lie to myself.

My attention catches on the guy standing two stations over. At first, it's the long black trench coat, worn over a gray hoodie, that stands out to me. Who wears that many layers in the middle of June? My curiosity is piqued. Granted, LAX's air-conditioning is no joke and I'm kinda wishing I had my own trench coat. I don't own a trench coat. I literally do not know one person who owns a trench coat. And his is *fancy*. I, fashion-impaired as I am, can even tell standing ten feet away.

I can't quite make out if he's handsome or not, since the bottom half of his face is covered with a black mask and his ball cap is pulled low so I can't see his eyes. But he exudes handsome. I bet he smells handsome too. It's the air of mystery. Today I'm realizing that a possible international jewel thief or potential con artist is my type apparently because I'm very curious.

It would be fun to be seated next to a cute guy on the plane, exchanging witty banter, flirting to distract from my fear of free falling thirty thousand feet to my demise. I wonder where this guy is going.

He tosses his passport at the airline worker, talking to her without even looking up from his phone.

Welp, there goes that fantasy. Rude to customer service workers means likely rude to his mother and would definitely be rude to me, his brief daydream girlfriend. And considering the possible lines of work I've assigned to him, I don't think rude adds much charm to being a felon either.

"You're all set," Julie From Tampa says, holding out my ID and boarding pass.

I watch as my bag is none-too-gently tossed onto a conveyer. Goodbye bag. See you in New York. Have a safe flight. Be nice to the other bags. Somehow I get the feeling even if possibly-cute-mysterious guy isn't up to no good, he definitely wouldn't be interested in me, the Luggage Whisperer. Go figure.

"The Preferred security line is to the right."

I smile and nod. It was nice of Julie to tell me which line she prefers. I grab the documents and place them carefully into a folder in my new Coach tote bag. It's my most precious possession. It was a miracle find at the Coach outlet store. Even though it was already marked down and the salesperson offered me an extra fifteen percent off because of the barely noticeable black scuff on the back of the tan leather, I spent more on it than I have on anything. I need a serious bag for my serious internship.

"This can't be right," I hear the frustrated trench coat guy say to the airline worker as I pass by. He has an expensive-looking backpack with a large triangle logo reading "Prada" hanging loosely from one shoulder, the front pocket unzipped. I have the urge to tap him on the arm and let him know before his stuff falls out.

But he seems upset.

He has a Korean passport in his hand. We're likely not on the same flight after all. A sense of relief washes over me. I'm nervous enough as it is. I don't want angry passengers bringing bad mojo onto the plane.

The security line is surprisingly short and the process a lot easier than I recall from the few times my family has flown together for summer vacations. Julie really knew what she was talking about when she directed me to this line. I see why she prefers it.

I smile at the TSA agent and hand over my boarding pass and ID. To get a head start, I bend over to untie my sneakers.

"Shoes stay on. Everything stays in the bag."

I look up from my crouched position, confused.

"You don't have to take your shoes off here. You can keep everything in your carry-on. Just place it in a bin on the conveyer."

"But I got a see-through case for all my liquids," I explain. "I made sure they were all under three ounces and whatever I couldn't fit, I plan to purchase at my closest Duane Reade drugstore when I reach New York City since there is reportedly one on every third corner."

Oversharing. It's a gift.

"Good practice for next time," the agent says, waving me through.

I feel a bit uncomfortable that TSA isn't doing their job as thoroughly as they're supposed to. Should I report this? See something, say something. But the agent was so kind to me— why is it my responsibility to call him out?

The other people in the line ahead of me, mostly older men in business suits, seem unbothered. They know this process like clockwork. They take more risks with their lives, apparently.

Plus, who's gonna listen to an eighteen-year-old who has only flown three times in her life? I should trust those who know better and follow the lead of my elders. Sometimes I surprise myself at how old-school and Korean I really am despite not having been there since I was a kid.

I make it to my gate with fifty-four minutes to spare before boarding, my anxiety spiking when I realize I'm six minutes behind my carefully crafted airport plan. I won't be the standout of the intern class by being late.

Always be the first to arrive and the last to leave. I hear my mom's calming voice and words of wisdom in my head. It's quickly pushed to the side by a vision of the disappointed look on my father's face. He doesn't even need to say a word and I know I've messed up. My heart immediately starts beating faster.

I'll need to walk places quicker. Be more direct in my communication, waste no time chitchatting. And when in doubt, stand straighter, lift my chin, and purse my lips with confidence. It's my fake-it-till-you-make-it stance.

I'm top three in my graduating class, secretary of the student government, and a varsity tennis player. I have done everything to make sure I'd be considered outstanding. And now it's time to show up for this internship.

Because there's nothing special about where I come from. Nothing to set me apart from kids who have privilege and opportunity. I've got no name or bank balance to throw around and impress like other kids getting into the best schools. This internship is my one shot to get a step ahead, even if it's a tiny one.

Terrified, sure. But capable, one hundred percent, I remind myself. And when all else fails, like I tell myself at least ten times a day, fake it till you make it.

And one day, I'll eventually get to the place in my life where there's a lot less faking it and a lot more making it.

I'm hoping this summer is exactly where that journey begins.

chapter two

elijah

"Can you check again? Try Lee Yoo-Jin instead. Or maybe Yoo-Jin Lee."

Maybe I should have taken my mom up on her offer to come with me. What made me think I could do this on my own?

I attempt to mirror my mom's voice instead of my dad's. Mom's tone can, when she wants it to, be sweet and persuasive. Dad has never been sweet in his life. His way of speaking is condescending, insulting, scary as hell.

I don't think that's gonna work in my favor here.

I should have used a "please" and a "thank you" as well. Those words feel like the most foreign of English words I've ever learned. People don't expect that from me. I am my father's son in everyone's eyes.

At least those who know our family.

I track the brows of the airline worker as they slowly furrow their way into a point in the middle of her forehead. Like skinny worms meeting for a kiss. She, clearly, does not know our family.

"You said your name was Elijah Ri...with a *R*." She says the letter *R* like it's code for "fuck off."

All I've ever wanted was for some space between me and my birth name. I even went as far as to go by "Ri" instead of "Lee" in my family name's English form. All for it to now be the thing that will likely get me dragged away in handcuffs for identity theft or something.

"Yes, um, but that's my English name. And you said I wasn't listed on the flight. Here." I reach over into the open pocket of my backpack and pull out my Korean passport. "This is my passport with my Korean name. Let me check my email and see if I have a confirmation number or something. My dad's travel assistant made the reservation so she may have done so with my Korean information. Sorry." I scan my email, a bead of sweat trickling down my back, and I'm too nervous to even look up at the disapproving expression on this stranger's face. I drop the passport on the counter and try and find the email with my information on my phone.

I'm beginning to think Betty Sue Airline Worker thinks something fishy is going on. Just because I'm standing here wearing a long black trench coat, in June, in LA, with a black ball cap pulled low over my face and a black face mask on, handing over two forms of ID with different names on them...doesn't make this suspicious, does it?

Shit.

Where is that email?

I should have just booked the flight myself. But my dad, always so certain I will fuck everything up, wouldn't hear of it. And he for sure would have a field day if I miss this flight.

I'm nineteen years old and can't do the most basic things on my own. I'm not *allowed* to do stuff for myself. We have people who work for us to do almost anything and everything we need. I don't even wipe my own ass. We have a high-tech bidet for that, complete with warm air for drying.

Do not get me started on how irritated this makes me.

So here I stand, my future in the hands of an airline worker's opinion on if my multiple identities are believable enough. Her whim will determine whether or not I get on that plane to New York and spend the summer bored to death in the Executive Training Program at my dad's company.

I look down at my wallet and pull out my VVIP card. This usually works in Korea as auto-entry into just about anywhere. But I push it back into its spot. Somehow, I doubt it would work here. In fact, it will likely piss her off even more.

Maybe this is all a sign. Maybe my ancestors are smiling down on me and laughing behind my dad's back.

I don't know if I even want her to let me through or not, to be honest. Spending the summer working for a bunch of miserable executives at Haneul Corporation is not my idea of a good time. But at least no one will know I'm the CEO's son and heir apparent to the company throne. I couldn't stand having them kiss my ass while talking behind my back about how incompetent I am. I get that to my face from my dad on the regular. Thankfully, my mom and sister helped me convince him to let me work from the New York office instead of the headquarters in Seoul, where he'd be breathing down my neck the whole time.

"Your boarding pass," Betty Sue says, holding out a slip of paper tucked in my passport.

Seat 34B. Almost all of my flights are on my dad's private jet. I rarely fly commercial and when I do, it's in first class where the rows are usually single digits. "This can't be right," I say. "Do planes even have this many seats?"

I consider pulling this trench coat over my head and hiding the moment I see her face. The eye roll, the snarl, the something-smells-like-shit expression. It's another one of those times when I come across like a total privileged asshole and don't realize it. I'm usually better at being aware of these moments and remember to say exactly the opposite of what I'm thinking.

It's why I want to do this internship on my own in New York this summer. I need to experience a life less sheltered than the one I have in Korea. I hate being so privileged that I don't even have the basic understanding of how people do things and behave in certain situations. It's like I'm from another planet sometimes. And though every person in Korea knows of the Lee family of Haneul Corp—we're considered chaebol, the wealthiest and most connected of families, after all—I doubt anyone even knows or cares about that here in America.

"Security check-in is to the left."

I nod and smile, though I'm sure it's lost behind my mask. Well, as my dad always says, "If they're not gonna be important to you later, they don't need to be important to you now."

Wow, come to think of it, that motto's a lot dickier than I ever realized. If I'm not careful, those kinds of thoughts are gonna stick and I'll turn into the junior version of Chairman Jung Hyun Lee after all.

I can't control the shiver of horror. I'm terrified that it could become a reality.

I put my passport back into my backpack and head toward security.

The line zigzags back and forth for as far as I can see. I don't think I've ever seen this many people at an airport before. Where are they all going at the exact same time?

I eventually get to the front and hand my ticket over to the stern-faced worker seated there.

"Lower your mask," she says without inflection.

I pull my mask down and try another of those "look, I'm just like everyone else" smiles on for size.

She barely spares a glance at me before looking back down at my ID, nods, and waves me into yet another long line of impatient people. I'm not quite sure why they're all taking off their shoes, removing jackets, placing everything in dirty gray bins. But I just follow their lead.

It suddenly occurs to me that all of this might be my dad's form of punishment for my less-than-enthusiastic reaction to the summer job. It would be just like him to book me a trip that any average person would take rather than that of a Korean chaebol, foreign royal, or K-pop star.

Well, that's fine with me. I'm in no hurry. I can stand in line with everyone else. In fact, I enjoy being just like anyone else with no special treatment. I pop my earbuds in and turn up my Seventeen playlist, waiting for my turn to go through security machines.

It's not like this plane is going to leave without me, right?

★ ★ ★

I'm dripping in sweat and gasping for air by the time I reach the gate. I was putting my Jordans back on at the security screening when the first announcement of my flight's boarding came over the intercom. By the time the final announcement was made, I was still twenty gates away. I started to run.

I'm going to murder my stylist for putting me in this black wool trench coat during summer in LA.

I hand my boarding pass to the attendant who beeps me in and hurries me down the jet bridge. I step on the plane just as they close the doors behind me.

I walk down the narrow aisle passing the unhappy faces of basically every passenger on this plane. My eye catches on a girl in row four, her long black hair tied up in a messy bun, bangs cut slightly crooked. I notice her wide-eyed and smiling out the window. She couldn't be more out of place. I doubt anyone else on this plane is smiling.

What makes someone that happy?

After the first few rows, the aisle gets even narrower and the faces unhappier. I almost stop in my tracks at what I see.

How can so many people be piled in like sardines into the back of this airplane? This flight is over five hours long. People of all sizes, mothers holding crying babies, others fanning themselves with the airplane's brochures, and not a glass of champagne or pillow in sight.

I keep walking, finally reaching the back of the plane and row thirty-four, seat B. The only empty spot is the one in between a man who looks like he may be training for Olympic weightlifting, and a very tall Asian guy about my age whose one leg is jammed up against the seat in front of him and the other straightened out into the aisle.

I point to the empty seat next to him. "Um, that's me," I say.

He frowns but unbuckles his seat belt and stands up to let me through. I take a moment to figure out if it's even possible for me to get past, and if I should scootch in facing toward him or facing away. I choose the latter. I'd rather risk an awkward ass rubbing than an almost kiss with a stranger.

I squeeze my way through and collapse into my chair, my knees hitting the one in front of me. "Sorry," I say to the back of a head. I push my backpack under the seat at my feet and tuck my elbows in since the passengers on both sides of me have draped their own arms over each armrest. I'm sweating like crazy and all I want to do is take off my coat. But there's no way. I can't even move an inch.

Okay Dad, you win. Lesson learned.

I press the button to lean my seat back but realize there's a wall behind me blocking it. Great. I knew my dad was a tyrant, but this is crueler than I ever imagined.

This is going to be a very long flight. But I can survive five hours in a cramped seat that doesn't recline with the chemical odor of the bathroom wafting in the air.

At least I'm not heading home to Korea to face a summer working with my dad. If this is as bad as it gets, I'll be okay. I'm tougher than he thinks.

But, if I had known then how much worse this summer would get, I would never have gotten on this plane.

chapter three

——

jessica

I've never flown first class before and the difference is remarkable. I have enough room in my seat to tuck my legs up under my blanket and relax. I didn't want to be a burden to the flight attendant, but since she comes around asking regularly if I want anything to drink, I try each of the different kinds of juices they have stocked onboard: orange, apple, cran-apple, grapefruit. Which makes having a bathroom for just the first class cabin, one that rarely has a line, super convenient.

It's best not to get too used to it all, though.

I'm not sure what's gotten into my dad to make such an extravagant purchase. We're not first class people. We're most definitely of the economy, nonrefundable, every-restriction-possible variety. But maybe he's feeling guilty for being so resistant to the internship in the first place. Maybe it's his way

of telling me he's proud of me. I swallow back the lump in
my throat just thinking about it.

The email from Haneul's Internship Coordinator, Mira
Im, mentioned that a shuttle would be waiting to take all
the interns to our accommodations. After landing, I look up
all the other interns' flights and calculate that I'll likely have
to wait about two hours for the rest of the cohort to arrive
from their respective cities. I could explore all the sights and
sounds of Newark Liberty Airport, but I'm just too tired and
don't want to get lost. So I decide to search for the shuttle
driver and wait it out.

When I make my way down the escalator to the arrivals
area, I look for anyone holding a Haneul Corporation sign
as instructed. What I don't expect to see while scanning the
group of men dressed in black holding various different signs
is a tablet screen held up reading "Lee Yoo-Jin."

I shake my head and do a double take. Yes, that's my name.
But that driver can't possibly be just for me. Why would I
have a separate driver?

But who else would it be for? My name is right there. My
face stretches into a smile. Haneul Corp is going all out for
their interns. Nice. My dad has always complained about this
company. How they never respect his hard work, or anyone's
for that matter. But maybe he's just grouchy and exaggerat-
ing. I feel like they're giving me the royal treatment. And if
they treat their interns like this, it's a pretty good sign that
it's a great place to work.

"Hi," I say, trying to put on my most confident smile.
"That's me." I point to his tablet. "Lee Yoo-Jin. Would you
like to see some ID? My American name is Jessica Lee but my

all my IDs still list me as Yoo-Jin Lee, my Korean name, so I'm sure they'll validate that I'm who you're here to pick up. I also have the address of the accommodations if you want me to show you that as well. But I'm guessing you already know where we're going. At least I hope so. This is my first time in New York City and I would be useless in helping direct you. Though, I could type the destination into Google Maps if you'd like me to help navigate."

The handsome driver's face remains blank as he stares at me. I think I've stunned him. It wouldn't be the first time. He nods once and reaches for my Coach tote.

"Oh, um, I can carry this," I say, holding on tightly to the straps. "I, um, checked a bag as well."

"Baggage Claim is over here," he says gruffly. I hope I didn't hurt his feelings. It's awfully nice of him to want to carry all my stuff, but the most important things like my wallet, phone, and paperwork are in this bag. It's safest if it stays with me at all times.

He starts to walk briskly toward the carousels. It's like he's gaining speed with each step and my short little legs struggle to keep up. I focus on picking up the pace...

...and run right into a human wall.

"Oof, sorry," I say as I watch the entire contents of my bag spill to the ground in slow motion, and a searing pain shoots up my arm. Ouch, that's gonna leave a mark.

I drop to my knees and start grabbing anything and everything off the floor, trying not to think about how many feet, many of which have just come out of public bathrooms, have walked this ground.

The worst horror imaginable is having the world see what

one decides to put in their bag for travel. Well, I'm sure I can actually imagine worse horrors, but in this moment, this is what I've got.

I stuff my wallet, my travel-sized hand sanitizer, two granola bars, an extra pair of socks, my knock-off brand AirPods, and the ginseng candy I hate but my mom insists I keep for any and all ailments ranging from indigestion to the flu back into my purse. That would leave just...

Why is it when you're about to face the most humiliating moment in your life, everything slows down to super slo-mo? It's like life just wants you to never forget how very embarrassing this moment is going to be. You know, that moment when you glance over at the black Nike gym shoes, track upward to the perfectly torn knees of the slim fit black jeans, and finally, to an outstretched hand...holding your in-case-of-emergency extra pair of undies.

Or is it just me?

I grab them quickly and jam my hand into my purse. "Watch where you're going," I try to say curtly. But it comes across instead like I'm about to cry. Come to think of it, I just might die of embarrassment here and now and that surely will be accompanied by some tears.

"Sorry," a voice says. I expected something deeper from a man in all black. Apparently all-black means Darth Vader in my mind. But the voice is surprisingly soft, melodic. I squeeze my eyes shut for one breath, wishing for this day to start over. Maybe just from after we got off the plane since I wouldn't want to miss out on the first-class experience.

Then I open my eyes and brave a glance.

I pull back in surprise as I recognize him as the guy from

the airport back in LA. The international jewel thief. Renowned con artist. Rude to his mother. Damn, he *does* smell good.

"I was distracted and not paying attention to where I was going," he says. He reaches out his hand—did he even retract it after offering me back my undies (ohmigod)? I stare at his long fingers and perfectly manicured nails. Maybe not a jewel thief, since these hands have clearly never scaled the wall of a Sotheby's or meticulously tried to crack open a safe ever. These are the hands of someone definitely rich and pampered. Not a hangnail or callus in sight.

I look up into his eyes. They're the only things I can see between the black of his ball cap and the black of his face mask. They're warm, smiling eyes, with eyelashes that look as long and thick as a camel's.

So, I'm never gonna be a poet, okay?

I reach to grab the offered hand and wait for him to help me up. But as I remain on the floor, fingers wrapped around his, he doesn't stand or pull or even give me a tug. Instead, he lifts his chin toward my other hand. I look down to see that I'm holding a phone. Not my phone.

Oh shit. His phone.

He wasn't trying to help me at all.

Chivalry is truly dead these days.

"Oh sorry, is this yours? How did it end up in my hand? It's not even the same as mine. I still have the version from two years ago. It's a lot smaller. I don't think I can have one of the bigger ones like these. I can barely hold it. Good luck trying to take a selfie. Does this even fit in the pocket of your jeans?"

I wait for the eye roll or stitching of the brows that usually follows one of my verbal regurgitations. It's the slight laugh that I hear behind his mask that makes my cheeks blush.

He takes his phone out of my hand and then actually does help me to my feet.

"Miss Lee, are you ready to go?" the driver asks. He looks between me and the guy currently still holding my hand. I pull away. I miss the warmth immediately.

"Oh, we're not together. I mean, he's not coming with us," I stammer. "You, um, have someone picking you up, right?"

I don't know why I ask. Maybe because he seems a little lost. Like maybe this is his first time traveling on his own too. But, then again, he's wearing expensive clothing and has the most recent iPhone in tow. He likely has access to the kind of funds that allow for plenty of ride options.

He pulls his cap off and runs his fingers through his hair. His hairline is slightly damp and I get it. We're in Newark in the middle of summer and he's dressed entirely wrong for the weather.

But then again, I'm in a plain white T-shirt and jeans and I'm feeling a little heated right now too. Nope, that's the New York summer hitting me. And that sheen of sweat starting to form on my forehead? Humidity, I tell you, humidity. Definitely not because of a cute guy in front of me.

"Yeah, I'll be okay. Thanks for asking… *Miss Lee*," he says. The corners of his eyes lift again as he smiles behind the mask. But I don't get the sense that he's making fun of me. He's laughing *with* me. Like *oh how ridiculous at our age to be referred to so formally.*

I smile back and nod. "Okay, well, then, I'll be going along on my way now." If I could slap my forehead in a way that wouldn't draw attention to myself, I would. *I'll be going along on my way now?*

I start walking and tell myself not to look back. *Do NOT look back.*

But when I do look back, because of course I do, he's gone.

And the feeling of disappointment lingers. What? Did I think he'd be standing there watching me walk away?

Apparently so, because an entire summer romance plays through my imagination in a matter of seconds. Good to get that out of the way now. I do not have time for romance, for friendships, for anything of the sort for that matter. I have to focus on my internship, working my ass off, and standing out among the rest of the cohort. If I'm impressive enough, memorable enough, maybe I can get a letter of recommendation from Haneul Corp for future school and scholarship applications. So that after my first year at junior college, I'll have more options.

The entirety of higher education is built for a world of the rich-get-richer. I've never stepped foot in that world. But I consider this internship my invitation to enter, or at least dip my big toe in. And this may be my only chance ever.

I turn to the driver who, with arms crossed and a couple peeks at his watch, is clearly losing patience. He probably hates driving around teenagers. Am I supposed to tip him after he drops me off? How much is an acceptable tip? I could just feign ignorance and hope Haneul took care of that already.

"I'm sorry. Yes, I'm ready to go," I say. I point out my bag as it makes its way around the carousel. He picks it up and starts walking without a word. I follow as he leads the way out the doors, through the parking garage, to his black SUV.

Damn, this car is nice. It can easily fit six people, maybe more. And it's really here just for me? I mentally chide myself to stop acting so shocked and amazed like everything is new to me. This car likely costs the entirety of a first year's tuition at school. What a waste. Don't be impressed.

Still, I can't help but take in a deep breath of the leather scent in the SUV. So this is what rich smells like. I let out a breath and remind myself not to get too used to it. It's likely a onetime treat to kick off my internship in style.

I decide to store the memory of this experience away in the back of my mind to be pulled out one day when I've finally made it. Because once I get there, I'll know this internship was my first step. And when I do, I want a car that smells exactly like this.

chapter four

elijah

Cute.

It's the first thing I think when I run into the girl at the airport. No, *bony elbows*, that's the first thing actually. I'm still feeling the sting of her knobby arm knocking the wind out of me. Though I think I had the less embarrassing of things knocked out.

I'd normally think an extra pair of panties in a girl's purse was hot. But those cotton briefs were way more for practical usage. Not that I'm some kind of expert when it comes to girls' panties. Still hot, not gonna lie.

But what I don't think I'm going to forget any time soon is the way she made sure to ask me if I had a ride. In my life, things are given to me. No one asks me about what I want or need. In fact, I'm usually told what to want or need. I rub my chest trying to get rid of the odd sensation—not pain, but something else—happening there.

I watch as she walks away with her personal driver. Nothing about her screams that she comes from money, what with her no-name clothes, worn gym shoes, and cheap bag. Everything is generic. But she's the girl I saw in first class. And she has a driver…all that's promising. I wonder what family she's from. How they made their money. She looks Korean and I think the driver called her Miss Lee. I'd know her already if she was chaebol. But maybe her parents immigrated and made their money here in the States.

I shake my head to rid myself of this entire train of thought. Why do I even think shit like this? It's how my dad sizes up everyone, that's why. Always looking at how they're dressed, what labels they wear to indicate what they can afford, what situations they're in, how much they're likely worth and where that money comes from. Most kids get their parents' eyes or their sense of humor. I, unfortunately, have gotten my father's internal money meter. But what I won't allow myself to become is the judgmental prick he is.

Every relationship in my dad's life is carefully strategized. Who he married. Who he's friends with. Who he plays golf with. Who he eats lunch with. All planned to maximize partnerships, publicity, and the bottom line. Every play date I had as a kid was with some spoiled rich brat I couldn't stand. And I won't be surprised if my future love life is already arranged for me as a part of a huge business deal.

What I would give to just not have everything in my life organized according to some business plan. Not have my future already determined for me. Not be told I can't just figure out who I am, what I want to do, who I want to be with on my own terms.

My eyes catch on a handwritten sign held up by a frazzled-looking Korean woman. "Haneul Corporation." That must be *my* driver. I walk up to her and lower my voice from its normal higher register. Make it seem like I know what I'm doing instead of having spent the last thirty minutes lost at the airport trying to find this person who has been standing right in front of me all along.

"Hi, I think you're my driver."

"Name," she says as she looks down at her clipboard.

"Elijah Ri," I say. Is it not obvious I'm the person she's here to pick up? I won't let that irritate me. I'm in no hurry. Though, I'd love to change out of my travel outfit and into something clean and less arctic-appropriate. I hope whatever's waiting for me at the brownstone is lightweight because I'm a sweaty beast right now. The personal shoppers assigned to my travels have impeccable taste and never get it wrong. *Well*, I think as I squirm in my too-hot-for-the-season trench coat, *almost never*.

I watch as the woman looks at her clipboard and furrows her brow in confusion. Not this again. "Lee Yoo-Jin, maybe?" I don't need to explain Korean vs English names to her, apparently, because she immediately nods, checks the name off and looks up.

"Please stand to the side while we wait for the others."

"The others? I don't have any staff with me this trip," I say.

But she's not listening. She just lifts the sign back up and ignores me.

Maybe this is why my dad is such a tyrant when it comes

to work. When he isn't paying attention, his staff slacks off or doesn't treat people the way he would expect, especially his own family. But I kinda like that she clearly doesn't know who I am, who she's here to pick up. This is what I wanted, to be incognito this summer. I'll just hang out and people watch and see whoever it is she thinks we need to wait for. No skin off my back.

Two hours later, I'm stuffed into a van with weak air-conditioning and a handful of other Korean kids who all seem around my age. From what I gathered in bits and pieces of eavesdropping, they're all here for some summer internship program at, you guessed it, Haneul Corp.

The chatter in the van is low, everyone still sizing each other up. Or maybe it's just me doing the sizing up while the others go through the roll call of introducing themselves. James from St. Louis, second year at Stanford. Grace from Dallas, third year, Harvard. Jason from Irvine in his second year at UCLA. I recognize him from my flight. He was sitting next to me but he gave up his aisle seat to a mother with a baby and took her middle seat in another row. Which left me next to a crying child for five hours.

Jason's a fucking saint apparently.

And I'm clearly in the wrong ride.

But at this point, I'm too tired and too annoyed to try and explain it to anyone. Just drop me off at my home for the summer and I'll sort it all out later. The rest of these people can go on their merry way.

By the time we get on a highway, it's loud and buzzy in the van. I'm not used to being around this many people. I'm tempted to put my AirPods in and ignore them. But I'm curious to hear what they all have to say. And it's kinda cool being a part of a group of people and not stand out in any way.

"Hey man, saw you on the flight over. I'm Jason," he says to me. He's sitting in the bench seat in front of mine and reaches his arm over for me to shake his hand. "I didn't get your name."

"Hey, I'm Elijah. Um, I'm not sure where I'm going to school yet, to be honest. Still working through the details." The details being I'd rather study abroad in the States than go to Seoul National University. But that isn't an option in my dad's mind.

The plan for my life, made for me entirely by my father, is to graduate from Seoul National and then step into an upper management role at Haneul. Follow in my family's legacy. My dad is the third-generation CEO of the company. My older sister has even taken this route and now is second in command. But since the company reins will only go to the first son of the family, she'll never be in charge. I hate how misogynistic Korean culture can be.

I hate it for her. And I hate it for me.

We pull up to a nondescript building and everyone files out of the van. "Are we in the Upper East Side?" I ask the driver.

"Sure, something like that," she says with a laugh. "Shut the door behind you. Remind everyone there will not be transport provided to work tomorrow or from this point on. Every year, the interns think they're gonna get a ride every day." She shakes her head and faces forward, waiting for me to shut the door. I do so and within seconds she takes off and folds into the heavy New York traffic.

One of the interns, Sarah, I think it is, hands me her bag.

"Hold this, would you? I have the apartment info in my phone." She looks down at her screen and reads the instructions. "We're on the fifth floor and the door code is pound four five nine nine pound."

One of the others punches in the numbers and buzzes us in. We make the trek up the four flights of stairs. Though the sun has set by now, it's still pretty hot and definitely humid.

"Oh shit, dude. Did the airline lose your luggage? I'm always freaked out that's gonna happen to me for some reason. That sucks," Jason says.

All eyes turn to me and take notice that I have only my backpack and the unseasonable black trench coat draped over my arm. I just nod as, truthfully, I am way too out of breath to talk as we're climbing these stairs. Why is there no elevator in this building?

"Where'd you get your dupe?" Grace asks me. "It's decent quality. You wouldn't be able to tell from far away, though I see some of the inconsistencies in the stitching up close." She reaches out for my backpack and examines it closely. "I have an awesome Gucci dupe I got in some hole in the wall deep down an alley in Itaewon."

I want to protest that my backpack is, in fact, genuine, current season Prada and quite expensive, but I hold my tongue.

We open the door to the apartment and everyone immediately scatters to check it out. Each room has four bunk beds. The entire apartment has only one bathroom. In what is presumably the living area, there is another set of bunk beds. I remind myself to close my mouth. I can't believe ten people are expected to live in this one small apartment.

"This is awesome," Roy from Ames, third year at Yale, says.

"It's like fucking sleepaway camp, but without counselors," someone else says excitedly.

I've never shared a room with anyone in my life. In fact, in our home in Korea, I have an entire wing of the house to myself.

"Is this the Upper East Side?" I ask again, this time to anyone who will listen.

"Not even close," Sarah says. "We're like a hundred blocks away. This is the Lower East Side. No way Haneul Corp is putting us peons up in that part of town."

I nod slowly as I look around at the tiny accommodations, the sparse furniture, the unfamiliar faces with their off-the-rack clothing. We may all be here for a summer gig at Haneul, but we are not the same. This is not where I'm supposed to be.

My irritation spikes, yet again, as I realize how vastly different the summer my father has planned for me is from anyone else my age. I never get to have an experience like everyone else. I'm not stupid nor do I need to be sheltered. But for some reason, that's how I always feel like I'm being treated. With kid gloves.

I should call my dad's assistant and have the situation cleared up. But instead, I take a seat on one of the beds in the living room. Despite my exhaustion from the journey, I'm also kinda energized by all of this.

"You and me on this set?" Jason asks.

Without even thinking, I nod. "Sure, I'm good with that."

Whoever the tenth intern is supposed to be is not here. So even if it's just for tonight, it won't hurt anyone for me to hang out and play along in their place. I like the chatter. And though it sometimes feels like they're speaking a foreign language, what with my English learned almost entirely in class settings outside of the States. But it's not how they talk as much as it is the things they talk about that I'm not familiar with.

They go over the plans for shopping for groceries, toiletries, sharing, bunking, cooking. I just keep my mouth shut and listen, nodding when it feels like the right time to do so. I must look like a deer caught in headlights. But it's all such a trip.

Jason hands me a T-shirt. "Here, you can borrow this until we figure out what happened to your luggage. I'm sure someone at the company can help you get it all tracked down. The humidity here is no joke, right? I mean, it's not as bad as in Korea, that's for sure. I've spent almost every summer in Seoul growing up, so I know how bad it can get."

I appreciate Jason's effort trying to engage me and also bringing up Korea to make me feel more at home. He seems like a pretty cool guy.

"Thanks," I say, grabbing the shirt. I head to the bathroom to change. I catch Jason glancing my way and shaking his head. Did he just expect me to take off my clothes right here in front of everyone? They're strangers. And there are girls here.

I turn the water on and rinse my face. I wish I had my essence, serums, and moisturizer with me. My skin always gets so dry on airplanes.

I look at myself in the mirror. After a long travel day and being away from all my own stuff, I don't look that different from anyone else here. But I feel like the odd man out. I've never had to think about things like roommates, work schedules, budgets. I'm the one who doesn't quite fit.

A part of me really wants to, though.

When I return, I hear the group talking about going out and grabbing some dinner. "There's a really good soon tofu place around the corner if we're craving Korean food. Haneul serves Korean food in the cafeteria for lunch that's really good too, so we'll never be without," Jason tells us. It's his second year interning at the company, which makes him some kind of prodigy, considering how tough it is to get chosen for the program. He mentioned in the car that working at Haneul is not a cakewalk, but the name is so huge he's had multiple doors open up for him because of it. Jason knows more about the company than I do and I'm supposed to be the CEO one day.

It crosses my mind that if I were where I'm supposed to be, I'd likely be eating a meal made by a private chef, alone, followed by a mindless night of watching some Korean zombie movie on Netflix, and then going to bed.

Instead, I'm with a bunch of kids my age exploring the streets of New York.

Everything sounds louder here than in Seoul. People's voices, the honking of car horns, generators running food carts are all competing to be heard. And though the streets and storefronts are lit this time of night, nothing is quite bright enough to be seen clearly. Like there's a haze, an air of mystery, over everything, shadows around every corner.

We head out a few blocks from our apartment building, Jason leading the way. He stops for a second on a corner despite the walk signal. I stand off to the side to let people, all crossing the street with a purpose, pass me by. I feel something wet hit me on the forehead. I look up and another drop falls on me.

"Air conditioners," Soobin says.

"What?" I ask.

She pulls me aside a couple inches and then points up. Each of the windows of this building have white boxes precariously hanging out of them.

"Window unit air conditioners. Condensation builds and then they spit on you," she explains.

"Are those…safe?" I ask.

She shrugs.

"Let's cross," Jason says to the group, his head down looking at the map on his phone. He leads us across the street and then takes a turn down a suspiciously dark alleyway.

"Uh, I don't think this is the right way," Roy says, speaking exactly what's in my own mind. Well, what's actually in my own mind is that we're about to get mugged or murdered. If my ears aren't deceiving me, I hear faint high-pitched screeches and swear the shadows along the ground are moving—scurrying actually. It takes everything in me not to squeal and run away.

"Here it is," Jason says.

"Here what is?" Sarah asks, cautiously.

We stand in front of a door with a shockingly low-wattage light shining down on it. No sign. Just an X painted on the door.

"Home of the best soup dumplings you will ever have in your life," Jason says proudly.

"Do we even want to ask what's in these soup dumplings?" I ask.

"Trust me, everyone. I know it looks sketch, but it's legit. This restaurant is rumored to have been written up by the Michelin Guide itself, but they refused to let it be printed because they didn't want tourists and newbies to find their way here," Jason says.

"You mean like us?" Sarah asks.

"We're not tourists. We live here now, for the summer at least. We're locals. And this is our first local spot. Follow me," Jason says confidently, leading the way.

It's no brighter inside than it was outside. But the smells that come from wherever the kitchen is are so incredible, my stomach growls instinctively. And I almost let out a groan of appreciation. The place is packed with patrons, not one face non-Asian. Heads down, not a lot of chatter, just people appreciating the good food in front of them.

None of this is anything I've experienced before. In fact, this entire day has been the weirdest day of my life, but the truly weirdest part of it all is the feeling loosening in my chest.

I don't know what's gonna happen tomorrow. What I do know is that once training starts, I likely won't be around anyone under the age of fifty and below the one percent. So for tonight, I'm gonna sit with a group of strangers who have bonded over long flights, cramped van rides, a tiny apartment, and apparently the best soup dumplings we'll ever eat.

And I'm going to let myself, just this once, not worry what my dad would say about it all and have some fun.

chapter five

jessica

I should have guessed something was wrong from the moment I tried to check into my flight. I definitely should have known when I saw that my seat was in first class. Why I didn't admit it to myself when I was picked up by a personal driver at the airport, I'm not sure. But now, as I stand in the foyer of a three-story brownstone in one of the swankiest parts of town, with a chandelier that looks like a cascade of diamonds sparkling over me, dread crawls up my spine.

There has been a terrible mistake.

I'm not supposed to be here. I wasn't supposed to be at any of the places I've somehow found myself in today. And I'm not sure how, why, or what to do about it.

I take out my phone and pull up my dad in my contacts. It's fine. Take a deep breath and get to the bottom of this. I didn't do anything wrong. I can't get in trouble for some mistake done *to* me, not *by* me...right?

But no matter what happened, in my dad's eyes, it will be my fault. I know how he operates. In times of stress, he over-reacts. And it's never pretty.

I wish he'd pick up golfing or something to relieve his stress instead of taking it out on me.

If I call him and tell him I'm standing in a stranger's house, a very rich stranger at that, he'll ask me what I did wrong and how I ended up here. I put my phone back in my pocket.

Think, Jessica. I could call Mira Im at Haneul Corpora-tion and see if she can possibly figure out the mistake. But it's already 10:00 p.m. on a Sunday night. And honestly, is this how I want to start off my internship? I already know it's gonna be incredibly difficult to stand out among the crowd with my performance alone. But the last thing I want is to be known for stealing someone's plane ticket, their ride, and now their home.

So I do what I always do when I have no idea what to do.

"Hi hi, tell me everything."

The face on the screen of my very best friend, Ella, makes everything better. Sort of. I release some tension from my shoulders and let out a breath.

"Okay, so..." I begin.

"Wait, where *are* you? Why are the ceilings so high? What is that massive chandelier?" Ella asks in awe.

"I was getting to that. But the story doesn't start here, Ella. It ends here. Or it ends in prison, one or the other," I say.

"Let me sit down and grab a back pillow. Do I need to

get a glass of water, too? Should I go to the bathroom first before you start?"

I ignore her. "You will never believe what happened to me. In fact, I don't even believe it. I think I'm in some deep trouble, Ella, and I need you to tell me how to get out of it."

I go over the entire ordeal and when I'm done, I wait anxiously for advice on what to do next. But I'm met with radio silence, Ella's head propped against her hand, eyes closed.

"Are you asleep?" I screech. "Ella! Wake up!"

"I'm awake, I'm awake. I heard it all, ev-er-y last detail. Jesus Jessica, one day we are really gonna have to deal with your oversharing. And though it's fascinating that the first-class seats in the newer planes don't have TV screens, that the car you were in had carpeted floor mats, and that this incredible house you're crashing at has a banister made of wrought iron you think might be imported from France, let's get to the actual problem. What are you gonna do?"

"Well, I was kinda hoping *you'd* have an idea," I whine.

"It's not like you have a lot of options at this time of night. I guess call your dad?"

I just stare at her.

"Okay, you're right. Bad idea. Remember when you were driving us home from church and that guy rear-ended us?"

"Yup, it wasn't even my fault, and yet he took away my driving privileges for six weeks. Mom tried to explain that he was so worried I'd been hurt and that was his way of releasing all his concerned energy. But I'm not in a place right now to handle his 'concerned energy.'" I use air quotes with my free hand to make my point.

"Honestly, I think you should just stay there and figure it

out in the morning. If no one finds out, no harm, no foul. If someone *does* find out, bat your lashes and play innocent. No one can stay mad at those Bambi eyes of yours," Ella reasons.

Can it really be as easy as Ella makes it sound? I mean, it would only be for tonight. I wish she was here with me. This house feels so massive, like all my fears and concerns are bouncing off the vaulted ceilings.

"Well, you're there now. And this may be the only chance either of us gets to see the inside of a McMansion like the one you're in. So, can you at least give me a tour? Let's put those years of HGTV marathons and your gift of oversharing to good use. Do not leave out even one tiny detail."

Ella shares my interest in homes we cannot afford. And she's the master at deflecting so my thoughts don't spiral to The Bad Place.

But my lack of matched enthusiasm must get my point across. Ella's eyes fill with compassion...or maybe just pity. I can't even be distracted with the one thing that makes me happiest: pretty homes. "Do you want me to ask my grandma to call your mom?"

I shake my head. "No, I don't want to bother my parents just yet. I'll figure it out. I think you're right. I'll just sleep here tonight and leave the place cleaner than I found it, if that's even possible. I'll sneak away in the morning and deal with it when I get to the office tomorrow. I'm sure it'll be fine. So what if they hate me, think I'm a total imposter, and this whole thing has thrown my entire future out the window. At least I won't be sleeping on the street, right?"

"Call me in the morning?" Ella asks.

"I'm three hours ahead. It'll be 5:00 a.m. your time," I remind her.

"Call me in the afternoon?"

A small smile tugs at the corner of my mouth. "Deal."

I hang up and immediately feel completely alone. I realize I haven't even stepped foot out of the foyer...which has such incredibly detailed tile work, I toe off my shoes for fear of dirtying the floors. I notice some leather house slippers lined up by the door, but they all look new and frankly, very expensive.

For the first time, I allow myself to look around the house. I've never been in a home this luxe before. It's not huge, though. It's narrower than the mansions I see on television in Beverly Hills and Malibu. But I know Manhattan is only thirty-three square miles, and a good chunk of that is Central Park, so land is scarce In New York, wealth is shown by where your home is and how you've decorated it, not by the square footage. At least that's what I heard them say on *Million Dollar Listing New York*.

The entire entryway and foyer is lined with the gorgeous tile I noticed earlier. The cherrywood built-ins and wrought iron banister give the house an old money feel. I wonder who owns this. Years of poring over *Architectural Digest* and watching shows on HGTV have made me a self-proclaimed design savant.

I walk further into the house, lightly brushing my fingers over the carved inlays of the arched entryways into each room. I stop in my tracks when I see the fireplace in the formal living room. It's bordered by a floor-to-ceiling stone mantel so grand, my jaw is on the ground.

Speaking of the ground, the wide-planked dark wood floors are perfectly stained while still showing the character of generations-old original knots and crevices. The oriental rugs covering parts of the floor look like restored antiques. The room has high ceilings exposing large expanses of wall covered with likely genuine pieces of fine art.

It feels more like a museum than a home.

I turn to my left and spot the kitchen. It's not an open concept home like you'll see in newer builds. The kitchen was clearly built to be separate for hired help to prepare meals and serve them in the formal dining room. And yet its floors are all marble, as are the countertops and the massive island in the center.

I walk through the door and freeze. "Whoa," I say, expecting a cavernous echo to respond to me. The kitchen is enormous, so large, it's likely bigger than the entire first floor of my home in Cerritos. On the island is a basket full of fresh fruit and the glass doors of the commercial grade refrigerator show a fully stocked selection of drinks and other necessities.

My stomach growls. My hand reaches out, the temptation to take a banana from the fruit basket almost too strong.

But this isn't my home, I remind myself, dropping my arm. Not even temporarily for the summer. And that's not my food. I feel a bit like Goldilocks in this moment, and I know how that story ends. I don't need a family of bears, or the police for that matter, to be showing up and arresting me for eating their food.

I head back to the foyer and grab my bag. I'll just have one of the two remaining granola bars I packed. Just as I reach the entryway, the front door opens and someone walks in.

A small yelp escapes my mouth just as a much louder scream escapes the older lady's.

"I'm so sorry," we both say at the same time.

"You startled me," in unison.

"You first," voices perfectly synchronized.

I shut my mouth and point to the older Korean woman.

Her eyes narrow and she tilts her head slightly, examining me. She knows I'm a stranger in her home. She probably has her finger on the emergency call button on her phone right now.

But she shakes her head and quickly replaces her expression with a polite smile.

"You must be Yoo-Jin-ssi. I'm Mrs. Choi. I'll be here to prepare your meals and help clean up after you. I usually come in the mornings, but when they mentioned you'd be arriving tonight, it occurred to me that you might be hungry when you got here. So I rushed over to make you a snack before bed."

This house isn't only the most gorgeous thing I've ever seen, but apparently it comes with a Mrs. Choi?

"I am Yoo-Jin," I say. "But…" But what? That I'm likely not the Yoo-Jin she thinks I am? But how does one explain something you yourself don't understand?

"Why don't you go and get washed up and I'll make you something to eat. You must be so hungry and tired. I'll have everything prepared and set out on a plate on the island in the kitchen and I'll leave quietly before you come back downstairs."

I don't move.

"Unless you'd prefer to eat in the formal dining room?" she asks.

"NO WAY. Oh, um, I mean, no, the kitchen is fine," I say. If she's gonna make food anyways, I might as well not let it go to waste. My very angry empty stomach will be happy.

I want to ask Mrs. Choi to stay. I want to ask her who she thinks I actually am and if she can help me figure out this mess. But she's already disappeared into the kitchen and the thought of washing the grime of the day off sounds too good right now.

She basically gave me permission to use the restroom, right? I'll take it. I grab my bag and lug it up the stairs. There are a bunch of closed doors down a hallway and one at the very end that's open, which leads to a huge bedroom with an attached bathroom. A four-poster bed is in the middle of the space, made up with crisp and clearly high-thread-count white linens, the initials *YJL* embroidered along the border of the duvet cover and the pillow shams. I walk through to the bathroom and it's bigger than my bedroom at home. White plush towels hang from the rods and top-end toiletries line the shower.

I take off my grubby, sweaty clothes and jump in.

What feels like an eternity later, I'm clean and feel more of sound mind and body. I've washed off the haze of fatigue and confusion and now I'm hungrier than I was before.

I go back into the bedroom to grab my luggage, but I notice it's not where I left it. I open the closet door and to my surprise, all my clothes have been put away already. I quickly throw on a clean pair of underwear, jeans, and a T-shirt, tie my wet hair in a messy bun, and rush downstairs.

I see Mrs. Choi about to leave, carrying a bunch of garment bags with her.

"Mrs. Choi," I call out.

She jumps, startled, looking like she's been caught.

"I'm so, so sorry for the mistake," she says.

Oh, thank goodness. She realizes it too. Now we can talk. "So am I, truly," I say. "I didn't realize…"

"We didn't realize you were a young lady. They mistakenly bought the wrong type of wardrobe for you. I packed everything up and I'll contact the company to make sure they have everything rectified and new clothes brought to you as soon as possible. Please leave any dishes in the sink and I'll be by in the morning to wash them and make you breakfast."

She bows and rushes out the door.

"Wait," I call out. But she's already gone.

I stand, yet again, in the foyer, stunned.

I walk into the kitchen to find a myriad of bowls laid out on the island with a glass of water, a cup of what looks like tea, and utensils all perfectly set.

The smell of the doenjangchigae and the colorful display of various banchan call me over. So much for *not* being Goldilocks. The thought of eating another granola bar when all this food is sitting *right there* waiting to be consumed is unbearable.

I take a seat and dig in.

By the time I've finished every last bit of food, I am so stuffed, and so sleepy, I can barely keep my eyes open. I put all the dishes into the sink and rinse them off. I also wipe down the island.

I let out a huge yawn and slap my cheeks a couple times.

Wake up Jessica. You need to make a plan and figure out what to do. I can't just sleep here in a stranger's house. Can I?

But it's now almost midnight on a Sunday night and even in the Upper East Side, I don't exactly feel safe roaming the streets of New York by myself.

Goldilocks, porridge, bed.

I take a seat on the plush couch in the casual family room. "Think, Jessica," I say to myself just as my eyes slowly close and I fall asleep.

I'm having the weirdest dream that someone is calling me by my dad's name.

"Mr. Lee," I hear the gentle voice say again and again.

"No Dad, it was all a mistake. They let me sit in first class. They drove me here. They gave me the keys."

I wake in a start.

"It is currently seven o'clock, Mr. Lee. Time to waken for your day." The voice is coming through the sound system of the home. Is it some programmed alarm for the house?

Oh no, it's seven o'clock.

I wanted to be at my internship by eight. We're technically not required to arrive until nine, but my plan is to be the first to arrive on the day one, check out the lay of the land, make a good impression.

Plus, I need to be out of here before Mrs. Choi returns with the authorities to kick me out.

I run up to the bedroom and quickly brush my teeth, wash my face, and change my clothes. I throw everything that Mrs. Choi put on hangers and placed into drawers last night back into my suitcase. No time to fold and pack. I gotta run.

I don't even put on any makeup. I just tie my hair into a low bun, grab all my things, and head for the front door. I take one last detour into the kitchen where I snatch an apple and an orange, stuffing them into my tote. How quickly my morals have faltered.

Just before I leave, I look around one last time. So this is how the "other half" lives, I think to myself. It's beautiful, but I can't help but feel its emptiness, its lack of life. It's a house, not a home.

What a waste.

Whoever this other half are, they're not people I'd ever understand or get along with. My envy would never allow it.

chapter six

jessica

I decide to walk to work this first day. I haven't had the chance to check out the subway and plan my route yet. I wanted to take a couple practice rides and see exactly how long it would take me to get to the office. Oh yeah, and there's the fact that I won't be coming from the Upper East Side again.

I drag my suitcase along behind me, the cheap wheels constantly getting turned around and stuck in every sidewalk crevice. This bag is older than I am…literally. My parents used it on their honeymoon.

The streets are packed with people and none are very happy about me bulldozing my way through with my roller bag.

"Fuck outta the way," someone says behind me.

"Get outta here," another yells.

"You can't be fuckin' serious," says a construction worker walking toward me.

By the time I make it five blocks, all the comments become like background music and I realize it's the New York way of saying "Good morning." At least that's what I tell myself to keep my people-pleasing, over-apologetic self from breaking into tears.

Still, as flustered as I am, I can't help but feel a little like Alice in her own big-city Wonderland. The mix of new and old, brick-built apartments with rickety fire escapes sandwiched between glass skyscrapers and their turnstile front doors, all take my breath away. And lucky for that since the smells of the city this early are quite shockingly pungent. Yet no one's nose is scrunched. Does one just get used to this odor?

Every sound, the honk of a taxi horn, the food vendors rolling their carts, the trash trucks grabbing bags of garbage left out on the curbs, people yelling and cursing at each other, construction and scaffolding on every block, each has its own moment in the symphony but play together to create the masterpiece titled "City."

I'm mesmerized.

"Geezus fucking ka-rist, whattarya new," someone screams at me with barely a second glance.

I drag my luggage off to the side and let the oncoming foot traffic have their own lane on this narrow sidewalk. "Sorry," I say to the back of the sea of heads walking in my same direction but three times faster than I am. Only one apology the entire walk to work so far. I'll be a New Yorker sooner than I expected.

By the time I reach the building that houses Haneul Corporation, I am slightly frazzled, but, surprisingly, incredibly energized. Is this what city living does to you?

I stop to look up and see how high the building goes. From where I stand on the street, I can barely even make out the top of the skyscraper. "Close your mouth, Jessica. You're not a fly catcher," my mom would say to me whenever I acted like I was too new, in awe of something that showed how inexperienced or uncultured I was. Even though we don't come from money, how we behave and carry ourselves has always been a priority in my Korean household.

Act like you're supposed to be here, I tell myself. I pull my shoulders back, lift my chin, and walk through the doors.

"Whoa," I say aloud, the moment I enter the lobby. So much for not being a noob.

It's fantastic, this lobby, a completely open space with floor-to-Heaven windows. And the way the sun's rays pierce through all the glass causing a light show effect is incredible. I could just stay here all day and admire all the big and little architectural choices made when designing this building.

But I have a job to get to.

I make a mental note to add ten more minutes to my morning buffer and maybe sit and enjoy a coffee in the lobby tomorrow, taking in the contrasts of light and dark, the hard and soft edges of the way the entryway is designed. I make an addendum note to my mental note that I don't know where I'll be walking from tomorrow so I'll need to add ten more minutes to my ten more minutes to my morning buffer. Listen, it all makes sense in my head.

I walk up to the information desk and smile as I approach the man in the suit with an earpiece.

"Can I help you?" he asks me.

"I'm here for my first day at Haneul Corporation," I say, trying to ooze confidence. I want to tell him about how the walk to work was longer than I expected and how walking an avenue block is twice as long as a street block and how this suitcase, despite having wheels, doesn't seem to be made for rolling at all and how it's hot in sunlight but going down certain blocks where the buildings block the sun and actually cause a bit of a wind tunnel makes it quite chilly and that I wish I'd worn a jacket but it would be a pain to take it on and off and on and off each block.

But I bite my tongue and hold that all back.

Yes, progress.

His sympathetic smile back at me makes it clear I've failed at my attempt to seem like I know what I'm doing. I mean, if I knew what I was doing, I wouldn't be stopping to ask him for help I guess. He knows I'm an imposter.

"First day. Good for you. Knock 'em dead. Name and ID please."

"Yoo-Jin Lee," I say, remembering that it seems most of my documents have been listed under my Korean name.

"Hmmm," he says, his brows stitched as he looks at the screen. He glances up to me again and then back at his computer.

I wait patiently, though my heartbeat picks up wondering if he'll tell me it's all been a big mistake, I'm not in the system, and I need to fly back home to LA immediately.

"I guess this one must be you." He inspects my ID one more time and nods. "Yes. Forty-third floor. Please look at this camera and we'll make you a temporary access badge for today until you get your permanent one."

I do as I'm told and wait as a very unflattering black-and-white picture of me prints up onto a sticker name badge. He points me in the direction of the entry to the elevators and some unseen scanner beeps letting me in.

I know I'm early, not as early as I hoped since I really misjudged the walk between the avenues, but where are the other interns? Didn't anyone else in this group of Korean American overachievers have the idea to arrive a little earlier than asked?

I get off the elevator and am immediately greeted by a stunning young woman, hair and curtain bangs meticulously blown out, makeup perfect, wearing a navy suit, skirt hitting exactly at the spot where it's still appropriate for work while being just short enough to be considered sexy.

"Lee Yoo-Jin?" she asks.

I bow in greeting. "Anyounghasaeyo," I say. "You must be Mira Im. Nice to meet you."

The woman smiles but shakes her head. "No, I'm Sunny Cho."

My cheeks heat immediately at my mistake. "Oh, I'm so sorry. I thought I was meeting Mira Im. I apologize."

"No, you're not the one who needs to apologize. I will be getting you all set up and will be managing your needs during your time here this summer," she says.

Oh, so she's my manager. I didn't expect to meet my boss right away for some reason. I also expected the entire intern cohort would be meeting her together.

"I'm looking forward to working for you," I say.

She cocks her head to the side, confused, but nods and leads the way through the glass doors. When she opens the door to what I assume is a corner conference room, I follow her in and try to discreetly push my bag into the corner.

"About the mistake…" she begins.

Thank goodness. I'm so grateful to be getting this all out in the open right away. I'll accept whatever punishment they see fit for yesterday—a dock in pay, less-interesting projects to work on, desk in the basement, whatever. Truthfully, I didn't do anything wrong. But, I'd rather stop walking on eggshells waiting to be called out and just get on with it.

"Yes, I'm so sorry. It was all my fault. I should have been clearer from the beginning," I say.

"No, no, it was our mistake. We're not given much information whenever we're assigned to a VIP. But they've always been male in the past. We assumed Lee Yoo-Jin was a boy, since 'Elijah' was written—well, that's no matter. It was an error. With what little detail we received about who you are and what your background is, we just tried our best. But this kind of mistake will never happen again. If you weren't too troubled by it, we'd appreciate if you don't bring it up to…" She leans in and gives me a knowing stare.

I give her a very unknowing stare back.

"To?" I ask. I'm not quite sure I follow.

"I assume your father is someone important in the company. Or possibly a grandfather? Sometimes it's helpful if we know who we're working for and with."

"Oh don't worry. My dad would hate it if you tried to give me preferential treatment," I try to explain. I don't go into how all the executives who pull strings to get their kids into these programs irritate the heck out of him. My father finds privilege to be incredibly unfair.

Sunny Cho stitches her brows together, leaving a barely-there wrinkle in her otherwise flawless complexion. "Well, okay then. As it is, we've already gone about and fixed everything from our misunderstanding. A new wardrobe will be waiting for you when you get home. I have an outfit more..." she looks me over from top to bottom, "appropriate for today being brought in and it should arrive momentarily. I apologize, as I didn't realize we would need hair and makeup to arrive this morning as well, but I'll get on that." She lifts her phone and begins barking orders to someone in Korean.

I run my hand along my head. I mean, I'm not glamorized like Sunny Cho is, but I kind of was in a hurry this morning escaping from luxury. Okay, so I messed up my bangs and didn't quite trim them straight last week. But it's hardly noticeable. When I make the effort, I think I present pretty impressively, if I do say so myself. And there's no way I'm spending any money on some glam squad to do my hair and makeup. I'm an intern for goodness' sake. What do they expect from me? They know how little their entry-level pay is, right?

"I really don't need..." I start to say.

But Sunny is in damage-control mode and is not listening to, nor asking about my needs. I don't want to question my manager, not on day one. But I also don't want to be put in a situation I can't handle, such as spending money to fit a visual expectation I don't agree with. She didn't even ask me what size I wear.

I think what I'll do is wait for the other interns to arrive, see how they're all dressed, and maybe we can approach the topic as a group with Sunny Cho. For now, I'll keep my mouth shut. Since this whole mess began, whenever I've tried to question what's been happening, I just get cut off like I have no idea what I'm talking about. And maybe I don't. But I can't be the only one who sees that something isn't adding up here, can I?

"Your office has a view of the park," she says. "Your laptop is all set up here. We were told you're more comfortable on a MacBook vs a Microsoft based machine, correct?"

I nod, because it's true. But how did they know all of this? I don't recall that being one of the questions on the application or any of my new hire paperwork I was given to fill out.

"Um, Ms. Cho? Where are the other interns?" I ask. My heart is pounding and I can hear it in my ears. I can't be this scared to ask a simple question to my manager and expect to succeed this summer. Get a grip, Jessica.

"The interns? Well, I would suspect they're going through orientation in the conference room on the lower level."

"Oh my gosh, am I late for orientation? Shouldn't we hurry? Or did you want me to just head down there on my own? I'm sorry, I was confused. I shouldn't have expected you to direct me there. I'll figure it out," I say. I'm panicked, late, and unprepared. This is not how I wanted this day to go.

"Yoo-Jin-ssi, you won't be joining the other interns. Your internship is in the Executive Training Program. This is a role reserved for someone connected to a company VIP such as yourself."

VIP? Is she talking about my dad? Has he downplayed his role at Haneul Corp all this time? He always made it seem like he was unimportant, unappreciated. None of it makes any sense in my head. It doesn't add up.

"If you're ready, I can show you around the office. I'd normally wait until the new clothes got here as to present you in the best way possible. But since none of the executives are here yet, just the support staff, it should be fine." Ms. Cho smiles at me as if all of these words aren't meant to be jabs at my looks and presentation. And maybe they aren't. But they sure feel like it.

I'm taken around on a tour of the forty-third floor. It's all impressive and though everyone I meet is curious about who I am and what I'll be doing as this executive training intern, they mostly just politely smile and go about their business.

"We have a cafeteria on the tenth floor. It's for all employees, serving lunch and a light dinner. Mostly all Korean food, but some western options as well," Ms. Cho tells me as she leads me back to the elevators. "I'll show you that now before it gets busy."

"Does Haneul have all the floors in this building?" I ask.

"No, we have the tenth for the cafeteria and the gym, and then we occupy from the thirty-second up to the forty-third floors."

The elevator stops at the thirty-second floor. The door opens and a group of young people is waiting on the other side.

They all pile in the spacious elevator. It gets noticeably quiet when they see us and realize we're riding together. Ms. Cho has an air of "I'm in charge" that exudes from her posture, her appearance, her vibe. No one says a word. I must

look like her frazzled assistant or someone who is lost, clearly
in the wrong elevator.

And…it's at this moment that my stomach decides to remind me I didn't have breakfast. Loudly. I grab it, wishing
for it to shut up and stop growling.

But it's too late. I hear the giggles.

"Luckily we're all heading to the cafeteria," a voice behind
me says. That voice.

I look over my shoulder and my eyes widen as I recognize him. I'm met with an equally surprised expression as he
clearly recognizes me. It's the guy I ran into, literally, at the
airport. He's here too.

Without the hat and the mask and the expensive clothes,
he looks younger. He was handsome in a mysterious, dashing
way before. Here, in this elevator filled with people where it
would be entirely inappropriate for me to check out this softer,
cuter version from head to toe, it's all I seem to want to do.

A banana appears in front of my face. The tall, skinny boy
next to airport fella reaches out to offer me one. "Here," he
says.

I shake my head. "Oh, um, no thank you," I say. It's not
like I can just peel it and start eating right here on the elevator in front of my boss. That would be inappropriate.

He shrugs a shoulder and rescinds the offer.

My stomach growls again in protest.

"So, like I was saying, they're usually a lot more organized
than they've been this year. Elijah, it sucks that your clothes
didn't get here. But it's hilarious that they had you listed down
as a Jessica. Weird. Gonna call you 'Jess' for the summer," he
says, breaking the silence.

I freeze. What did he just say?

I turn back toward the tall guy talking to see he's addressing the guy from the airport.

"Really wish you wouldn't," the airport guy replies.

"Fine, then, *Yoo-Jin*," tall guy says.

"I told you, I prefer to be called Elijah."

What? Did he just say his name was Elijah? Didn't Ms. Cho mention an 'Elijah' earlier?

I can't take it anymore. Names are being thrown around in this conversation, one that I'm not a part of, mind you, when some are actually *my* names. And another name I've now heard multiple times in passing. It's like the answer to this mix-up is right in front of me but I can't quite grasp it.

"I would call you Elijah if it didn't sound like you just made up that name on the spot."

"Elijah's a person in the Bible," a girl says, joining the conversation.

"I get that. But do you know of any Koreans named Elijah?" tall guy asks.

"There was a guy in my freshman Chem class named Elijah Kim," someone says.

"I know an Elijah Song," someone else adds.

"Okay, okay, so I'm wrong. Apparently there are a lot of Korean Elijahs. My bad. I will call you Elijah and you can be just some generic dude out of many."

Everyone starts to laugh and the camaraderie warms me a little. I hope I get to work with everyone and get to know them too. I crave this kind of environment, a group of people thrown together by circumstance.

But I'm confused where I'm supposed to fit in this puzzle. Or if I'm an errant piece that has no place here.

"I'm sorry," I say, "but did you say your name is Elijah? Is your last name 'Lee' by chance?"

His eyes narrow.

The elevator dings and Ms. Cho, without hesitation, walks off. I want to ask her to wait but she doesn't even spare me a glance. I have to get to the bottom of this, and this Elijah definitely has the answers.

But what if I don't see him again?

Without thinking, I grab Elijah's hand, take the cap off my fancy new Haneul Corporation pen, and scribble my phone number on it before rushing off the elevator.

"Please, this is very important," I say to him as the doors begin to close. "Weird, but important. You have to call me later when you get off work. Please."

And with that I scramble after Ms. Cho and leave Elijah and the answers behind.

chapter seven

---

elijah

I look down at the phone number hastily scribbled onto my palm. The first thought that pops into my head is that my manicurist would have a field day seeing ink recklessly marking my well-cared-for hands. The second thought: What are the odds I'd run into the pretty girl from the airport here at Haneul?

"Whoa, what just happened? Did that girl just give you her number right here in a packed elevator?" Jason asks. "Damn, that's like straight out of a K-drama or something. And here I was trying to get her attention with a banana."

"I'm not sure," I say. Though obviously, there's a number written right here on my skin.

There were twelve people in this elevator including myself and she just took my hand and gave me her number. That took some guts. But I get the sense it wasn't an act of flirtation. I mean, it's kinda weird that it's now the second time we've run into each other. And there definitely was something about the wild, almost desperate look in her eyes when she asked me to contact her that doesn't sit right with me. That situation is not what it seemed.

"I wish I was that badass sometimes," Grace says.

"Same," Roy agrees.

"Badass like our boy Elijah here, who got himself a number after one day of being in New York?" Jason adds. "Or badass like the girl who gave it to him and peaces out without a goodbye?"

I can't get the expression on her face as the doors of the elevator closed out of my head.

She didn't look badass or confident.

No. She looked freaked out.

She also seemed like she needed answers as much as I did after everything that went down yesterday. It was obvious something, everything, was off.

But I was just having too good of a time to worry about it.

These strangers all took me under their wing. They seemed to like having me around, and I like being around them. So much so that I slept in a bunk bed in a stranger's generic T-shirt. I got up at an ungodly hour and rode the subway to the office this morning, seated next to someone who may, in fact, call the subway his home. And I let myself be pushed around, not even blinking twice when I was asked to get coffee for the Intern Coordinator this morning.

Listening to people my age talk about how this internship could be life-changing for their futures, planning years ahead and hustling to make their dreams happen, it's so different from everything I've known. And here I am doing anything and everything to hide all my privilege, not wanting any of these responsibilities, and hoping I won't get found out, at least for just a little while longer, so I can enjoy the summer.

And having zero interest in my dad's company.

I honestly thought the jig was up when our intern leader did roll call and asked for a Jessica Lee. I knew there was no Jessica in our group as of last night. And there wasn't going to be an Elijah Ri on her list. So I raised my hand and took a chance, asking if she meant Yoo-Jin Lee. And there it was, passing my lie off as someone else's mistake. Even letting her apologize for it. The list must have been wrong, she tries to explain.

I let everyone teasingly call me Jessica.

How much do you wanna bet that the girl from the elevator is Jessica Lee. Double or nothing that her Korean name is Yoo-Jin Lee.

Just like mine.

I'm not sure how this happened, but I wouldn't be surprised if she happened to wake up in an Upper East Side brownstone this morning about as scared of being found out as I was.

Whatever is going on, I'll make it through this day and then give her a call after work so we can get to the bottom of it all and figure out a plan on how to explain it to everyone we've met today.

All I know is, if it's anything like what life has been like so far for me here in New York, I'd be happy living out a role like Jessica's this summer.

I text the number Jessica left on my hand and suggest we meet for coffee around the corner from the office.

"I hear this halal cart is the best in the city. You sure you don't want to grab dinner with us?" Jason asks.

The way Jason and the others are making sure to include me in plans, like we as a group move as one, is so new to me. I have friends back in Seoul. Kind of. But not like this. I'm not sure if I'm made uncomfortable by it because I like it or because it creeps me out.

"Thanks, man. But I've got something important I need to take care of tonight," I say. Jason looks down at my hand where I'm mindlessly rubbing the phone number I've already saved onto my phone.

"Uh-huh. I'm sure you do have something important to take care of tonight," he says with a laugh. He shoves me on the shoulder, but before I can try to deny whatever ideas are going through his head, he takes off with the rest of the interns. "Have fun, Yoo-Jin-ah, I mean, Elijah," he says over his shoulder playfully.

I watch the group walk away and not once do I take inventory on what brands they're wearing or what their parents do for a living.

I walk to the coffee shop around the corner and through the window, I see Jessica already sitting inside. Her hair is no longer pulled back into the messy ponytail like earlier. It's down in long waves cascading down her back. If I'm not mistaken, she also looks like she has makeup on. At the airport yesterday, and in the elevator earlier, there was a charm to her simplicity and natural beauty. All done up like this, she's pretty, sure. But she looks a lot like the Korean girls back home.

She has her hands clasped in front of her, her back ramrod

straight, looking capable and confident. The giveaway is her knee bouncing uncontrollably under the table. She's nervous.

I'm surprised my own heartbeat is racing, too. I don't have designer clothes to hide behind. I'm wearing Jason's borrowed T-shirt and generic underwear I bought at a store called Duane Reade where I tried to ignore that my friends also bought food, household cleaners, and toilet paper from the same place as my undergarments.

I don't have a name to drop for a sought-after reservation. We're at an empty diner that looks like it has about twenty years of grime stuck to the table.

I don't even know why I'm trying to impress a girl who shouldn't mean anything to me. I just need to get some answers, figure out whatever game of switched identities is going on, and then be on my merry way.

"Hey," I say as I reach the table, pulling out the chair and sitting down.

She looks up at me and tucks her lip under her teeth, biting down nervously. Her eyes are wide and round, and in this moment, I know that whatever fallout there will be for this, if any, I'm not letting Jessica Lee take any blame for it. It's all on me.

My thoughts surprise me. I'm normally a selfish sonofabitch. But there's something about this girl.

"Elijah Lee?" she asks.

"Ri, actually. Long story. But close enough, I guess," I say. "I think what matters is, my Korean name is Lee Yoo-Jin."

She closes her eyes and nods her head slowly as understanding washes over her features.

"What a coincidence," she whispers and opens her eyes again, looking straight into mine. "I'm Yoo-Jin Lee, too."

"Also known as Jessica?" I ask.

She nods again.

I don't know how I thought this conversation would go, but I'd hoped it would be something we could laugh about and move on from. But Jessica looks straight-up traumatized by this. I wonder if she's ever made a mistake or broken a rule in her life.

"Seems our shared name is like a magnet for the two of us," I say. "I was wondering why I kept running into you. I was beginning to think it had the makings of a summer romance or something."

That was the in for her to laugh easily and break the tension. She didn't take the cue. My cheeks flood with heat. So not smooth, Elijah.

"I guess I kinda hoped it all really was for me..." She stops as if she's just caught herself talking to the wrong person. Maybe that's exactly what she realized. "Never mind. Look, I know I'm not in the right place and I'm guessing you've figured out that you're not either," she says. "But I'll pay for anything and everything I used last night. It was an honest mistake. I'd really like to be able to stay on with my internship at Haneul Corp."

"Hey, hey," I say quickly, raising my hands in an effort to show I come in peace. "It's no skin off my back, seriously. No one even has to know about last night. And you don't need to pay for anything."

"I think they bought me a new wardrobe," she mumbles.

"Ah yeah, let me guess, the clothes waiting at the house

were all men's styles?" I smile. "Not that I don't think you could rock that look. Androgynous fashion is really having a moment."

There it was. The first small smile to appear on her face. "I can't even pronounce the names of the designers who made the clothes they brought me to wear. If anything is having a moment in fashion, I wouldn't know unless it's happening in the Target clothing section."

"I'm wearing underwear that I bought at a drugstore last night that was displayed between the hairbrushes and office supplies," I confess.

She lets out a husky laugh and her entire face lights up. I thought she was cute before, but I was wrong. She's a fucking stunner. It feels like an iceberg has been broken in half between us and I let out a sigh of relief.

But the smile fades from her face quickly. "When I think about yesterday, everything was fishy starting way back at the airport in Los Angeles. But there's no way I could've guessed it was this."

"Right? I mean, shouldn't the airline be more careful when checking people in for their flights? This is how dangerous things can happen." Truly, if we're going to assign blame, let's go all the way back to the beginning.

"No one's really to blame. Or, at least not just one person. Maybe we're all at fault," she says in a voice much kinder than the one I went with.

So maybe I *should* have said something sooner when I knew something wasn't right. But no one here knows who I am, or at least, they don't care. They only see a teenage kid and decide I have no idea what's right or wrong.

"How's the apartment? How's the internship? Are the people nice?" Jessica asks.

"Yeah, everyone's really cool, actually. The apartment, well, it's small for one person so you can only imagine how cramped it is with ten of us. Um, of you. But it's not bad."

"Well, the brownstone is huge. Three floors. Just, um, for you," she says.

"Yeah, my dad bought it and a house in the Hamptons last year when he needed to invest some cash in the States," I admit.

"Your dad is rich?" she asks, immediately blushing and covering her mouth with her hand. "I'm sorry, that's rude. Ignore me."

"My dad is Lee Jung-Hyun, chairman and CEO of Haneul Corporation." Might as well get it all out in the open now.

"What? Oh my god, I've been impersonating the CEO's son?" Jessica shrieks. "Can they put me in jail for this? Oh god, I need a lawyer. I have to call my dad. I…"

I reach over and put my hand on top of hers. I hope she doesn't mind how clammy it is. "Jessica, it's okay. We can explain the mistake. You didn't do anything wrong. If anything, we can blame the driver, Mira Im, the security guy giving out badges—all of them fucked up too. And it's their *job* to get this shit right."

"We can't do that. They were just following orders. They could lose their jobs if we put it on them. No way," she insists.

Why is she trying to protect people she doesn't even know? Except, here I am trying to protect her, a complete stranger.

"Okay, fine. Then I'll just tell them I was the one who planned it all. Trust me, my dad will believe that. He thinks

I'm a royal screwup anyways. It's on me," I say. "I can't get in trouble with Haneul Corp since I'm going to be in charge of it one day."

"But your dad..."

"As long as we didn't lose any money or tarnish his reputation, he won't give a shit about what I've done," I say.

This much I know for sure.

She nods but seems unconvinced as she goes back to working on that bottom lip of hers.

"Look, I don't know a lot about this internship world, or even about Haneul Corp. But I know Lee Jung-Hyun. I've been dealing with my dad for nineteen years. He will not take notice unless it's something that impacts him directly."

This is one thing I can say with one hundred percent certainty. It's exactly how my life and relationship with my dad has been up until this point, after all.

And I don't see that changing anytime soon.

chapter eight

elijah

We move from the coffee shop to an Italian restaurant next door to grab dinner. The restaurant is dim and the dark wood booths give a sense of privacy, as if this place was made for mobsters and criminal activity. It's cool how every part of New York, new or old, feels like it's telling a story.

As I look over at Jessica, I wonder what's *her* story. I oddly want to know every part of it. I don't think I've ever given a shit about anyone else's life before.

Jessica carefully pores over the menu, reading the prices under her breath.

"Are you ready to order?" the waiter, in a crisp white shirt and black bowtie with heavy Italian accent, asks.

I point to Jessica to go first.

"I'll, um, have the side salad with ranch dressing please.

And a cup of the Italian wedding soup. Does that come with any bread?"

"Yes, I can bring a bread basket," the waiter says.

"Thank you." Jessica hands the menu back to the waiter who seems confused at her lack of entree in her order.

I pretend not to notice and quickly make changes in my head for my own order.

"I'll take the chicken parmesan and…also the vegetarian lasagna. And can you start us off with the calamari with marinara sauce?" I figure if I order a lot, Jessica will be forced to share with me but not have to worry about the cost. I ask her, "Will you help me eat some of this if it's too much food?"

Her eyes light up. "Yeah, for sure. I mean, if there's too much food that is."

I nod and hand my menu to the waiter and he walks away.

"Okay, get me caught up. How was your first day? Was it awful? Did they walk on eggshells around you, treat you like a princess, act like your shit doesn't stink?" I ask.

Jessica scrunches her nose. Cute.

"They may think my, um, poop, doesn't stink. But they sure did think my clothes and hair and overall look were an offense to mankind. Other than getting primped, poked, and prodded without my permission, it was actually an awesome day. You're so lucky you get to do this executive training. Sounds like it's going to be pretty cool. You'll work with the Marketing department on the upcoming Sky High Conference and apparently be in charge of a pretty important project. They'll go over that with me, I mean *you*, later." Jessica's demeanor changes immediately as she begins talking about the work, sounding genuinely excited.

"And you met Sunny Cho in the elevator. She'll be your manager," she continues.

"Um, Jessica? Sunny is not your boss," I say.

"Yes, she is. Well, no, you're right. She's not *my* boss. She'll be your boss," she says, lowering her head and hiding behind her bangs.

"No, what I mean is, I'm fairly certain her role is to be your manager, in the sense that she works *for* you, to do all the things you want or need. Like, an assistant. Not a manager like a boss."

"What? Why would I need an assistant? I'm just a... I mean, I'm just an intern. I guess you might need an assistant in your role, though."

"Not gonna lie, nothing you've told me about your time here so far sounds exciting at all. I hate being followed around, checked-in on, having stuff done for me because someone is anticipating my needs. It's suffocating. And those projects just sound like...a lot of work." I laugh. Honestly, Jessica's dream role is exactly the kind of misery I thought this executive training would be. The two of us couldn't want anything more different.

"Well, it's gotta be better than what you've been doing, right?" she asks.

"No way. We walked around and hit up Greenwich Village and Washington Square Park. Did you know NYU is just *right there*, in the middle of the city, not behind some gate or tucked away on a perfectly manicured campus? Then we spent like an hour at Duane Reade to shop. I've never seen so many different types of candy. This morning we went to some tiny, messy corner market called a 'bodega' and grabbed bagels for breakfast. The dude was yelling at us because we didn't know what we wanted to order, it was hilarious. And then at the office we just hung out and signed some paperwork and went through a couple boring presentations. But it was all kinda cool, ya know? Like, I didn't realize how competitive it was to get into this program. So the other interns are all these impressive people who are here to learn a lot of shit. But they're also down to do nothing during this internship and just having it on their résumé."

I finish going through the list of memories I stored in my head from just the first two days in New York and realize how quiet it's gotten at our table. I look over at Jessica and she's staring back at me with a small smile on her face and a sparkle in her eyes.

"Most people come to New York City to see the Statue of Liberty or Central Park. But you go to a bodega and Duane Reade and make it sound like it's the best time ever."

Heat hits my cheeks and I pray I'm not turning red. I sound ridiculous, going on and on about places the average person doesn't give a second thought to.

Thankfully, she continues, her voice warm and kind. "You make it all sound so fun. And it's awesome you all get to hang out on top of working and living together."

"I've actually never had a job. Or a roommate. And here I am sleeping on the bottom bunk in a living room in an apartment with ten people. I guess I was just taking it all in," I say.

Jessica's eyes are smiling, and I can tell that she's really listening to what I have to say. There's a surge of anxiety in my chest as I realize that I've never actually shared feelings and shit with anyone, let alone a complete stranger. And here I am spilling it all out to Jessica. My dad likes us to keep things behind closed doors, away from anyone not within our inner circle or hushed by a non-disclosure agreement.

"It all sounds great. I mean, other than the ten people to an apartment and the sitting around all day doing nothing," she teases. "But I'm glad you had a good time. For me, it's like, well, I'll never get an opportunity like this again. So even though I knew in the back of my mind it was some sort of mistake, I just wanted to enjoy it for one day you know? To experience how the other half lives."

"Yeah," I say. "I know exactly how you feel."

My mind is racing. What could a summer in New York be like on my own? Not as the rich son to a chaebol family. Not having the future of Haneul Corp hanging over my head. Just laughing with friends over ten-dollar meals. Wearing regular clothes that I picked out for myself and learning to do my own laundry. Being around people my own age instead of ancient executives who hate me for who I represent.

"So here's a wild thought," I say before I can think twice about it.

Jessica's eyebrows raise over her water glass as she takes a sip.

"What if we just don't tell anyone what's going on? What if we keep going over the entire summer like we did for this first day? I think today went pretty well. Other than a few hiccups no one even seemed to think twice about it. There's no one in this office that knows me or you," I suggest.

"What are you saying? How could we pull this off? There's no way." Her words all say no, but she's leaning in further toward me. She's listening. She's interested in the possibility.

She smells good. Not like the expensive, overpowering perfume my mom or sister wear. Something simple but clean. Is it the possibility of doing something nefarious and having Jessica as my partner in crime that's making me this drawn to her?

She's not my style at all. One, she's not a chaebol, that's obvious. Two, despite the clothes and hair and makeup Sunny Cho has given her today, she looks uncomfortable in Dior. I would never think that possible. Gucci, maybe. But everyone should enjoy Dior. And three, well, my dad would never let it happen. Though if he knew how dedicated Jessica Lee is to doing good work for Haneul Corp, he *might* think differently. Doubtful. He'd hire her as an assistant to some mediocre man, but he'd never let me date her.

I shake my head. Now I'm thinking about dating her? Our worlds are way too different. Get back to business, Elijah.

"Look, it's simple. You do you, but in my place. I'll do me, but in your place. Everyone already thinks they've fucked up in the planning and organizing. They're all too scared to fuck up again. So we've pretty much bought ourselves each a golden ticket to the summers of our own making. Keep going as you are and so will I," I say.

"You're the son of the CEO and I'm…nobody. Someone is bound to notice. And I have to check in with my dad regularly. He's very…overprotective and in-my-business that way. He'll ask questions about the internship and will know if I'm lying because I often get red in the neck and start to sweat and when I get nervous I overshare and he'll suspect it right away as he's seen this happen since the time I first started to speak, which happened to be in church in the middle of the pastor's sermon and I said out loud, dramatically, in front of the whole congregation that I was bored to death."

I'm speechless. But then I can't help it, I bust out laughing.

"Don't make fun of me. Oversharing is my nervous habit. See? I'll never be able to fool my dad. I don't even know what types of things I'd be doing on a daily basis in the job I'm supposed to have."

"Okay, then, I'll tell you. We can share all the pertinent information about what we do in our roles and be armed with the intel we need to update our dads," I urge.

"There's no way I can pull this off," she says.

"Yes, you can. I know you can. I'll help you. We'll help each other. Trust me."

She looks me straight in the eye and holds my gaze, searching for answers, for assurance. She's convinced this can work, that I'm gonna make it work. She trusts me, I know it.

"Yeah, there's no way. It'll never work," she says.

Or not.

"Look, my dad knows I don't want to do this. It's exactly why he's making me. He thinks one summer in executive training will make me decide I actually *want* to take over the company some day."

"You're supposed to take over the company?" she exclaims, eyes huge. Jessica looks around to see how much attention her scream has just brought us. She acts like we're planning a heist or a murder or something. Someone needs to get this girl a Xanax.

"Here's the deal. Haneul was started by my great-grandfather. My grandfather was the next CEO, and now my dad. Dad has big plans for how to keep taking this company into the twenty-first century. All of those ideas have come from my genius sister. She's the brains and the vision behind what

Haneul is today. She's also the wrong gender, according to my dad and the board of directors. So they all think I can just step into the role. But one, I have no desire to be a figurehead of a company that I don't give two shits about and two, how messed up would that be if I took all the credit and made my sister do all the work?"

I stop and take a breath. This time I look around to see if I've invited any interest from the other patrons. We're not far from the office. I need to be more careful about what I say. This is something I've been taught, that eyes are always on the rich and powerful, waiting for them to fuck up and fall.

"If you don't want to take over Haneul Corp, what do you want to do?" Jessica asks me.

Nobody's asked me this. Ever.

And honestly, I have no idea.

"I just want to play video games all day and live a life of leisure off my family money," I say. But my voice betrays me with a mild tremor. I'm shaken by this conversation.

"The thought that we're supposed to already know what we want to do with our lives and make huge choices like college and majors at this age baffles me," she says. "And even if we do have even some idea of what we want, the system is set up to make it impossible for most of us to get it."

I'm not sure what system she's talking about. But Jessica's words feel like she's physically come and pushed a huge weight off my back. Someone understands. Even someone as clearly driven and ambitious as Jessica agrees and gets it. Gets me, maybe, even. She deserves this more than I do. And she wants it. I just have to convince her to take a risk and go for it.

"Jessica, no one at the company knows who I am. I made

sure of it before coming here. We've already explained away the 'mistake.' Just go with it. My dad is expecting me to fail. So any work you put into this role will be a pleasant surprise to him."

"Someone will find out and when they do, you won't be the one in trouble. Because you didn't take anything from me. In the eyes of everyone, I was the one who benefited, who pretended to be someone I'm not, someone I can never be. No one cares if you fake downward. But if you dare to fake upward, I mean, look at all the con men and women on Netflix documentaries. Everyone gets pissed because they faked riches and fame. People feel duped. It's easy for you to make the switch. But I'll have to work twice as hard, and I'll be the one to take the fall. And anyways, why would you do this? What do you get out of it?"

"I get to spend the summer here in New York. I get to make some friends. I get to decide what I want to eat and how I want to dress and not have someone tell me I can't. I get to be me, whoever that is, without the Lee family crest hanging over my head. I'll work hard. I won't make you look bad. I'll do what's expected of me in your role," I say. I don't know if I'm trying to convince her or myself of this. I haven't actually ever worked hard a day in my life. But I'm willing to give it a shot if it'll convince Jessica.

"I'm not worried about that. I know you will," she says, looking lost in her thoughts.

This girl doesn't even know me, but she seems so sure that I won't fuck up for her. Why? How? And why does it make me feel like I want to prove myself to her even more?

"It's just, my dad works for this company. And I know that

you're not worried about what your dad thinks of you, but regrettably, I do care what mine thinks of me. I care that he sees I can do this. He hates his job and this company." She pauses. "Um, no offense."

I shrug my shoulders. "Everyone hates their jobs and Haneul Corp. It's an awful place to work, apparently. Didn't you see the faces of everyone walking the hallways today? Poor chumps." I pause this time. "No offense to your dad."

She smiles. "Still, I don't want to put him at risk of getting into trouble."

"Listen, I know you don't know me. And I'm kinda glad for that because my reputation may make it seem otherwise. But I swear to you, I won't fuck this up."

"Why do you keep trying to convince me? How are you so sure *I* won't be the one to, um, 'fuck it up'?" She uses actual air quotes when swearing.

Fucking cute.

"Because you've already shown you give a shit," I say.

"Well, so have you. Just with a lot more profanity," she says, but her smile spreads across her face, and I don't know how serious she is about the rebuke, but I don't take it personally. Though I do make a mental note to try and cut back on the swearing.

Jesus, I usually don't give a shit—erm, a shoot?—about what anyone thinks. But, if I'm gonna convince Jessica, and if I'm gonna make this switching thing work, I gotta focus and try to care, or at least pretend to.

"What are we gonna tell the other interns? What are we gonna tell Mrs. Choi, the housekeeper?" Jessica asks.

"Why do we have to tell them anything?" I ask back.

"Um, because when we move into our correct apartments, trust me, someone's gonna notice I'm not...you."

"What are you talking about? Why would we move? Do you not like the house?"

"Are you kidding me? I love the house, every single thing about it. All the marble, oh my god. And the detail in the woodworking. The arches." She clasps her hands in front of her and lifts her shoulders as if she's Cinderella getting magically ready for the ball. I push the plate of lasagna closer in front of her and she puts her fork in and takes a bite. "And the artwork. Not to mention the state-of-the-art kitchen and whatever else smart home features it has. And then there's Mrs. Choi, who apparently is there to take care of my every need. Food, clothes, laundry..."

She looks down as if just noticing that she's been eating the lasagna. "This is incredible," she says, glancing up at me, eyes filled with wonder.

"The lasagna or the house?" I tease.

"Well, both are pretty amazing."

"Okay then, they're both yours. Knock yourself out. You and Mrs. Choi can be besties. And you and Sunny Cho too. And you can enjoy having everyone in the company kiss your ass all day long."

"And you...?"

"And I will punch in and out, do the work, not have any expectations put on me, be around people my own age and explore the city. A dream come true." And I mean it. A dream I didn't know I had, but one I'm kinda excited to live out. "Jessica, take advantage of the opportunity, learn from it, make a name for yourself, impress the shit, um, socks off of them. And then, at the end, if we have to, we'll come up with an excuse as to how it happened. I'll say I forced you, blackmailed you, or something. Or we can even play dumb and say we never even knew, didn't even realize the mistake."

"No one's gonna believe that," Jessica says with an eye roll.

"People will believe anything that makes young people look foolish. It's their default to believe that we aren't capable."

I can see the wheels in her head spinning. And she keeps nodding, faster with every argument I give her. She's caving.

"And as I said, we'll do it together. When I report to my dad, you can tell me the things that you're learning every day…"

"…and when I report to my dad, you can tell me the things that you're learning every day…"

"Exactly. Foolproof."

It's too tempting an opportunity for her to walk away from. She sees it as clearly as I do…she's never going to get a chance for this level of exposure again, around executives of a huge and successful corporation.

And this will be my one and only chance to have a free summer. Because at the end of all this, we will likely need to come clean. And I will take the blame completely, as I promised her. Once that happens, my dad will put me on lockdown and control every step of the rest of my life. And he won't let me forget about my family responsibilities for one second.

So I gotta make this summer worth it.

"Whattaya say? Are you in? You ready to step into the role as the newest executive trainee for Haneul Corporation?" I ask her.

She bites down on her lower lip, gnawing, thinking, considering.

My eyes are focused on her mouth, my breath held waiting for an answer.

"Okay, I'm in. Let's do it," she says, eyes wide as if she's surprised even herself with her answer. "Oh my god, I can't believe I just said that." She covers her face with her hands. But the corners of her smile peek through. Maybe Jessica Lee isn't as big of a prude as I made her out to be. Looks like there's a risk taker in there somewhere.

"And you're sure about the house? I'm totally willing to part ways with that element of the agreement," she says.

"Yeah, the hope in your eyes that you'll get to stay there says different," I laugh. "And the shithole on the Lower East Side is part of what I'm looking forward to this summer. Weird, I know. But it's true. Oh, but I probably should grab some clean clothes out of the closet though. I didn't bring anything else with me."

"Um, okay, well here's the thing. They kinda came and took them all away the moment they thought they'd made a mistake. Apparently, I've got a new wardrobe waiting for me when I get home." I hear her trying to hide the squeal in her voice.

"Okay, fine. It's probably best I don't draw attention to myself by wearing the newest collections straight off of Milan's runways anyways. So, tell me, where can I get a bunch of T-shirts and jeans and stuff that will help me fit in?"

"I'm sure there's a Gap around here in the city somewhere?"

"Gap?" Never heard of it.

"Yeah, it'll have everything you need there. Just don't look at the labels. You won't find your luxury name brands at the Gap," she says.

"I don't need that. I just need to not stink or borrow Jason's T-shirts. Or buy anything in Duane Reade ever again."

We both laugh.

"I'm nervous," she says.

"It'll be fine. If at any time someone gets suspicious, just do the name drop," I suggest.

"The name drop?" she asks.

"Lee Yoo-Jin. *Our* name," I say, pointing between the two of us. "It's the easiest way to confirm we're who we're supposed to be. Or have a foolproof excuse for why we're *not* who we're supposed to be."

"Okay then. Sounds like Operation Name Drop has begun," she says.

This is gonna be an experience. And one I can't wait to live out.

Operation Name Drop starts now.

chapter nine

jessica

"Tell me this is the most asinine idea of all time," I say into the phone. I called Ella in one of the hundred moments of panic I had after leaving Elijah last night and told her the entire plan.

Then I called her again this morning from my desk, still way too early back in California, but I need to be talked off the ledge. I steal glances left and right to make sure no one is around, speaking only in a frantic whisper. But I guess on the scale of misdemeanors, identity fraud far outweighs making a personal call during work hours.

"You are correct. Everything you've just told me is completely bonkers," she says sleepily.

I don't know if I'm relieved or disappointed that she agrees.

"...and it's absolutely brilliant," she finishes.

"Ella, I need you to be my voice of reason," I plead.

"You are a loud enough voice of reason for yourself. I'm your voice of what could be. I'm the one who is here to say this is an opportunity you might not have otherwise gotten, and it's been served to you on a silver platter by a very rich and hopefully very hot boy, though that's yet to be confirmed because you will not answer any of my questions about this guy. Take it and run with it, Jessica. Now, call me back at a decent hour and be ready with some salacious details about said rich boy to make penance for calling me this early."

"Wait—" I say into the phone, but the other end is silent and cold.

Well, I guess that's enough convincing to get me at least through to the afternoon.

I put my phone down and open up the calendar app on my laptop. I should schedule a standing meeting with Elijah for us to share intel about our jobs.

"Jessica, can you come in here please."

I look up, but no one's waiting for my answer. All I see is the back of a short man in a slightly rumpled suit walking past my office. I get up from my desk and quickly follow who I think is Mr. Song, introduced to me yesterday as the Communications Director, into the conference room. There are a lot of very important and stern-faced people sitting around the table and my heart starts to race. They know. They found out about me and Elijah and any moment now the police are going to come in and take me downtown or wherever they take criminals.

"We need a notetaker for the meeting," Mr. Song says, passing me a pad and pen.

Oh, okay, fine. I mean, note-taking seems a little below

an executive trainee, and doing it on a laptop would make more sense.

I don't want to be seen as a problem. But I also don't want to be a doormat or a yes person, agreeing to everything. The only way to really set myself apart is to make sure they notice me for my work ethic but also my confidence and my leadership qualities. Still, it's only the second day. Maybe not the time, just yet, to pull the "it's not my job" card and ask someone else to take notes.

"Please use feminine cursive handwriting to make it look lovely and pleasing for us to read later," Mr. Song adds.

"I'm sorry, what?" I look up and around in panic, but luckily no one is even paying attention to me. As a rule, I try not to question the way people like to have things done, especially if they're the experts. But this feels downright odd, old-fashioned, misogynistic, even.

My cheeks heat as my irritation spikes and I bite down on my tongue to keep my mouth shut. *Just do it*, I tell myself. Luckily, I do happen to have pretty nice penmanship. Even though I don't remember the last time I've written anything by hand longer than scribbled notes on a random napkin.

I take the seat in the corner with my pen and paper. The entire meeting is spoken in a mix of both English and Korean, but curiously, not everyone at the table is Korean. I wonder if they all are required to learn Korean as part of their jobs here. I make a mental note to ask Sunny about this later.

I try my best to keep up, but I don't know exactly what the most important bits are, and I'm worried about my Korean spelling since I'm unfamiliar with this level of business vocabulary.

If Elijah was the one here, would he have been asked to take notes and to do so in "feminine" writing? I highly doubt it. I tamp down the irritation growing within me.

When the meeting ends and everyone begins to disperse, I walk up to Mr. Song and hold out the pad. "Here you go. I think I got everything that was discussed," I say.

He looks down as if I'm offering him trash. He raises his chin to Ms. Kang, who, if I remember correctly from the company organization chart I studied, is the Head of Marketing and in a more senior role than he is. But she hustles over and grabs the notes from me. "I'll take those," she says almost apologetically. "Why don't you go around and collect the papers left on the table and put them through the shredder."

I nod and do as I'm told. Why people print out so much information for a meeting only for it to be left behind and shredded later is beyond me. How many trees could have been saved if we just all used digital notes?

I notice the sheets are all stamped with "Confidential" across the top, and just below it, "Haneul Gaming: Fall Titles." There are ten new video game titles with short descriptions and developer names listed. The final one reads "To Be Determined, Male, 13+." These days, categorizing a game based on a binary gender system seems odd. My cousin Jasmine was recruited to UC Irvine's E-sports team, full ride. Games aren't just for those who identify as "male" anymore. But this isn't the first time Haneul Corp has come across as outdated and out-of-touch. And it's only day two.

Mr. Song turns to leave but just before he does, he looks over his shoulder. "Oh, and Miss Lee. The way you had your hair and makeup done on your first day is what's appropriate and expected. Please make sure to keep that high standard of appearance in the workplace." And he walks out.

My entire body freezes. Yesterday, my hair was worn down and curled. I had on more makeup than I've ever used except for when I went to prom. Oh, and both were done by a professional glam squad. What about that amount of overkill is more appropriate for the workplace?

"Korean beauty standards are as important here in the New York office as they are in the Seoul one," Ms. Kang says. "If you have any questions, you can ask me. Or refer to Sunny to get the help you need." I want to challenge this, or at the very least question it, but I remember what Elijah said last night. That no one cares what people our age think.

I'm not quite as pessimistic as he is. But I'll also pick and choose my battles. Especially since I'm trying to lay low and not cause any trouble. I'm not going to HR and complain on my second day. I just want to impress everyone and finish the summer with my recommendation letters in hand.

But am I really willing to be treated like this?

"Jessica?" Ms. Kang calls out, pulling me from my thoughts.

"Yes?"

"If you have a moment..." Ms. Kang steps on to the elevator, signaling me to follow her. When the doors close, she remains facing forward but begins to speak in a low tone. "I'd like to go over your project assignment with you." She turns her head ever so slightly so her eyes meet mine. "They wanted to give it to one of the junior execs, a guy with no drive or experience, but I insisted it would be better for you. We women get so few opportunities here, so make the most of it."

My jaw is on the ground. A big project. Assigned to me
instead of one of the men. This is all a lot to absorb. "Absolutely. I'm looking forward to hearing all the details and getting to work, Ms. Kang," I say.

I sound like a butt-kisser, but I don't care. It's all true. I
can't wait to prove what I can do.

If I'm not mistaken, I catch a whisper of a smile from the
very corner of Ms. Kang's mouth. I amuse her. Great.

When the elevator doors open, any hint of emotion is
erased from her face and she power walks down the hall to
her office. I scuttle along behind her trying to keep up.

"So you'll be in charge of what we call the AIP, the Annual Internship Project." She drops the bomb as she closes
the door then settles herself in her sleek leather office chair
behind her all-glass executive desk. I'd whistle subtly under
my breath...if I knew how to whistle...or how to do anything subtly. And then it hits me exactly what she just said.

"The Annual Internship Project? What is that exactly?"
I ask.

"Well, it can be anything you want it to be, really. Last year
they planned a black-tie fundraiser for all the executives, the
proceeds going toward donating computers to some school
somewhere. The year before that, I believe the project was a
park cleanup day along the river. It's up to you, and you'll be
managing all the other interns to pull it together."

"A fundraiser? A park cleanup? Those are things the clubs
at my high school could pull off. Haneul is a huge technology company. Surely we can aim bigger." I cover my mouth
with my hand. I didn't mean to say that out loud.

Ms. Kang raises an eyebrow but then she shakes her head

and smiles. "Well, Jessica, I look forward to seeing what you can come up with. As far as details go, here's the business plan that was pulled together last year as an example. There's a lot of potential to, as you say, aim bigger, to do better. There should be some information about budget and timelines that might be useful to you." Ms. Kang pushes a very thin binder across her desk toward me.

I'm still standing but suddenly feel like my legs might give out on me. This is a lot of responsibility for someone who's been in a fake identity for all of two days. But it's also the kind of project I've been dreaming about to prove what I'm capable of.

I take the binder and open it, ghosting my fingers down the tabs—there's not much here. Ms. Kang continues. "It was written by last year's executive trainee who truly did not care about the role or the project. He just wanted a summer in New York away from whoever his VIP father was. That seems to be the case every year. I'm hoping that you'll be the one to finally break the mold, to try and come up with something fresh, nimble, creative. Show us what the next generation of Haneul Corp could look like."

My eyes widen at the blank slate before me, at all the possibilities. What could we do to bring something new to Haneul Corp? My mind immediately recalls this morning's meeting. Maybe some digital note-taking with a lot less misogyny for one. But that's not what this is about.

"I'm expecting a lot from you. I'll do whatever I can to set you up for success, but the rest is on you. You'll be given the support of Mira Im, the Intern Coordinator, and of course, this summer's internship cohort to get everything done. Use them and abuse them. That's what they're here for. If not for the Haneul internship program, I think most of these kids would go on to have pretty unimpressive careers and lives."

The discomfort rolls around in my chest and lodges itself in my throat at the way she's speaking about the interns, as if they're second-class citizens and Haneul some kind of savior for their sad lives. I am supposed to be one of those interns, I remind myself.

"I need to be honest. No one's expecting anything from this. But, if it's done well—" Ms. Kang pauses to look me straight in the eye and I make sure to hold her gaze, to make it clear that I'm paying attention "—and someone notices the impact, it could be a huge breakout for the person in charge of it all."

I nod slowly, taking in the gravity of her words. They may not be expecting much, but if I can deliver something meaningful, something memorable, I can land squarely on the radar of someone that has the power and the connections to pave the way for my future. And that's all I want, all I need.

Because then the hard choice of going to junior college this year will have been worth it. Applying at Haneul despite my father being against it will have been worth it. Taking the risk and switching places with Elijah this summer will have been worth it.

"I'll look all of this information over and get back to you with any questions I have," I say.

"No, I'm not available for questions. I have a full plate of other projects that need to be done before we put on the Sky High Convention."

"What is the Sky High Convention? No one's really told me," I say.

"Well, it's only the biggest annual tech convention put on by a Korean company. Think E3, the Apple Developers Conference, and Dreamforce all mixed in one, but highlighting the best in what's coming out of Korea in biotech, telecom, and gaming. It's the most ambitious undertaking for our company to continue to prove itself as a leader in the tech space. It's also where we announce our new gaming titles for the following year. There's a lot riding on this. So, I need you to take that information," she says, pointing to the binder in my hands, "and figure it out on your own. Report back to me next week once you have a timeline and budget." With that, Ms. Kang turns her gaze to her computer screen, typing at an impressive speed. It's clearly the signal for me to leave.

As I walk back toward my desk, I can feel my heart rate climbing. Yes, I've been waiting for this kind of opportunity to prove myself, but how am I supposed to actually do this? Where do I even start? For all my talk about Haneul being capable of something more than the past AIPs, I've never done anything like this before, let alone at this scale. Should an eighteen-year-old whose only work experience is shift manager at her local ice cream shop Scoops de-Loop be given this much responsibility?

What was my motto again? Fake it till I make it? More like, fake it till I totally fall on my face and crawl into a hole.

This is your chance, I remind myself. *You can do this. You have to.*

chapter ten

---

jessica

Instead of returning to my desk, I turn back around and head to the elevators. I go down to what everyone refers to as the "ground floor" of Haneul, technically the thirty-second floor of the building, where I remember the interns have their workspace. I knock gently on the door and open it to find the ten of them sitting around a long, communal desk. The volume is loud in the room and something that looks like a peanut M&M flies across the room and hits one of the boys in the head. I look for Mira Im but don't see her anywhere.

"You are so gonna pay for that you mutherfucker. You made me lose my last life with that distraction," one of them says, all focus on the Nintendo Switch in his hands.

"Just give up now. You'll never crack my high score," another says.

"I have all summer to try."

I stand there, frozen. If this is what the interns do all day, there's no way they're gonna want to work their butts off for an annual project that none of the higher-ups even care about.

"Hey, Jessica, right?" The tall boy from the elevator yesterday calls out. How does he know my name? Elijah, from his spot next to him, whips his head around, clearly as surprised as I am.

"Jason, um, you just gonna call everyone Jessica now?" Elijah asks.

"Nah. I just asked Sunny Cho who she was working for this summer. I wanted to get the name of the girl who gave you her phone number," the tall boy—Jason—says, sending a wink my way. "Don't be mad at Sunny. She and I were in the internship program together last year and after she graduated, she landed the coveted spot of working for some hotshot new executive trainee, Jessica Lee. Which must be you."

I stand glued to my spot, afraid to move and draw any more attention. I notice Elijah sit up a little straighter. Why is anyone looking into me and the Executive Training Program? If someone looks too closely, they're certain to find I'm not who's supposed to be in the role.

The jig is up. We're doomed.

"There was some clerical error in HR and that's why Jessica's name was on the intern roster and Sunny thought Elijah here was gonna be her boss," Jason explains. He gives Elijah a pat on the back, which causes him to nearly jump out of his skin. He must be as tense as I am. "They mixed the two names up. This dude doesn't even know how to make toast. As if he could be an executive trainee."

"Thanks, Jason. Appreciate your confidence in my abilities," Elijah says. His shoulders drop in relief, as do mine. Eljiah was right, if we wait it out and pretend like we have no idea what was going on, other people will take the blame for the "mistake," or, more likely, blame HR.

I don't like the bitter taste in my mouth at the thought. Innocent people, just trying to do their best at work, being scapegoats. I truly hope no one gets into too much trouble over it.

But I guess we're here now and I have a job to do.

"Hey everyone, can I get your attention?" I try to make my voice even, loud, stern, but not demanding. I want their interest and respect, not their derision. "I'm Jessica Lee. I work in the Executive Training Program here at Haneul. I've been given the task of leading the Annual Internship Project. I... don't know much more than that, but we can figure it out together. And Jason, since you were in the program last year, maybe you can help us decipher these notes?" I ask, holding up the binder. "Wouldn't it be cool if we could put together something truly impressive, come up with an idea that's really groundbreaking?"

Good job, Jessica. Inspire the team, let them know they're part of something big.

"Grunt work," one of them says.

"Haneul hasn't come up with a groundbreaking piece of technology in years. Getting desperate for new ideas, I bet," someone else scoffs.

I see Elijah fold in on himself a bit. I can tell he's not comfortable talking about the company, nor having the company spoken about. What a weird conundrum to not care, but to also care a lot.

"Look, I get the sense that they think this is a throwaway project, too. But, I'd like to prove them wrong. I know this Haneul internship was not easy to come by. So let's show them why we were—I mean, um, *you* were the best of the bunch," I say.

Nobody moves, nobody speaks. That's either a good sign or a really bad one.

"What about a hackathon?" Elijah says. The room quiets. I can't tell if they think the idea is outrageous and they're rendered speechless, or if their interest is piqued.

I, myself, am enamored by Elijah's voice and his air of self-assurance. I mean, I'm, um, impressed by his ballsy idea, even though I have no idea what that means. "A hackathon?"

"It's when you get a bunch of programmers in a room and give them a problem to solve, or an assignment to complete. They work around-the-clock for a set amount of time and then present their solutions," Elijah explains. "It could be really awesome. We could blow their minds with this thing and give some young programmers a chance to do something cool too. Maybe we focus on gaming, like, have them come up with a new game concept. And maybe the winner could have it produced by Haneul." Elijah's voice grows louder and his animated hands betray the excitement he's clearly feeling by the idea. He throws a glance my way, like he's suddenly realized all eyes are on him and is anxious about what we'll think of his idea. I give him a small smile, hoping he knows how much I appreciate his enthusiasm.

"I just heard they're announcing next year's game titles at the Sky High Convention. Maybe we can get the hackathon winner on to that list," I add.

To be determined. Male. 13+. What if this hackathon helped determine that game title? Minus the limitation of "male." I have no intention of putting on a program that doesn't give opportunity to anyone and everyone.

"Elijah's right," Jason says. Of course, when a guy makes a suggestion, he's a genius and he's *right.* No one seemed to be that excited when it was my idea to do something groundbreaking. Figures.

But honestly, it's already clear that Elijah is a natural born leader. People listen to what he has to say.

I mean, even I agreed to this bonkers idea of his to trade places, right?

"Okay, let's do it," I say, pulling out the only empty seat. Elijah, currently at the head of the table, gets up, gathers his things, and moves to the chair I was going to sit in. He nods his chin at his now vacated spot. I want to decline—I'm not here to force myself as the leader down anyone's throats—but I appreciate the gesture.

"This binder of info is all we have to start with, and it's pretty sparse. That said, we've been given a bit of a blank slate to do what we want. I've never planned a hackathon. But—" I look around at everyone seated with me "—if we can pull it off, it'll look great on our résumés, it's an impressive talking point in interviews, and we'll have the experience of having worked on something bigger than I think any of us have done before. And it'll be a big win for Haneul Corp, too."

I hoped for everyone to cheer at the end of my little pep talk, but I'll settle for the few nods and smiles I get from my peers. It still feels like a step in the right direction.

I realize that other than Elijah and his friend Jason, I don't know anyone else's names. "Oh, and just by way of formal introduction, I'm Jessica, as I mentioned. I'm from Cerritos, California, and I'm, well, I'm going to Cerritos Community College next year before deciding on where to apply for transfer."

That intro will get easier one day, won't it?

"Rich kid," someone mutters under their breath, but loud enough that I can hear it. I freeze at the words, the accusation. Heat makes its way through my body, and I feel the burn of it as it reaches my neck.

They think I'm going to junior college because I'm taking some kind of easy way out. That money affords this choice for me. But it's the complete opposite. I want to tell this room of my peers that I'm not a rich kid. I didn't buy my way into this role. Okay, so technically, I lied my way in. But I need this as much as the rest of them, if not more. I have to work harder than anyone else just for the *chance* to get noticed and even then, I had to deceive everyone to do it.

My eyes turn to Elijah. His head is down, shoulders slumped, like he's trying to hide. I don't know why I thought he'd say something, defend me even. But I realize that although the "rich kid" comment was aimed at me, it was actually meant for him. He *is* the rich kid. And maybe for the first time in his life, it's not a compliment.

Someone clears their throat, breaking the silence. "Yeah, okay, so I'm Jason. I'm from SoCal too," he says. He's the type of guy that puts everyone at ease, I'm coming to find, and his words release the tension gripping at my shoulders. "We must've been on the same flight over here."

I give a weak smile and nod, trying to convey my gratitude to him in a look. Jason gives me a barely noticeable lift of the chin.

I glance over at Elijah and he's watching the silent exchange between me and Jason. His lips are tight, eyes narrowed.

"I'm Grace," the girl next to Jason says, and we go around the table making introductions. I repeat each person's name in my head three times along with whatever bits of information they share to be sure I remember everything. *Grace, Grace, Grace studying law. Roy, Roy, Roy from Iowa where there are surprisingly a lot of Koreans.* And so on.

"I'm Elijah. I'm here for the summer from Korea." And he leaves it at that.

I smile his way, but his head is still down and he doesn't catch it.

"Nice to meet all of you. Okay, well, there's not a lot of helpful information in here so that can either be a good thing or a bad thing. Let's divvy it up, review the info and prepare a quick presentation of what we have to start with. What are the expectations, the cost, the metrics and then share with the group as a whole so we can then strategize how we move forward in planning and execution."

We go around and split the topics based on interest and expertise: marketing to Soobin who reviews spicy romance books on Tiktok with over a million followers, design to Henry who builds websites for small businesses in his free time, finance to Jason who apparently has a love affair with spreadsheets, and so on.

"And that leaves logistics to me," I say.

"I didn't take a section," Elijah mumbles.

"Well, what are you good at?" Jason asks.

"Nothing," he says.

I want to reach out and shake him, tell him to stop being this way, pretending to be lazy and not caring, when it's obvious he's hungry to figure out who he is and what he wants. Plus, we agreed. It's his job to make me look like I didn't fail at my internship.

"That's not true," I say, instead of resorting to physical violence. "I know it isn't."

"Fine, whatever. I'll help with logistics too then," Elijah says.

A hundred butterflies take flight in my belly. What the heck? It's logistics we're talking about here. I don't even know exactly what that will entail, but it's most likely the least interesting and sexy part of this whole project. And this is Elijah, my partner in crime...likely an actual crime. What's there to get excited about?

Not that soft voice that makes my skin feel clammy any time he talks to me. Nothing exciting about that.

Or those freaking mile-long lashes he always seems to be looking up from under. Nope, that's not exciting AT ALL.

Knock it off, butterflies, I say internally, glaring at my belly, before getting back to business.

"Okay, so maybe we all spread out, find a quiet place to review the materials, and meet back here by...four o'clock? Is a couple hours enough for everyone to gather initial thoughts, questions, and ideas?"

All eyes turn to me.

"You're letting us leave the ground floor?" Sarah asks.

"Um, well, there are a bunch of unused conference rooms and I'm guessing this is the kind of work they're supposed to

be utilized for. And we need separate space to discuss, don't
we? Or if you'd rather go outside and try and get inspiration
from the city itself, I'm okay with that too."

"Mira hasn't even shown us anywhere above this level,"
Roy says.

"You heard Jessica," Elijah says. "Get out of here. Spread
out. Find a room or leave the building. If anyone looks at you
weird, look at them back even weirder. We're employees here
too and we're doing work for the company."

I can relate to their feeling of waiting for permission to do
something, of fearing reprimand. It's because we have something to lose. But Elijah is different, with all his confidence,
maybe from being born from privilege. He acts like he owns
the place. And you know what? He literally does.

"See you back here at four," I repeat. And with that, everyone disperses. I turn to Elijah. "This is gonna sound super
annoying, but we can go work in my office, if you want. It's
pretty private up there."

He furrows his brow at the suggestion. "Let's find somewhere else. I have no interest in being up in the executive
floor at all this summer if I can avoid it. How about we take
a walk?"

"Sure." I'm not sure exactly what Elijah is going through
and why. But I want to respect his boundaries. And I also
kinda wanna make sure he's okay this summer. That he gets
what he wants and needs from this experience. It's the least I
can do, since that's exactly what he seems to be doing for me.

The moment we leave the building, Elijah's entire disposition changes. Energy courses through him as he looks left

and then right and then left again. He nods a few times as if having a conversation with himself as to where we should go.

"Let's head this way," he says. I follow and pick up my walking pace to keep up. "Have you had the chance to take in much of the city yet?"

"Not really. Yesterday was a lot so I went straight home to the brownstone after we talked. I kinda just snooped around the house," I admit. My cheeks heat as I realize what a creeper that makes me sound like. "Sorry."

He shrugs. "It's not my house. I don't care. I bet my dad had it all decorated with things that seem like they should fit, but he has no idea what any of it is or where it came from. You're fine."

"It's big. It's weird being able to talk out loud to myself if I want to since I'm alone, but also feeling like I shouldn't be making a sound."

"Huh, I never thought of it that way, but I totally get what you're saying."

We turn the corner and I stop in my tracks. The person walking behind me runs into me and says some profanity-laced curse under his breath. But I'm too distracted to apologize. My mouth is on the ground. Before me is the most vibrant place I've ever seen. The colors of all the flags of other nations. Bushes and trees and flowers next to yellow cabs. The iconic red and blue of the sign that reads "Radio City Music Hall." I'd only ever seen Rockefeller Center on television. I wasn't ready to take it in with my own eyes.

"You just stepped in gum, Jessica. And those are some expensive new Hermès loafers you've got on," Elijah informs me.

I turn to him just as he gently pulls us both off to the side, out of the way of busy city goers with places to be.

"It's beautiful," I say, taking it all in. Even gum on my shoe can't take away from this moment.

"Yeah, it's pretty cool," he agrees, a small smile spreading across his face. "New York is just a city, but it's not like anywhere else. I mean, in Seoul, it feels like everything is lit up to shine bright outwardly. Here, it's like everything has a different glow, like the city is lit up to shine inward. That each of these city blocks and the buildings and even this busy corner all have secrets. And everyone has a place to be other than where they're at. I love that energy."

My attention is pulled away from the sights onto Elijah. He is mesmerizing as he talks, even more so than the view in front of us. And I know exactly what he means. I love this energy too.

"If I promise I'll be around to talk about logistics with you later, will you come with me somewhere right now? I wanna show you something." His eyes are wide with wonder and I can't help but want to know what he's up to. "Trust me," he says, holding his hand out to me.

I'd go anywhere with you. Whoa there, tiger. Where'd *that* thought come from? Elijah is nice and all. And he's potentially the only friend I'll make this summer, seeing how it's going thus far. But I need to be careful not to let myself get too attached. I have to stay focused. Eyes on the prize…and that prize is *not* a rich, handsome Korean guy who's *way* out of my league.

"I guess," I say instead. Replying in the affirmative without showing too much enthusiasm. Good choice.

But Elijah doesn't hesitate. He grabs my hand and leads me down the block. I try not to focus on the fact that we're holding hands…or the fact that my hands are embarrassingly clammy. In my defense, it's hot and humid out.

We stop at a building with a line of people waiting outside. He drops my hand and moves his to the small of my back, gently guiding me past the line and straight up to an Asian man in a uniform standing at the door. Elijah offers him a handshake, and afterward, the man looks down at his palm, smiling. He unhooks the stanchion to let me and Elijah through, past the others waiting.

"Wow, I've never seen that trick in real life," I say. "How much did you give him?"

"Hundred."

"One hundred dollars?" I meant to whisper. I failed.

Elijah's eyes bug out and he puts his finger to his lips. "That's nothing."

"Don't shush me," I say. "And it most definitely *is* something. I'd rather save the hundred for something more useful and just wait in line like everyone else. Who just throws around that kind of money?"

I want to continue this conversation, but we're shuffled into an elevator jam-packed with other people, all who likely actually did wait in line. The elevator shows an informational video about some history of New York, but I'm distracted doing mental math, realizing I'd have to work an entire shift at the ice cream shop to make a hundred dollars. And Eljiah just hands it off to a stranger in order to forego waiting a few minutes.

The elevator stops and the doors open. I'm ready to continue giving Elijah an earful on wasteful spending—wow, I really am my father's daughter. But as soon as I follow him off the elevator, every thought leaves my brain. All I see is sky, water, and the tops of the thousands of buildings that make up New York City. My feet lead me to the edge of the observation deck, where glass walls stand to protect me without obstructing the view.

"Wow," I whisper in awe.

"Top of the Rock," Elijah says, standing slightly behind me. "Everyone goes to the Empire State Building to see all of New York. But Top of the Rock is supposed to be the better view. From here, you can see all of New York *and* the Empire State Building." He points off to the side and I follow his finger, looking at the majestic building I'd only ever seen before in pictures.

"It's incredible," I say.

"Sure, it's just the skyline of a city. But there's something magical here," Elijah says. I feel the breath of his words gently ghost past my ear.

"It's like the past, the present, and the future all coexist in this one place," I say.

"Exactly. I think that's why it feels like anything can happen here. Like we can reimagine and recreate what our life is like, what it's supposed to be," he says.

His words resonate deep in my bones. I know he's talking about something for himself. But I feel the same way. I came to New York City worried about my future. And now, just a couple days later, standing here with the cityscape unfolding before me, it's like I've actually got a chance to claim something better for myself.

Two days ago, I didn't know this guy. But now, we're a team. We're here in this city, in this company, in this plan we've concocted…together. We haven't spoken one word about logistics or the hackathon, and yet it feels like we've been incredibly productive just by walking, by looking, by being.

Before I can stop myself, before I overthink it, I lean back a fraction, just a couple inches and my body makes contact with his. He gently puts his hand on my waist to steady me. The feeling is warm, strong, safe.

I have no idea what I'm doing. But for this brief moment, it doesn't matter. We're standing over the greatest city in the world and anything feels possible.

There's a familiar flutter in my belly and I don't hold back this time.

Release the butterflies.

chapter eleven

jessica

It's been a couple days since we ditched work and went to the Top of the Rock. But I've barely had a chance to check in with the interns about the hackathon. I've just been so busy taking needless notes and making wasteful copies of things for the Sky High Conference. It's not like I've been avoiding Elijah—and those pesky feelings that keep bubbling up when I think about him. I swear.

But we're almost at the end of our first week at Haneul Corp and I promised my dad I'd call to check in. That means I need to touch base with Eljiah.

I'm fine.

It's fine.

All is fine.

Elijah and I agree to meet at the brownstone at seven o'clock after work. Mrs. Choi will be gone by then. He's never met her and she doesn't have any idea who he really is. But still, I worry. Elijah doesn't think we need to sneak around like we're doing something nefarious. To which I reminded him that exchanging identities from a mere intern to an uber-rich-child-of-the-CEO-executive-training-intern was, indeed, nefarious. In fact, it was about as nefarious as one harebrained idea could get.

Why am I sweating so much?

And why is Elijah four minutes late? Was he caught and taken away in handcuffs to the nearest precinct? Or worse, kidnapped by the Korean mafia?

The knock on the door comes at seven-oh-five.

I rush to open it and freeze as I see Elijah's face. He's here. He's safe.

And I'm oddly comforted by the fact. I sag against the doorframe, letting out a massive sigh of relief.

His eyes widen. "Are you okay?" he asks.

I drag the back of my hand across my forehead, wiping the moisture off on my shorts. It's in these moments it makes sense to me why old-timey folks carry around handkerchiefs. "I sweat easily. It's genetic. Once I start, there's no stopping it. And I don't want to use the air-conditioning in the house because the energy costs will skyrocket and it'll bring attention on to my presence here as an interloper."

He purses his lips, like he's holding back a laugh, and nods once as if it all makes sense before entering the house.

"I brought us pizza. It was only a dollar a slice. Can you believe that? One dollar for an entire slice of pizza. Jason says we need to pat some of the oil off the top, but not too much that it dries it out. Where are the napkins?" He slides right past me in the doorway.

I wait for the *ooh*'s and *aah*'s as he takes in the massive home. Silence.

I turn around to find him exiting the kitchen with an apple in hand.

"I left the pizza on the kitchen counter for now. Hey, can you do me a favor and ask the housekeeper to stock some Asian pears and bring them to me at work? I went to some place called Whole Foods and they were trying to charge me five dollars for one. Do you know I only make fifteen dollars per hour in this internship? That's twenty minutes' work for a pear."

"Maybe you shouldn't be slipping a hundred-dollar bill to security guards then," I remind him.

"You're still on that? What, it wasn't worth it?" he asks, a cocky smile tugging at the corner of his mouth.

We stare at each other. It's like I can almost feel the heat from the other night, my back pressed against his front, his hand on my waist, just by memory alone.

I don't answer because honestly, it was so worth it.

"Anyways, this is all gonna take some getting used to," he says eventually. "I've already blown through most of the US dollars I brought with me to New York. And I'm pretty certain my pathetic paychecks aren't gonna support my usual lifestyle."

I nod in agreement.

"But seriously, you can use the air conditioner. Please don't worry about the electricity costs. Make yourself at home here," he says.

"We don't ever use the air conditioner at home because, well, we worry about the electricity costs," I admit.

"Well then, promise me you'll try to make yourself *comfortable* here. I mean, if I'm gonna suddenly start calculating the costs of items, you might as well not be burdened by any financial implications this summer."

It would be nice to not worry about money for once. But it's all easier said than done. I'm still in Cinderella mode, waiting for the clock to strike midnight and suddenly have rats running around my feet. We're in New York, after all.

But I give in this one time, walk over to the thermostat, and lower the temperature to let the A/C kick in.

Heaven.

"So, how's it been for you so far?" I ask Elijah. He's made himself comfortable on the white velvet couch in the sitting room that I have been too afraid to sit on and risk leaving a middle-class stain.

Elijah clearly doesn't share those concerns. He's leaned back and draped an arm over the headrest, casually as can be. All I can think about is that his hand is palm down on the luxurious material, the oils and city dirt transferring on to the white linen couch. How much would it cost to clean that fabric?

"It's fine, I guess. I mean, there wasn't anything on the to-do list today for the hackathon, so I took off and wandered around the city. I went to the New York Public Library of all places. It's gorgeous there. Everything felt so old and historic, not like all the new and modern buildings in Korea. And then I had a street hot dog with sauerkraut, which reminds me a little bit of kimchi."

"Um, you did all of this while you were supposed to be working?" I ask.

The eye-roll response is impossible to miss.

"I'm not trying to be all Miss Responsible here, but you're in a prestigious internship. And you're being paid to work," I remind him.

"Okay, about that. You accepted a job at fifteen dollars an hour? One of the others said that McDonald's pays more than that. How does anyone afford to buy anything? It would take me one hundred hours of work to afford the new Celine bomber jacket, I think."

I don't have it in me to explain taxes to this naive, privileged soul.

"As I mentioned, it's a prestigious internship. We're lucky to be making anything. A lot of internships are actually unpaid. And you're the future CEO. Now that you understand how low you're paying, do something about it. Tell your dad about it."

"Yeah, that's the last thing he cares about. You all agreed to fifteen dollars an hour, why would he pay more?"

Not for the first time, it's crystal clear that we could not be from two more different worlds. We don't even see things like obligations and doing what's right in the same way.

I collapse into the leather chair at the antique oak writing desk in the corner instead of answering him. I love this desk. I wish I could take it home with me and put it in my room, never mind that the shipping alone would cost more than my entire savings. And the desk itself is likely worth more than my family's house.

"Can we not talk about money?" Elijah asks.

"Easy for you to say. When you have it, you can choose not to talk about it, not to think about it. When you don't, well, that's kinda all you think about," I say.

Elijah nods his head, lost in thought.

My phone rings and I leap to my feet when I see who's calling.

"Oh my god, it's my dad," I announce in a panic. "Quick, hide," I whisper.

"What?"

"Get down! Hurry! Here, under the desk," I say pointing to the floor under the desk.

"Why?"

"It's my dad! He won't understand why I have a boy in the house at this hour," I say, frantic.

"Uh, but he's on the phone, it's not like he's here at the door. I'll just stand out of the way. He won't see me." Elijah is too calm for this moment.

I am very not calm.

My dad is a traditional man. And he is extremely protective. He would most certainly not like to have a boy in the home his daughter lives after the sun has set, unchaperoned.

"But, I'll see you. And I'll get flustered. And I'll turn red and splotchy, and not from heat since I turned on the air conditioner, likely jacking up the electric bill that I don't even know who pays for. But from panic. And I'll slip up somehow and with one raised eyebrow from my dad, I'll be admitting to it all, confessing everything that we're doing and…"

"Fine. FINE!" he says, throwing up his hands. He starts crawling under the desk and I shove his head down and flatten his back with my foot as I sit back down and accept the call.

My dad's face fills the small screen of my phone. There are the familiar lines around his eyes and dark circles beneath. His overdue-for-a-cut hair seems to have sprung a few more grays. Has it really only been a week since I saw him last?

"Hi Dad," I say, a little too out of breath.

"Hi Jessica. Is this a bad time? Were you exercising?"

"No, no, it's fine. How are you? How's Mom?" I want to ask him why he looks so tired. Ask how work is going. Ask if he can't sleep at night worried about me being away from home. But as much as I love my dad, he's not a *feelings* kind of guy.

"Oh, we're all good here. How's the internship? Have you been working hard? Have you been speaking only when spoken to? Raising your hand before offering an opinion? Taking on all the responsibilities that no one else wants to volunteer for? Making your name known but in a good way?"

"Dad, I just got here."

"No time can be wasted, Jessica. I know how things are at Haneul. It's very cutthroat and they won't hesitate to disregard you. You make one bad impression and it stays with you. You have to be on top of your game all the time. As you know, I wouldn't have chosen this company for you, but that's your decision and all I want is for you to do well."

The guilt trip hits the intended target. Me.

"Dad, I promise I won't let you down," I mumble.

"Jessica, enunciate your words," he says.

"Don't worry about me, Dad. I'm going to kill it this summer. You watch." This time I speak clearly and make sure we both believe my words.

"Well, I hope it's worth it in the end. Now tell me, what have you done so far?" he asks.

My heart rate skyrockets again. I can't tell him I've been assigned to run the hackathon. I can't tell him about taking notes in the executive team meeting. He'll wonder why I was even involved in stuff this high-profile.

What did Elijah say he's been up to? "I, uh, went to the New York Public Library. For...research. It's very historic there, not like the more modern buildings in Korea," I say, regurgitating Elijah's words. But the lie coats my tongue like the layer of grease that floats at the top of a bowl of pho.

"What kind of research?" my dad asks.

"For an event they're putting on. Looking for possible locations." I feel the heat rise in my neck. I hate this.

But then it hits me: the New York Public Library could be the perfect location for the hackathon. There's something that makes sense about it. Mixing the old architecture and history with new ideas and innovations. Do they rent the space out for events? What would that cost? Could we afford it in our budget?

"Well, that sounds like a waste of time," he says. "But hopefully they were impressed with your willingness to take on the challenge. I'm glad it's going well. Be good, Jessica. Don't get into any trouble." My dad has been saying this to me since I was old enough to walk. Like I'm the kind of kid who gets into trouble. I don't even jaywalk.

"I won't, Dad. Say hi to Mom. I'll talk to you later," I reply.

"Oh Jessica, one more thing," he adds. "You got a letter from UC San Diego. Turns out it was just some junk mail. But it reminded me to put on your radar to look into financial aid and scholarship options now for the following year. I think you'll have a better chance if you start much earlier this time."

Timing wasn't the issue. But I don't say that to my dad. I can't get scholarships without recommendations, which take connections. And whatever financial aid I get will still cost my family more than we can afford.

"Okay," I say just to appease him. Going down this road would make me have to lay out all my nonexistent options, and that tends to make me spiral into a pit of despair afterward. Best not to get into it with him.

"Maybe if you'd started earlier this year, you could have accepted UCSD's offer..."

"I told you, I'm going to junior college this first year to save up some money and fill out my résumé before applying again to bigger schools. This internship is the first step. No regrets."

"Jessica..."

"Dad, I don't want to be a burden on the family financially, saddling us with debt for years to come. I'm fine with this decision. I'm actually relieved. It's the right choice," I say, looking him straight in the eyes, so he can see that I'm telling the truth.

But it's my dad who turns away first.

It's not your fault, I want to tell him. The last thing I want is for my father to believe he failed me in some way. He works hard enough as it is. There's nothing he could do differently. It's on me now.

"Let me crunch some numbers and we'll discuss it on our next call," he says. Dad's solution to everything is crunching the numbers. But the numbers don't lie.

"Okay," I say. "Love you, Dad." I disconnect the call. Short and predictable, like clockwork. I take out a sheet of paper from the desk drawer and start to scribble down my notes about the library, pushing any thoughts of money and finances to the back of my mind.

"Uh, can you stop stepping on me and let me out now?"

I look down under the desk, my eyes wide with surprise.

"Oh shoot, I totally forgot you were down there," I say.

I push my chair back and make room for Elijah to get out and stand up.

"Nice save with your dad, about the library. Wouldn't want him thinking you're not working hard and just roaming the streets of New York while getting paid a whopping fifteen dollars an hour," he says, a satisfied smirk on his face.

"I needed an excuse. Isn't that what these meetings between us are for? To get info to tell our dads what we're supposed to be doing each day?"

"I thought I was just here to clear out your fridge to stock mine." Elijah reaches his arm to his back and starts punching it. "Oh, and maybe work on that nervous habit of yours. You know, the pounding of your foot, the one that was squarely on my back."

"Oh my god, I'm so sorry. Yeah, it drives my mom crazy when I do that. She thinks it's so unladylike."

"I don't know about that. But it's brutal, that's for sure."

I walk over to Elijah and grab him by the shoulders to turn him around so he's facing away from me. Using my thumbs, I start applying pressure to his lower back.

"Ow," he says, jumping away at my touch.

"Stay still," I say, pulling him back toward me.

I start massaging again, adding additional pressure, but then switch to using the heel of my palm, rubbing circles where his muscles are.

Gulp. Why is my throat so dry?

Elijah's head drops forward and he lets out a groan. "God, that feels fantastic. Almost as good as the massage the merciless ajumma gives me at my favorite jjimjilbang back home."

I find it hard to believe that the very rich Elijah Lee visits the very modest bathhouses in Korea. I can't help it, I let out a huff in disbelief.

He turns his head to look at me over his shoulder. "There's an old one down a side alley in Sinsa-dong that I stumbled upon a few summers ago. It's kinda become my hideaway." His voice sounds almost apologetic, like he's admitting to something he shouldn't. I immediately feel guilty for my errant huff.

The silence draws out and the air around us feels heavy. There's something intimate about Elijah letting his guard down, and me, letting my overthinking brain shut off, giving him a back massage in the middle of a house that isn't mine. I don't realize it when my hands stop moving and instead mold themselves to hold Elijah at his waist, only a couple inches separating our bodies.

He lets out a deep, slow breath. I match it.

We both jump as the humongous grandfather clock in the room chimes.

Dong. Oh crap what just happened?

Dong. Why is it so hot in here?

Dong. Is Elijah's waist slimmer than mine?

Elijah suddenly steps out of my reach and clears his throat.

"Um, so, your dad really hates Haneul, huh?" He walks over to the thermostat on the wall and pounds the down arrow a few times, cranking up the A/C.

"Oh, sorry about that. He tends to complain about his job a lot." I cringe a little thinking of Elijah, the future CEO of this company, listening to my disgruntled father. Especially since Dad didn't know he had an audience besides me.

"It's fine. I don't take it personally. What does he do for the company?" he asks.

"He's a Finance Director. I don't know much else about it, except that he says he doesn't get paid nearly enough for what he does."

"Yeah, I can relate," Elijah says, a small smirk ghosting his mouth. "So, that's why you can't go to the school you want to?"

"There are a lot of reasons I can't go to most of the schools I want to. We don't have enough money for me to go without putting both my family and my future into debt. It just doesn't seem worth it. I have to find a different path to success." These are words I've repeated to myself over and over again for my own convincing.

"Like Operation Name Drop," he says.

I nod. "Yeah, I guess so. I need connections to get recommendations."

"By the way, your dad's job sounds kind of like an awful one to have." Elijah says it so matter-of-factly. I know he's not trying to be a jerk about my dad. I actually appreciate that Elijah doesn't always have a filter. I tend to be around people who are very careful about what they say depending on who is listening. It's one of the things that frustrates my parents the most about me, that I'm not nearly careful enough with my words. I tend to speak my mind, unless I remember in time that my parents would prefer me not to. Maybe that's what money buys you—the ability to not care.

"Well, he used to work at Microsoft, and so when he came over to Haneul, I think he thought it would be a lot more organized. But, I guess, well, it's kind of a mess. So he gets frustrated." I sneak another peek at Elijah, back in that habit of worrying what he might think of what I've just said.

"Why are you looking at me like that?" he asks me.

"Well, I mean, you're gonna take over the company one day, right? Don't you wanna know what needs to be fixed and what can be improved? This is insider information. If it were me, I'd take this all and figure out how to make things better," I say.

"Yeah, no, I'm not gonna do any of that," he says. He plops back down on the white sofa and puts his feet up on the coffee table, messing up the carefully stacked coffee table books. "I'm gonna hire people to do that stuff," he adds, crossing his arms behind his head.

I roll my eyes at him. Must be nice.

"Then hire me." The words come out before I even think about what I'm saying. But honestly, Elijah and I are basically partners, definitely colleagues, and I don't know, maybe even friends at this point. Why wouldn't I ask him to hire me? And, frankly, why wouldn't he give me a job when I graduate?

Before I can start on a monologue of reasons to defend my request, he says, "Sure. Why not." Without a moment's hesitation.

"Really? You'd hire me? But I don't have any experience."

"Clearly none of the other interns do and yet you've got us putting on one helluva hackathon." He smiles at me and my heart decides this is a great time to pick up speed. I take a quick glance down at the company-provided Apple Watch I'm wearing to ensure my bpm isn't showing on the screen.

"You're smart. You're a hard worker. You don't take any bullshit. People respect you. I like being around you. Why wouldn't I hire you? You're exactly the type of person that should work at these big companies," he says. And for a minute, I believe him. I believe that he believes in me, and that things like junior college and middle class and no connections don't matter. And for maybe the first time, I see something in Elijah, too. I see someone who's been bred his whole life to take charge. To make decisions without fear, without worrying about the pedigree of someone listed on a page.

"Thanks. That's nice. I don't get a lot of chances like that, so I'm gonna hold you to it." I say it teasingly, but I file this conversation away in my head. I absolutely will find a way to hold Elijah to this job offer, no matter how premature it is. "And…" I hesitate but decide to be brave. "I like being around you, too." I won't let him get away with admitting that without countering with my own confession.

"Yeah, well, I have a feeling I'm gonna be the lucky one in all of this. Or, um, I mean, Haneul Corp will be." He clears his throat. "Anyways, it's nicer than I expected. This whole thing we're doing together."

"I agree. It has been nice. I mean, the job and all this," I say, sweeping my arm in an arc to capture everything that is fantastic about this brownstone, trying not to betray that I've found time spent with Elijah has been nicest of all.

I need to be careful. Because it's already becoming very clear to me that I not only need Elijah this summer...but I want him around too.

"Anyways, I have an idea," I say. I tuck any thoughts about feelings for Elijah in the back of my head to overthink about later, along with the hundreds of other things from this day alone. For now, my mind keeps coming back to the library.

"Do I wanna know?" he asks, raising an eyebrow.

"You do. Because, Mr. Team Logistics, it's a doozy, and it's gonna be on you to make it happen."

He believes in me enough to hire me? Well, I believe in him enough to secure us the New York Public Library for the hackathon.

chapter twelve

elijah

I look up from my phone and scan the room. Everyone has their heads down, either staring at their computers or talking quietly with someone else. There's a buzz in the air.

The group is excited to be working on the hackathon.

What I don't get is...what are they actually working on? My to-do list today is completely blank. Eight hours is torture when there's nothing to do. I wonder if I can sneak out and find a PC Café to play some *League of Legends*.

But why is everyone so much busier than I am? What do motivated and ambitious people fill their time with?

If I was home in Korea, I'd probably go shopping, or have a personal stylist come and present some options to me for review and selection. Or maybe I'd hit up a museum and have photos taken of me there? Or meet an important someone with an important name and an important bank account at a trendy café?

That life feels so far away. And so…unimportant come to think of it.

"Does anyone need any help?"

The words leave my mouth before I can think through what I'm offering.

They also feel like a foreign language, as if my lips have never been formed into this phrase before. Have I ever offered my help in nineteen years?

The memory of standing on a kitchen chair next to my mother floods my mind. She's making something…mandu maybe? I'm too little to see above the kitchen island so she pulled the chair over for me to climb up on.

"Since you wanted to help me, Elijah, let me show you what to do. You use the egg mixture to wet the ends of the wrappers, pressing them together. It works like glue, holding everything inside so the filling doesn't spill out," she explains. Her delicate hands show me once before letting me and my clumsy little fingers try it.

"What are you doing in here? Where is the cook?"

I can't help but tremble at the sound of my father's loud, commanding voice. I drop the bowl. It shatters, scattering shards and the eggs all over the floor. I'm too afraid to look up and see my dad's fury on his face. I swallow my tears.

"Dangshin, I told the staff they could have the night off. Elijah was hungry for mandu and I was in the mood to make some. Can't I cook for my own son?"

I've never heard my mother talk back to my father.

"Call the staff in to clean up this mess and to make us some dinner before I fire them all," my dad barks. His word final. He turns and leaves as my mom sighs.

"Your Appa likes my mandu, actually," she says to me softly. She bends down to pick up the pieces of the shattered bowl. I see red mixed in with the yellow eggs and the white of the broken ceramic before she even notices.

"Umma," I say, panicked, "your finger is bleeding."

It's like I pulled her from a distant memory. She looks at her bleeding finger and wraps it in her apron. She picks me up and carries me over to the other side of the kitchen. "Elijah, go up to your room. It's not safe in here," she says.

I want to apologize for breaking the bowl. I want to get a Band-Aid for my mom's finger. But instead, I drop my head and drag my feet as I walk away.

"Elijah?" I hear my mom call out to me gently.

"Yes, Umma," I say, looking back over my shoulder.

"Thank you so much for helping me. I wish we could have finished. Next time, we'll wait for Appa to be on a business trip and we'll make mandu together without him, okay?" She smiles, but I see the sadness in her eyes.

"Okay," I say. I walk away to my room, knowing there won't be a next time.

"Dude, did I just hear my savior offer to help? Because I'm drowning," Jason says, pulling me from my stroll down memory lane.

I scan the room and all eyes are on me. Maybe everyone's as surprised at my offer as I am. Or maybe no one believes there's anything I'm capable of doing to help.

And then they all begin talking at once.

"Can you look up the phone number for the printing company?"

"Can you contact the IT department and put in a help ticket for setting up the offsite network?"

"Can you ask Ann in the Travel department who she wants to be the point of contact for the hackers?"

I grab my phone and start typing in all the requests into my notes app. I hadn't realized there was so much to do and people were dying for an extra set of hands.

None of this sounds too awful. So once I finish jotting down the list, I get to work.

It takes me all morning to get through just the first task, but the time goes by way quicker than I expected. I lift my arms up above my head and stretch out the knots between my shoulders.

"You're acting like you've never worked a day in your life," Jason says to me, patting my back. I let out what sounds like a painful huff rather than a laugh. I don't say anything, though, knowing this is one area I can't fake my way through. If anyone asks me what kinds of after-school jobs I've had, I wouldn't even know what to say.

"Elijah, you're with me this afternoon, if that's okay." Jessica stands and closes her laptop, gathering her things. Her eyebrow raises in question.

"Uh, yeah, sure," I say, trying to tamp down the jolt of excitement I feel. I don't know what we're doing, but the thought of spending the entire afternoon with Jessica has my pulse racing. I was planning on exploring the High Line today. Maybe she'd want to go with me, and we could discover the city together. I can't get the look of wonder that was on her face when I took her to Rockefeller Center out of my head. I keep thinking of things I can show Jessica around town that might spark that same magic for her.

Next thing I know, I'll be suggesting matching couple outfits and key chains. Get your shit together, Elijah.

"The rest of you, please make sure you take a break for lunch and don't stay too late. We'll be gone the rest of the day," she says. "Jason, you're in charge while I'm gone."

Jason lifts his chin and gives a quick nod, his face spreading into a cocky smile. I swear I see Jessica's cheeks pinken. Dudes like Jason are such the obvious choice. Tall, funny, charming, smart. Whatever.

I stuff my phone into my back pocket and jam my fists into the front ones, waiting for Jessica to lead the way. When we get to the elevators I finally ask. "So, where we going?"

"I told you. You and I are Team Logistics. So today, we've gotta secure the New York Public Library as our venue. I can't get it out of my head, all the possibilities. I even looked at pictures online and planned out how we could use the space for the hackathon. Can you imagine? Hosting some of the best young engineering minds to come up with new programming in one of the oldest, most majestic venues in the city?"

Well, when Jessica puts it that way, I'm intrigued. The contradiction. I imagine myself sitting at a workstation set up in the high-ceilinged hall, the warm wooden floors creaking on their own, as I type code for a new real-time strategy game. Very cool. A part of me wishes I could take part in the hackathon rather than help organize it.

"They, um, didn't have any appointments available today

so—" she hesitates, dropping her voice and letting out a small breath "—we'll just have to go there and convince them to see us."

I detect a fake confidence in her voice. I know that sound, like when our house staff acts like they're happy to do whatever we ask of them. Or when Dad's business partners talk to him like they respect him for asking them to wipe his ass. She's not sure she wants to do this. Or maybe she's not sure that she can.

But Jessica's voice has something else underlying it. Determination? Stubbornness? A need to prove herself? Maybe all of the above. Her back is ramrod straight and she's lifted her chin a little bit too high to be natural. A practiced position.

Why this location is so important to her, I'm not sure. If this doesn't work out, there are plenty of other places in the city we could secure. But it seems Jessica is gearing up for a fight and I'm not about to miss out on the show. "Alright then, Boss Lady," I say, "let's do this." I wink at Jessica and she rolls her eyes. But the corner of her mouth twitches a tiny bit.

It should be fun to watch. I guess the High Line can wait a couple hours.

"Let me do the talking," Jessica says. "Okay?"

We stand at the top of the steps outside the entrance of the library.

"What am I gonna say?" I ask.

She shakes her head, but her eyes are focused on the front door and whatever lies behind it. Her lips move ever so slightly but the rest of her is frozen on the spot.

"We gonna do this or are you gonna practice your speech the rest of the afternoon? Library closes at six." I make a show of looking down and tapping my nonexistent watch. "That only gives you a little under seven hours to talk yourself into it."

Jessica slowly turns her eyes to meet mine. And they're murderous. Good, guess that fire inside her has been lit. I hold back my smile and instead reach to open the door. "After you," I say, waving my arm for her to walk through.

"Jerk," she says under her breath. "I was about to go in anyways…"

"Hello," I say, approaching the woman at the information desk. "Is there someone we can talk to about hosting an event here?"

I feel Jessica's eyes burning a hole into the back of my head. I know she asked me not to say anything, but at this rate, we'll be here all day. I'm just gonna get us started. This is the one thing I can do, charm people into giving me what I want.

The woman sizes me up and I'm reminded of the way the lady at the airline counter also looked at me, as if reviewing me, as if judging me for my age, my race, my social status. As much as I want to wipe that expression off her face, tell her who I am, who my father is, what my family owns, I remind myself that I'm incognito this summer. And if everyone else in that intern cohort, including Jessica, can accomplish shit without having a pedigree and a Black Amex, than so can I.

"It would depend on how many people, the day of the event, and what kind of event we're talking about. We don't host after-school clubs or proms here," she says, face blank, voice dripping with I-don't-have-time-for-this. I narrow my eyes at her and clench my jaw. Heat rises from my neck to my cheeks. I can't help it—I reach into my back pocket for my wallet. The contents within it are everything I need to prove who I am, how I'm better than she is, and how she needs to grovel for forgiveness for not bending over backward to accommodate me.

"Hello, my name is Yoo-Jin Lee and we're here with Haneul Corporation." Jessica steps in front of me and reaches her hand out to address the rude-as-fuck woman. There's that tone and that chin raise again.

She leans back slightly to just cross over into my space, a warning for me to back off.

Fine. Go for it. Have fun.

I take a step away but keep my eyes lasered on the woman as I look over Jessica's head.

"Do you have an appointment?" she asks Jessica.

"We don't, but we'd like to speak to the person overseeing event space rental here. We have a very large-scale event that we'd like to discuss hosting at the library. It's the perfect venue you see..."

"You can make an appointment through our contact form on our website." She looks back at her computer as if she has no time or patience left for us. "We're booked solid for the remainder of the summer..."

That's it. I shift closer, trying to face the woman at the desk and protect Jessica from her rudeness. But Jessica's faster than I am, blocking me and lifting her chin even higher toward the raised desk.

"So what you're saying is that you're the person I should be speaking to? Or are you prescreening me in some discriminatory way? Because I do believe I asked if there was someone I could speak to about hosting an event here and I don't appreciate being dismissed."

It's no longer a fake voice. It's no longer a practiced polite-but-firm voice. It's a pissed-off voice. I sneak a peek at Jessica's face and it has take-no-prisoners written all over it. If we weren't locked in a battle to be taken seriously right now, I'd pull my phone out and snap a picture. Show her she doesn't have to fake it—she's had it in her all along.

"What I am saying is, you can make an inquiry through our contact form on the website and someone will get back to you, though we're booked through the summer."

Jessica's shoulders drop, defeated. The fire in her eyes extinguished. She went to war with a seasoned librarian and lost. She turns around and walks toward the exit.

That's it? That's all the fight she's got?

I take one last look at the lady at the desk who has already forgotten about us, chatting away on her phone. I grab a business card from the holder and follow Jessica out the door.

I was kinda hoping it would be easier than this. But if this morning's to-do list is any indication, nothing is easy. Every single thing takes ten phone calls, followed up by two emails, cc'ing twenty other people. It's days like today that I actually really respect my sister and my dad and the successes they've had in business. Though I doubt my dad has written his own emails even once in his life.

"Hey, give me a sec. I need to make a quick phone call," I say. Jessica nods absently, her gaze locked out into the street, not saying a word, disappointment painted on her face.

I take out my phone and call the number on the card. I get the voice mail of Rebecca Jenkins, the Event Manager for the New York Public Library. Her voice is professional, stoic, no-nonsense. It's not accommodating like the staff who work for me. It's not ass-kissing like the people who want something from me because of my family name and position. It's not judgmental like my father's.

Yet, what good is it being the son of Lee Jung-Hyun and the future leader of Haneul Corp if I can't use it when I need to? I may be playing someone else this summer, but no one has to know.

It's a small act, a phone call, a name drop, to make something okay for Jessica. To get her foot in the door, she needs connections. She's said it herself. And this is the only thing I know how to do—throw my name and my money around to get what I want.

So in that split second from when the beep of the voice mail sounds and I open my mouth to leave a message, I make a decision. I picture my dad's face and channel his air of authority.

"Hello, Ms. Jenkins, this is Elijah Lee, Chief of Staff at Haneul Corporation. I'm calling on behalf of the CEO, Mr. Lee. We'd like to rent out the library for an event we're hosting. Cost is not an issue, and to be clear, we can't take no as an answer. Please call me back at this number as soon as possible."

I hang up and swallow back my doubt. It's one voice mail. And though my entire body tingles as if the skin it's in doesn't fit quite right, I'll live with it. I made a decision. One that I hope will help Jessica and the hackathon.

One that I had no idea might come back to bite us all in the ass later.

I pocket my phone and walk up to Jessica, nudging her gently with my shoulder. "Hey, don't worry. It's gonna all work out. I'm sure of it." I'll *make* sure of it.

She doesn't look at me, she doesn't respond right away. But then, as if shaking it off to fight another day, she nods her head a few times and turns to me. "You're right. We'll figure something out. And if not here at the library, we'll come up with someplace else to hold the hackathon. No big deal."

But I see it in her eyes, the frustration, the disappointment.

My hands itch to reach out to her, to pull her close, to stare into those eyes and tell her I'm going to get us this venue no matter what. But if I tell her what I've done, what I'm willing to do, she'd never agree. She got mad when I spent pocket change for us to skip the line at Top of the Rock. Imagine how pissed she'd be if she found out I'm throwing serious money at this problem?

"Hey, wanna get a hot dog from a street vendor for lunch?" I ask. Anything to get her mind off what happened inside the library today. And to get my mind off of the call I just made. "I'm craving more of that sauerkraut."

The corner of her downturned mouth lifts a bit and I consider it a win. "Yeah. A hot dog sounds perfect. I've been wanting to try one ever since you raved about it the first time." She turns to lead the way to the closest vendor on the corner.

And without hesitation, I follow.

chapter thirteen

---

jessica

"I can't believe you're here," I squeal as I wrap my arms around my emotional support person.

"I told you, you didn't have to come all the way out to the airport to pick me up," Ella says. Originally, we'd talked about Ella maybe visiting at the end of the summer, once my internship is over, so we could spend a week together in the city before heading back to California. But some drama at home had Ella begging her grandma to let her come out for an impromptu weekend trip—though she's been pretty tight-lipped about what happened. So I fully intend to 1) absorb as much of her best friend energy as possible and 2) get to the bottom of what's going on with her and give her some of my BFF-love right back.

"Like I'd let you try to navigate the trains on your own. You barely remember where you park your car at the mall,"

I tease. "The driver will be here in a second. He went to get the car."

"Ohhh, fancy, a driver," she singsongs.

I roll my eyes at her. "One of the perks of the job, I guess."

"And this new fit is another perk I am *so* feeling on you. Let me see the whole thing." She pushes me to arm's length, gesturing for me to spin in a circle so she can take me in top to bottom, nodding and humming in appreciation. "Very nice. Is this Chanel?"

I shrug. "I have no idea. Is that what the tag says?" I pull at my collar, contorting myself to try and read it.

She swats my hand away. "That is not how you treat Chanel, Jessica."

Ella and I met as kids when we were in church youth group together. Just before we started high school, Ella's parents moved back to Korea, but luckily, she was able to stay with her grandmother in California to finish off her schooling.

Her family is not Elijah-level rich, but well-off enough that Ella was able to fly out to New York on a moment's notice. And though she doesn't have a closet full of designer clothing, she's clearly familiar enough with my outfit to clock the brand.

Our black Escalade pulls up and the two of us pile into the back seat.

"So, are you going to tell me what's going on? Why did you need to suddenly escape to New York?" I ask.

"What? I can't just come out to visit you? I'm not waiting till the end of summer to see that brownstone with my own eyes. Anything could go wrong before then."

"Uh, thanks for the vote of confidence," I say. "But you're avoiding the question. What's going on?"

She sighs. "Okay, CliffsNotes version is I found out Scott was cheating on me. And nope," she says, pointing at my open mouth, ready to speak, "I will not be taking questions or accepting any sympathies. I was going to break up with him eventually anyways. He was only ever gonna be a summer fling. You know I like clean lines... I have to end something before starting something new. So this would have been over before I started USC in the fall anyways."

I reach over and squeeze her hand. She squeezes back. She's putting on a brave front. Whether she was going to end it or not, the situation hurt enough for her to have to escape to New York. And selfishly, I'm glad she's here.

"Well, I'm happy to be your distraction for the weekend. Anything in particular you were hoping to do while in the city? One World Trade? Brooklyn Bridge?" I ask.

"I've only got one thing on my 'must do' list," she says.

"Yeah? What is it?"

A very large smile with just a hint of wickedness spreads across her face.

Oh no.

"Meet Elijah Ri," she says slowly.

That's exactly what I was afraid of. She's taking way too much pleasure in whatever romance she's concocted in her head.

"Well, uh, your wish is my command, I guess. I've invited the interns to meet us for a water taxi ride to the Statue of Liberty. A lot of us had been talking about it and haven't had the chance to go yet. It's gonna be our first stop today."

"Sweet. I'm excited to meet him."

"*Them*, Ella. There is going to be more than one person there," I say in a slight panic.

That hint of wickedness becomes a full-blown face of mischief.

"Please please please please please don't embarrass me. Reminder, you're my best friend. You're supposed to be on my side," I plead.

"Oh, don't worry. I'm one hundred percent on your side. Which means I only want what's best for you. And I, for the life of me, can't fathom why a very rich, very cute Korean boy isn't exactly that."

"I never said he was cute," I mumble.

"I've seen your face when you talk about him. You didn't have to," she says.

"It doesn't matter. Elijah and I are in a business relationship. A partnership. We need each other this summer." *Meaning, don't make this complicated, Jessica.*

"Uh-huh," Ella draws out. "Look, you've got nothing to worry about. I'll play it cool."

Ella hasn't played anything cool a day in her life. It's why I love her. She's so much more outgoing and effusive and forward than I am.

Yeah, right, I've got nothing to worry about, nothing at all.

We arrive near the very bottom of Manhattan by Battery Park and pull up to the curb where a long line has already formed to board the next water taxi. I see Jason first, his tall head standing out above the rest. Elijah is next to him, along with Roy and Soobin. I'm relieved that some of them could actually make it on such short notice.

Jason waves the moment he sees us. I wave back, but my eyes slide immediately to Elijah. He gives a small side smile and lifts his hand slightly before dropping it.

"Hey everyone, this is my best friend, Ella, who's visiting for the weekend."

Ella goes around the circle shaking hands and introducing herself to everyone. Jason, Roy, Soobin, and finally...

"And you must be Elijah Ri," she says. She goes in for the hug, wrapping her arms around him like he's her long-lost brother. Elijah stiffens and awkwardly pats her back.

So much for playing it cool.

Kill me now.

"Jessica has told me a lot about you—" I clear my throat loudly. "...you know, since you both work on Team Logistics," she says. Terrible save.

"Uh, yeah, that's me. Mr. Logistics," he says.

If I wasn't so mortified, I'd probably laugh at how off guard Ella has made the usually very cool Elijah.

"I already ordered our tickets online, so we don't have to wait in this line. Let's go board the boat," I say, eager to escape this torture.

"I didn't bring cash, so can I Venmo you?" Soobin asks.

"Oh, don't worry. Today's ride is on me," I say.

Everyone tries to decline the offer, but I don't let them.

Ella raises an eyebrow at me in question. I pretend not to see it. I understand her confusion. I'm normally incredibly frugal. But I haven't had to use any of my savings since coming to New York, everything's provided for me. It's the least I can do. It's just not something I want to talk about right here.

As my mom always says, we never discuss religion, politics, or finances in public.

"Well, thanks for the ticket, Jessica. I'm excited," Roy says. "I wonder what it'll be like up close since the Statue seems so small from here."

"I know, right? Honestly, it's the coolest thing. It looks tiny up until the very last minute when you get really close, and then you're *right there* and you look up and the majesty of it all just hits you." Jason's eyes light up, matching the wonder in his voice. "When we came last year, I don't think I was ready for it. No matter how fucked-up it is sometimes living in the States these days, seeing the Statue of Liberty and all it represents, and the hardships our families went through to secure the right to live here, it's awe-inspiring."

We nod in silence, lost in thought.

I turn to Ella but her eyes are narrowed, focused on something. I follow her gaze and see her cock her head at Jason, trying to figure him out. He's not Ella's type—she usually likes a bad boy. The kind of boy who ends up cheating on her, I guess. This could get very interesting.

We all find a spot along the boat's railing. I go to stand next to Elijah.

"Are you excited?" I ask.

He shrugs a shoulder. "I never really thought about it, ya know? In Korea, this statue isn't significant to us. We're not taught about it in school. It's not a symbol of anything. So seeing you so pumped about it is a trip," he says.

"Huh. I guess I never considered how foreign it must be for you here in America," I say.

"It's not that different to be honest. You grew up with

some influence from Korean culture, I'm sure. But there are some things that catch me off guard. Like whenever anyone talks about 'being Korean' specifically, I don't know exactly what they mean. That's just something we *are* back in Korea. I don't know if that makes any sense." He shakes his head as if apologizing for what he's said.

"No, no, I totally understand. 'Being Korean' as you put it, here in the States, is something we have to think about constantly because it's what makes us different, I guess. But I can imagine it's nothing like that when you're like actually *in* Korea," I say. "I haven't been to Korea since I was a kid. But I remember the culture shock, even in just the little things. It surprised me at first. I just figured we were all the same."

"Oh the motherland is way more traditional," Soobin says, joining us.

"Totally. And stuff like respecting your elders and formal speech are a must," Jason adds. "I'm into that, though. I wish we applied that more broadly here in the US."

"Is it true that arranged marriages are still a thing in Korea?" Roy asks.

"It's Korea, not the Joseon Dynasty," Ella teases.

"Actually, as shocking as it may seem, they do still happen," Elijah says. "I know a lot of people who have been formally set up by their parents." He puts both hands into his pockets, clearly uncomfortable with this topic. "And you're right, Jason. Defying or disobeying someone older than you is not allowed. Complete strangers will berate you for your behavior on the street if you're not showing respect. And that's still nothing compared to what's expected of young people from their own family." He turns his head away from us, looking out over the water.

I think of how Elijah's described his father, how the plan for his life and future seem non-negotiable. I guess I've been surprised that he won't just tell his dad how he feels. But it makes sense now, why he doesn't. Why he feels like he can't.

It doesn't seem fair. I mean, my dad isn't always the easiest to talk to about things. But I know that if I need to say something important, he'll listen and at least *try* to understand where I'm coming from.

I rest my elbows on the railing and nudge Elijah a little with my hip. "Well, if nothing else, it's a great day for a boat ride," I say.

"Welcome home, Yoo-Jin-ssi." Mrs. Choi greets us at the door taking our coats.

We're back at the brownstone, ready for pajamas, food, and a girls' night in.

Turns out that it really was a great day for a boat ride. Everyone had an amazing time and Ella hit it off with my friends. Friends. I'm not sure when I stopped seeing them as coworkers and started seeing them as more. But here we are.

"Ella-ssi, I took the liberty of unpacking your bag in the first guest room. The towel warmers have also been turned on should you want a shower." Mrs. Choi turns back to face me. I try to ignore a surprised Ella, eyes wide, mouthing, "Are you kidding me?" behind her.

"Would you like me to serve your meals in the formal dining room, the breakfast room, or on trays in your respective bedrooms?" Mrs. Choi asks.

"We'll take them in the breakfast room, please," I say. She nods and shuffles away to the kitchen to get everything prepared.

"The breakfast room? You have a separate room. For breakfast." Ella nods her head, impressed.

"It's not really just for eating breakfast," I say. But it does have some more privacy. Knowing the interrogation I'm about to get about Elijah, I'd like to be as far away from earshot of Mrs. Choi as possible.

"I'm tripping that you have servants," Ella says, eyes following Mrs. Choi as she leaves to set up the table in the breakfast room.

"Just the one. But I don't really consider Mrs. Choi a servant."

"She's paid. To serve you."

"Okay, Ella, I get it. This lifestyle is very different from back in California. You don't have to drive home the obvious." A tiny bit of guilt creeps up threatening to lodge itself in my throat. Maybe I shouldn't be enjoying all of this as much as I have been. Especially not while Elijah, and all the other interns for that matter, are crammed into a tiny apartment.

She raises her hands. "Hey hey, I'm not judging. I'm all for you having your fairy tale summer. You deserve this."

"All I wanted was a shot to do something great. The rest of this is just gravy offered to me by a generous soul," I say.

"I like him," Ella says.

I know who she's talking about so I quickly try and redirect.

"Yeah, I can tell," I tease. "And it was obvious Jason was pretty into you, too. Your duet was iconic." I'd found Ella and Jason deep in conversation a few times throughout the day, both on the boat and afterwards when we all went to get cannolis in Little Italy. They even sang "Spring Day" together when we ended the night at karaoke. Not only did they both know the vocal line lyrics, but they also knew all the rap parts. They're a match made in BTS ARMY heaven.

Her cheeks pinken.

"I meant Elijah," she says, but she doesn't deny the connection I spotted between her and Jason. "Not much of a talker, but I'm into the air of mystery. Plus, he couldn't take his eyes off you."

"What are you talking about?" Ella's not the only one blushing now.

"Come on, Jess. You can't fool me. I'm your bestie, remember? He likes you. You like him. It's cute. And he fits in this whole fairy tale aesthetic. I Googled him, by the way, and he is most definitely loaded."

"You did not," I say, shaking my head at her brazenness. I'm way too afraid of having my search history tracked.

I let out a deep sigh, and with it all the confusing feelings I thought I was keeping hidden from everyone, including myself. "I won't deny it. I do like him. But I'm not going there. I can't. We're way too different. Plus, I really have to stay focused. There's a lot of work to do, and if all goes the way I've planned, it could change everything for me. I'm not willing to take the risk of getting distracted just because a guy's nice to me and makes me laugh."

"And is hot…" Ella adds.

"Okay, yes, he's hot," I admit.

"And has that quiet-confidence-but-with-a-heart-of-gold thing going on..." she continues.

"Yeah, and there's that," I agree.

"And can pull off a pair of jeans like it's nobody's business..."

"Alright, alright, I get it," I laugh.

Mrs. Choi enters with a large tray, setting two bowls of bibimbap down on the table, along with a bunch of other smaller bowls filled with various banchan. Ella and I take our seats and dig in.

It's quiet while we eat, which isn't really like Ella. She likes to fill any empty space up with her words.

"Everything okay?" I ask.

She nods, putting her spoon down and slowly looks up at me.

"I meant it when I said you deserve all this, Jess. But be careful, okay? Like, get in and get out. Do your thing this summer, make an impression, and earn those connections. But don't become too caught up in it all," Ella says.

"What do you mean?"

"I mean, remember who you are and where you come from. It's easy, I'm sure, to be swept up into a life of personal drivers, Chanel, a housekeeper-slash-chef. This brownstone." She waves her arms in the air as if to encompass it all.

"I'm well aware I'm on borrowed time," I say. It comes out sounding more defensive than I meant it to. But does Ella truly believe I'm kidding myself? I know none of this is mine.

But does it mean I can't enjoy it while I have it?

"I'm not trying to be harsh. I'm not. I'm all for this switch you and Elijah agreed to. You needed this shot. And honestly, he definitely seems like someone who could use a break. I've just seen too many of these Cinderella movies to know that if you get swept away by it, the clock is gonna strike midnight before you're ready and all you're left with is a pumpkin and some rats."

"That won't happen to me. When it's time for this to end, I'll be ready to give it all up. For sure," I say. I have to be. Because at the end of the day, what choice do I have?

chapter fourteen

---

elijah

"Two minutes," someone says to me, knocking on the bathroom door.

There are ten of us in this apartment with one full bathroom. To avoid any confusion or fighting, we have a strict schedule. In the mornings, we each are allotted twelve minutes to do what we need to do before we have to head to the office.

I have three bathrooms to myself in my part of the house in Korea. Until this summer, I don't think I've ever rushed to get ready or timed my showers in my life. But here, it's all about prioritization.

I look at myself in the mirror, check my jawline and cheeks. I can probably skip shaving for the next couple days. That'll buy me some time to actually do something with the overgrown mess on the top of my head. I put on deodorant, rub some gel in my hands and run my fingers through my wet hair. That will have to do. I take one last look, grab my dopp kit, and open the door.

Jason is waiting outside for his turn. He's whistling some song that he sang at karaoke last night, a ballad from a K-drama OST.

"Someone's in a good mood," I say.

"I had fun yesterday. I definitely want to try and hang out with her again. You need to make your way to California sometime soon. Maybe we can all go on a double date since the rest of us live there."

The suggestion catches me off guard. A double date? And who, exactly, does he have matched up in his head? Surely, Jason means he'd be with Ella and I'd be with Jessica. Right? Because if not, I might have to push him off the top bunk while he's sleeping. He'd probably only break a rib or an arm or something.

I need to chill.

Maybe I was a fool thinking I could do this, spend this much time with Jessica, without falling for her. But it's impossible to not be attracted to someone so smart, and driven, and freaking adorable. I want to be around her all the time.

I'm so screwed.

"Dude, outta the way. I only have eleven minutes now," Jason says, pushing past me into the bathroom. "Oh and I used the last of your milk in the fridge. Mine was expired."

So much for having cereal before work.

I drop my stuff on my bunk bed and grab my phone.

Me: Do you have any of those cereal bars left at your place?

I wait for Jessica to get my plea for some morning sugary carbs, and luckily she texts right back.

Jessica: Yup. Will 3 be enough? :)

Me: Perfect. And thanks.

Jessica: See you soon

It's all so easy. So domestic, even. I don't have to put my walls up or worry what someone will want from me in return when they offer me something. We've already laid all of that in the open right from the start when we made this arrangement. Maybe that's why everything feels safe with Jessica. I wipe the smile off my face before someone catches me.

Yeah, I gotta avoid any more talking or even thinking about dates. Not gonna happen.

And yet, on the subway ride heading to work, I find myself looking up places we could go and things we could do to show Jessica more of the city.

We all get to the office just before nine and head straight to our hackathon war room. There, on the table where I usually sit, three cereal bars wait for me. Of course Jessica got here early enough to drop these off for me.

I peel off the sticky note attached to one of them.

Elijah, per your request. :)

It's one stupid line, no hidden meaning behind them. But my stomach decides that it's flutter-worthy. My stomach is an asshole.

I take my wallet out of my back pocket and carefully fold the post-it in half and put it away. What I'm saving it for, I have no idea.

I shake my head and smile to myself as I sit, opening my laptop and ripping the wrapper off my breakfast.

Time flies as we all focus on the tasks assigned to us today. I look up at the clock and am shocked to see it's already five o'clock. Jessica has us working harder than I've honestly ever worked in my life.

And I'm having the best time. Go figure.

I'm not saying I'm giving up on a life of comfort and support at my fingertips. But there's something to be said for the accomplishment you feel at the end of the day when you've worked your ass off and gotten shit done.

The thought crosses my mind that maybe, just maybe, my dad would be proud of me for what I've done this summer. But then I remember that for one, my dad isn't impressed with hard work. He's more of a get-the-most-credit-with-the-least-effort type of man. And two, well, he's never been proud of me a day in my life. It does me no good hoping for any kind of validation from him.

Jessica stands and walks over to the whiteboard where we have all the plans for the hackathon event drawn out. She must look at that whiteboard a couple hundred times a day. "Hack It Until You Crack It" is written across the top. At first, I thought the name of the event we came up with was cheesy. But it's growing on me.

I honestly don't care about what this will do for Haneul. What matters to me is that this is something that this group of freaking geniuses wouldn't ever get the opportunity to participate in otherwise.

"It looks good," I tell her, joining Jessica at the board.

"It does. It's a solid plan," Jason adds.

I catch a glimpse of the three of us standing shoulder to shoulder reviewing the details. Does he have to be so tall? I feel like the kid brother whenever I'm next to him. It makes me want to cower and hide. Why I'm always looking for ways to remind myself how I fall short among this group, literally and figuratively, I'm not sure. I've never had a confidence problem before. Or maybe it's actually arrogance that I've never lacked. Belief in myself? Totally different issue.

I feel like Jessica would tell me it's just because I haven't found anything to be passionate about, or something like that. Maybe she's right.

"I presented to management today and they're on board. So that's a win," Jessica says. "Even though no one was really paying attention. I should have had one of you guys do it. I bet they'd be way more interested in what we're working on."

It's not the first time I've noticed Jessica make a side comment that seems an awful lot like throwing her hands up in surrender in the face of misogyny. This is a Korean company, and it's old-school in a lot of the ways. She's a girl and she's young. Two strikes against her. I've already seen how they've treated my sister in situations where she was clearly in the right or knew more about what was going on.

"But if we can just bring it all together, execute like we've planned, this hackathon will be a success for a lot of people," Jessica says.

"We'll make it happen," I say, more to myself than to anyone else.

"Fuck yeah, we will," Jason says.

Jessica nods at Jason and then turns to me with a small smile. She looks over her shoulder at the group of interns hard at work around the conference table.

"Thank you all for staying a little late. Dinner's on me," Jessica announces. "Well, it's on the company." She returns to her seat in front of her open laptop.

Jessica was afraid of making any decisions just a couple weeks ago. But now she's got us all organized and working pretty seamlessly, and she's taking care of us too. From what I know of her dad, he definitely *would* be proud of her.

I try to imagine what it would be like if Jessica and I were in the roles intended for us. I'd likely be hiding in my office and bossing Sunny Cho around to do all my work for me. But with Jessica as the executive intern, Sunny gets to go home to her boyfriend and cat at a decent hour because Jessica is on top of her shit. And Jessica maybe wouldn't have found this new confidence that suits her so well if she wasn't given this chance.

"Thanks, Jessica. How does everyone feel about Thai food?" Jason asks. He moves over toward Jessica, leaning over her shoulder to look at her laptop screen with the Grubhub home page pulled up.

All my hackles raise in alert. *Too close, too fucking close.*

I'm just being protective because I forced her into this role and fed her to the Haneul wolves. If Operation Name Drop goes to shit, she probably would have it worse off than

I would. I'd just have to deal with my dad. Still, he'd protect my, our, reputations at all costs. But I'm the only one who can protect Jessica…

Yeah, I'm like a bodyguard, that's why I'm acting like a caveman. Sure.

Except, my body remembers exactly what it feels like to be as close to Jessica as Jason currently is. It's like she's a magnet I'm drawn to, and any time she's in the same vicinity, my body decides the space between us ceases to exist. I think about how I held her waist ever-so-lightly at Top of the Rock. Or when we leaned into each other in the water taxi to the Statue of Liberty. I'd do anything to be the one that close to her now. But short of pushing Jason out of the way, that's not going to happen here.

"Elijah?" Jessica is calling my name, knocking me out of my thoughts. "Does Thai food sound okay with you?"

"Yeah, I'm good with whatever," I say.

"I'll take care of ordering," Jason offers, reaching his hand around her body to grab the laptop.

Heat crawls up my back. *Jeongsin charyeo*, I say to myself. I need to get my shit together. Enough with the jealous green beast making things out to be something they're not. All of these feelings are screwing with my head. I need some air.

I quickly turn, grab my backpack, and head for the door. I just need to get out of here for a little bit. I could really use some space right about now. I'm still not used to this lifestyle, after growing up isolated with every move planned for me and every want provided. It's a tough habit to break. But the most telling thing has been realizing that I truly am an introvert and actually need some alone time to process things, which has proven impossible living and working with nine other people.

I make it to the elevator before I hear someone call my name.

"Elijah?"

I beg for the doors to open but the counter indicates it's still twenty floors away.

I take a breath and then turn around to face her. I don't know why I'm suddenly acting this way. I need to get my shit in check.

"We were gonna hit up the Fabric District and pick up what we need to cover the booths and the participant tables," she says. "Remember they said stock is a lot better before the weekend."

"I can just go alone," I offer. "You should stay here in case anyone has any questions or something. I'm sure Jason would appreciate you sticking around." God, I can hear the jealous whine in my own voice and I hate the sound of it.

She purses her lips together, swallowing slowly and then nodding as if she can tell I'm trying to escape, that I need to get away. She drops her eyes and avoids looking at me.

Shit.

"Oh, um, okay then. Actually, why don't you go on and take care of whatever you were about to do. I can get it on my own. You don't have to hang around here if you have somewhere else to be," she says. She's lost all the confidence I'm used to hearing in her voice.

I am a dick.

The elevator dings but I follow Jessica where she's heading back to the war room. "Wait," I call out, reaching to take hold of her arm.

"There's no way I'm letting you go into Midtown on your own," is what comes out of my mouth. I might as well have pounded my chest and grunted a few times. The murderous glint in Jessica's eyes makes it seem like I have.

"I'm perfectly capable…" she starts.

"I just meant that you're right. It's a good idea if we went together since there's probably a lot to carry," I clarify.

She narrows her eyes at me, confirming that I'm not actually questioning her capability to traverse the city alone. I wonder if it's written all over my face that the real reason is that I'd do anything to spend more time with her, just the two of us.

"Fine. Meet me in the lobby at seven o'clock. I think the stores close by nine," she suggests.

"Yeah, sounds good."

"You're, um, not staying for dinner?" she asks.

Just then the elevator dings again and the doors open. A startled Grubhub delivery guy steps out. "Order for Jessica Lee?" he asks, first looking to me and then to Jessica.

"That's me. Thank you," she says. She reaches for the heavy-looking bag with all our dinners. But I grab it, and the second bag as well, from the delivery guy.

"I can take them if you have somewhere to be," she says.

"Nope, I got 'em," I say. "And I have nowhere else to be." And I mean it.

"But we called ahead and put all those yards of remnant fabric on hold. You can't sell them to someone else." The panic in Jessica's voice rises with her every word.

The fabric store is packed. Which is odd since there are like a hundred of similar looking stores lining the streets of this neighborhood. Who are all these people needing so much fabric this time of night?

A part of me just wants to step in and say we'll pay double what anyone else offered. I'm pretty sure this cashier wouldn't say no to that.

I see Jessica pull her shoulders back and stick her chin out. Here we go again. Her battle stance.

"I'd like to speak to your manager," she says.

"I am the manager."

"Great, well, then you must be aware that this is your mistake, not ours. I'd like to suggest you find us fifty yards of a replacement fabric, same color, of the same or higher weight, but at the amount quoted to us. And please make sure to include two copies of the receipt, one in the bag and I'll take the other copy."

The manager just stares at her.

"Why don't you go in the back and find some comparable fabric," I say to the manager as I pull out my wallet with its not-so-subtle Gucci emblem on the front. Money talks.

"Elijah, no..." Jessica reaches out trying to take my wallet out of my hand. "Can I speak to you over here please?" Jessica hisses and she grabs my arm, pulling me to a corner next to a ream of shockingly bright neon-pink leopard print velvet. "We're on a budget," she says, emphasizing each word.

"Fine, we're on a budget. But we also need fabric. So, how about we just, ya know, expand that budget a few hundred dollars? What's the big deal?"

"The big deal is that's not how this works," she says.

"Fuck, it's like what, the cost of one dinner at Nobu?"

Her eyes grow huge as she leans in and whispers, "A dinner at Nobu is a few hundred dollars?"

Cute. Again. Per usual, actually.

I meet her lean and raise her a whisper directly in her ear. She smells different than she did when I first met her at the airport. It's all those expensive bath products. I preferred her no-frills scent from before—simple and clean but so intoxicating. "No, come to think of it, that wouldn't even cover the first course," I tease.

I don't miss her full body shiver. She closes her eyes for a second, and when she pulls back and opens them again, I swear fire shoots straight at me. "Elijah, wake up. This is the real world. It's not your ivory castle. You can't just ignore cost and budget and money here."

Not gonna lie, that ivory castle comment stings a little. "I'm not so removed from the world that I'm naive to how it works. In fact, I may look at money differently, but I'd bet I'm more in tune with what makes the world go 'round than you are. I've traveled. I've seen it firsthand. From what I recall, you've barely ever left Southern California."

Her nostrils flare and I think for a second that I've crossed the line. It's not the first time she's been so caught up about finances. It's why I can't—I won't—tell her my secret...that I put a ten-thousand-dollar payment on my personal credit card to secure the library for the hackathon. I'll deal with that fallout later, after the event is over.

It's all just more reason why nothing could ever happen

between the two of us. She's infuriatingly uptight about money and it drives me nuts. Our worlds are just too different, farther apart than even the six thousand miles between Seoul and Southern California.

When she finally speaks, her words are like ice. "I may not have been given the privilege to travel the world, I may not be able to just carelessly spend hundreds of dollars on a meal. I have to earn what I get, and that doesn't make me any lesser than you. I have been working my butt off planning this hackathon, which includes sticking to the budget, because this job means something to me. How are you going to run this company one day if you don't understand the importance of balance sheets? This isn't some game for you to play—people's livelihoods are at stake."

She might as well have slapped me in the face. Does she really think that I believe I'm better than her because of the family I was born into? How do I explain that throwing money at a problem is all I know how to do? How do I explain that I'm in awe of her work ethic, of her relentlessness to make her vision for this event a reality?

I don't say anything. I just close my eyes and roll my head back, wishing I was anywhere but here. Wishing I was as far away from Haneul as possible. And here I was thinking I was actually enjoying working this summer.

When I open my eyes, Jessica has already returned to the register, negotiating the price and reducing the number of yards of fabric to remain in budget. And my envy of her capability curdles in my stomach. I accused her of not knowing how the world works, but really it's me who's too much of a pathetic, privileged asshole to accomplish the simplest of tasks.

I keep my distance until Jessica wraps up the sale. Then I grab the two bags of fabric she's secured, and without a word, the two of us leave the store.

chapter fifteen

—

elijah

It's eight o'clock by the time we're done at the fabric store and the other face of New York takes over. People gathered outside the hottest new restaurants waiting for a table for dinner. Couples walking hand in hand in extravagant outfits that seem to clash with the dirty city streets. The sounds and the energy are different in this city at night.

But in this taxi, it's dead silent. Jessica hasn't said a word.

My phone rings and I look down at the screen.

"Shit," I mutter.

Jessica turns to me as I press "reject."

I meet her eyes. "My dad. He's been trying to set up a check-in with me via his assistant. But I've ignored all the requests. I guess he's not too happy about that. He never calls me directly."

"Is everything okay?" she asks.

"Yes? No? Who knows? Don't worry, I'm sure it's not about work," I say. He could be calling about the charge on the credit card, but I don't think he'd notice it or care really. In his mental calculator, ten grand is chump change.

"I'm not worried about work. I'm worried about you," Jessica says.

It takes me a second to catch my breath. Every time she says something like this, it feels like a punch to the gut. And I'm starting to like that apparently.

"Thanks, but you don't have to. I'm good."

"Look, first, well, I'm sorry about the argument we had in the fabric store. I said some things out of frustration."

Her words loosen something in my chest—guilt, I think. "You don't have to apologize. I was the one being a total dick. I don't want to undermine your leadership. And I definitely don't think I'm better than you—it's the opposite, really."

"Thanks for that. It's hard not to fall in society's trap of thinking money equals value...people with more money thus have more value. Maybe I was projecting my own insecurities. I know I've been super aggro about the budget. I've always been this way. It's how I was raised. My dad is a stickler down to every penny."

"Sounds exactly like the type of person a company would want in a Finance role then," I say.

She shrugs a shoulder and turns to look out the window. "If you don't have plans tonight, maybe we can hang out and do a deep dive into everything we've been working on? I feel like I need the emotional support for next time my dad grills me about work. And maybe you'd be more prepared to answer next time your dad calls."

"I don't plan on answering the phone," I say with a chuckle. I don't find any of it amusing though. "But you're right, we really should get caught up to keep our dads believing everything."

She nods but still doesn't turn around to look at me.

"Jessica?" I say softly. What I don't say is: *Turn around. Let me see your expression when I ask you this. Let me make sure you want to be with me as much as I do with you. Let me know that everything else is just our excuse.*

She turns her face slowly away from the window and toward me. Her eyes are so soft, I have to ball my hands into fists to keep from touching her cheek and making a move.

It's been silent for too long. Any second, it's gonna be uncomfortable.

"Do you wanna walk around Central Park and talk?" I finally ask.

"Won't we get murdered?" she responds immediately.

Our taxi driver laughs and my cheeks heat at the thought of him hearing our entire conversation. He says, "Look, if you want, I could drop you kids off at Little Island over on the water. I hear it's pretty romantic this time of night and you're less likely to get murdered there." The rasp in his voice, paired with the smell in his cab, betrays years of a smoking habit he could never quite kick.

"Oh, no, sir, you've got this all wrong," Jessica tries to explain.

"Yeah, uh, we just work together," I add.

"Uh-huh," he draws out, not fooled one bit. "So, then, where am I taking you?"

"Fifty-fifth and Seventh Avenue," I tell him.

Jessica's shoulders drop when she hears the address of the office. She may not want to go to Central Park at night, but I think she still wants to spend time with me. Luckily, I have another idea.

"Let's drop these bags off at the office and then, if you don't mind, there's somewhere else I wanna take you. We can talk there," I say.

She raises her eyebrows in question, but I just smile back at her. "Sure, I don't mind at all," she says.

I crack the window of the taxi open just a little bit to let some of the cool night air in. And though we're quiet the rest of the ride back to the office, the sounds of the city act as the soundtrack to our anticipation of what's to come.

"I love it here, I don't ever want to leave," Jessica says.

"I think the trains eventually do stop running for the night and this place closes." Jessica and I sit on the stairs flanking the Main Concourse of Grand Central Station. It's bustling with commuters trying to get home from a long day at work or those coming into the city for a night on the town. I originally planned to come here because my mom raves about some oyster restaurant. But now that we're here, I'd rather just sit and people watch.

"I just wanna put down a blanket and lie here staring up at this gorgeous ceiling for hours." Jessica lets out a deep sigh of appreciation.

"I know. And it's wild that all these people have somewhere to go, somewhere to be. It blows my mind," I say.

"Is the train station in Seoul like this?" she asks.

"I don't know. I've never taken the train," I admit. "I have a driver who takes me everywhere. I jokingly refer to him as my best friend. Wow, that sounds more pathetic than I meant for it to."

She laughs, erasing my momentary embarrassment. "I totally get it. I'm beginning to think of Mrs. Choi as my summer BFF. I thought I'd love the lavish life and all the space to myself. But it's kinda secluded too."

"Welcome to my world," I say.

"Is your world..." she hesitates, "always this lonely? Because I kinda feel lonely. As much as I complain about living with my parents and not having enough space, I guess I don't love being alone as much as I thought I might."

"To be honest, I don't think I ever allowed myself to think of it as being lonely. Because that would suck. And there's not a lot I can do about it. But I have to admit that being around other people and making friends this summer has been pretty awesome. I just can't help but think that they're all...temporary? It's not like any of them are gonna want to be my friends once they find out who I really am. And honestly, would I even be able to be theirs? When I'm back to being myself, I don't think there's a way for me to keep anything about this summer other than memories."

She's quiet. Is she thinking what I'm thinking—that I wasn't just talking about the other interns?

I've made it awkward.

"Wanna take a train and just...go somewhere? Like, hop on the next one that's leaving, and see where it takes us?" Jessica's voice is high-pitched, animated, excited at the thought of a destination-less journey. It's a side of herself I don't think she lets people see, spontaneous, adventurous. I consider my-self lucky.

I look at the train schedules posted over the ticket windows. "It's late. I don't think we'd be able to catch a train back home if we leave now," I say. I hate being the voice of reason. It's rare for me. But there's no way I'm putting Jessica in a dangerous situation. And getting stuck at some out-there train station without a ride back into the city seems pretty sketchy.

"Then come over tonight," she suggests. "I'll make us peanut butter and jelly sandwiches and we'll watch a movie and we'll share stories to tell our dads and we won't think about all the work we have to do, all the things waiting for us after the summer, all the things we hate thinking about."

I can't possibly say no.

"Sounds like a plan," I say.

But neither of us moves to leave. We remain seated, shoulder to shoulder. And like I always want to do whenever she's near enough, I lean into her, nudging her, a wordless gesture to let her know I'm enjoying just being with her here.

She nudges me back.

Our bodies are touching now from our shoulders to our thighs to our feet. If I tilt my head just a little bit, we could be connected there as well. I lick my lips, wondering if I'm brave enough to make that move.

"Elijah?" Jessica's voice is just barely louder than a whisper. But we're so close, I can hear her clearly despite all the white noise of thousands of commuters.

"Yeah," I answer.

"Ella told me about this really cool spot in the park, but we didn't get to go while she was here. It's a bench that faces these huge rocks, and behind them in the distance is a perfect view of the city skyline. The contrast between nature and industry sounds so cool, and I really wanna see it. Will you go with me sometime, when it's not dark and we won't get killed?" Jessica turns and smiles at me before laying her head on my shoulder. I find it just a little bit harder to breathe. "I'd like to take *you* somewhere, show *you* something amazing next time."

No really, where's all the oxygen when you need it?

"It sounds incredible. We'll definitely have to go." My voice is low and raspy.

She lifts her head off my shoulder and I miss the contact immediately. Jessica nods at my answer with a satisfied look on her face and turns her focus back to all the activity of Grand Central Station in front of her. "And Elijah, just know that no matter what you say, I really hope we'll be able to stay friends after the summer. It's not like anyone else would understand all of this. And though that's our burden, I kinda also like that it's our secret, too."

I'm both surprised and touched by her honesty. But I don't know what to do with it. So I just answer with some honesty of my own.

"Me too," I tell her, turning my gaze to the bustle of commuters as well. I guess it's easier for us to admit these things without looking at each other. "To all of it."

chapter sixteen

———

jessica

"We've received over a thousand applications in just the first day," Roy announces.

The room erupts and I high-five the hands that are held up in front of me. "Way to go in getting the word out," I say to Soobin.

"Thanks to the designs Henry put together, they were so eye-catching," Soobin says.

I love to see the team giving each other the credit they all deserve. We're only a couple more weeks out before the hackathon and we're working the longest hours to date. But everyone is in great spirits. As expected, the rest of the company hasn't even taken notice of what we're doing. To them, we're just a bunch of kids working on a silly after-school project.

But that's not at all how we've approached it. The specs for the actual hackathon space are incredible. We're able to host twenty teams and put them up in a modest hotel for two days. We can't offer to pay for transportation, which is disappointing—I don't want people to be left out of the opportunity because of money. But we were able to secure an impressive cash prize for the winning team due to Jason's savvy accounting work, cutting back costs and finding ways for us to show savings in order to help make our case for the return on investment.

All of this done by "just a bunch of kids."

"Ms. Lee?" Sunny Cho peeks her head in. I'm not sure when Sunny started calling me "Ms." anything, but every time she does, my shoulders shoot up in a cringe. "You've been requested to come up to the executive conference room."

Her voice has a nervous twinge that I've never heard from her, not even on the first day when she thought she'd made a mistake about who I am. Sunny is usually calm and cool, exuding so much confidence that I initially thought she was my boss.

My palms start to sweat.

"Who's requesting?" I ask.

"The Executive."

Singular. But which one? And why?

"If you'll follow me," she says.

My eyes immediately scan the room for Elijah. He looks back at me and shakes his head in a barely perceptible move. What does that mean? Don't go? Don't worry? Run out the office and never return?

I widen my eyes at him, trying to convey my panic.

"The printer here keeps getting jammed. Jessica, can I use the one in your office upstairs?" Elijah asks out of the blue.

"Uh, sure?" I say.

"Cool, I'll go up with you then," he adds.

Ah, he's not letting me face the wolves on my own. Not if they've discovered the switch and are about to confront me and call the cops or something.

The three of us enter the elevator and I feel a light brush on my hand. I look down and Elijah's finger is stretched out to mine. Telling me that he's here. That it'll be okay.

I hook my finger around his. In any other situation, I might consider this romantic. Instead it feels tragic. Like I'm being sent off to my doom and my beloved is telling me to be brave as I face my demise.

When I started seeing Elijah as my "beloved," I'm not sure. It's got to be the anxiety, the panic, the pressure, the stress. But honestly, having him here beside me in this small elevator, makes me feel less worried. Less alone.

The ding of the elevator pulls me from my thoughts and I follow behind Sunny like a robot, not thinking or feeling anything. Numb. We turn the corner and she opens up the conference room door for me. Elijah hangs back in the hallway as to not draw attention. I walk in, and a lone, unfamiliar person stands gazing out the window, facing away from me.

She's slender and in a yellow dress with fabric that looks so delicate, like it would fly away in even the slightest breeze. Her hair is light brown with waves down her back, almost to her waist. There's an aura of beauty and of power coming from her. Like she's both a princess and a warrior. She looks over her shoulder and her profile reveals a perfect, small nose and a V jawline that is the epitome of Korean beauty standards.

"You might as well come in too," she says. She's not addressing me, but someone past me.

I don't turn my attention from her, but I hear Elijah step into the room. "What are you doing here?" he asks.

I'm so confused. What's going on? Does he know her? Who is she?

"Jessica, is it?" she asks.

"That's correct."

"It's so nice to finally meet you. I've heard a lot of great things about the work you've been doing here this summer."

Her voice is confident but lyrical, and I'm suddenly struck with déjà vu. It takes me a moment to figure out why, but I remember that this was how I felt about Elijah's voice the first time I heard it at the airport.

I've never seen anyone like her. I've only just met her but I'm completely mesmerized.

"Thank you?" I say. I don't mean to make it into a question. But I can't stop wondering who she is.

"Don't tell me you've been just playing video games and slacking off all summer, Elijah. I really don't want to believe this of you."

"This wasn't his fault," I say immediately. "And he's actually been working incredibly hard, even though he really doesn't have to. And his deep knowledge of gaming has been invaluable to the hackathon project."

A smile stretches across the woman's face. It's as if the whole room lights up. My eyes widen and my mouth opens as if I've been stunned by her presence.

"Oh god, Jessica is in awe of you, too. Figures," Elijah says, talking about me like I'm not even here. After I just spoke up and defended his honor? Sheesh. Men. "When did you get into town? And why are you even here? Did Dad send you? Or was it Mom?"

Dad? Mom?

"I'm sorry, but I'm feeling a little confused as to what's going on," I say.

The beautiful woman walks over to me—no, more accurately, she *glides*—and stretches out her hand. "How very rude of me to not introduce myself. Please forgive me, Jessica. I'm Lee Hee-Jin, Chief Operating Officer at Haneul Corporation. And I'm also this turkey's noona."

I shake her hand but turn my head to Elijah. "Your noona? The sister you said basically runs everything at Haneul?"

"Elijah said that, did he? Well, looks like you do pay attention, little brother. And I think we might need to draw out the family tree along with the org chart so Jessica can see exactly how screwed up this whole thing you've dragged her into actually is," Hee-Jin says.

"It's not screwed up," Elijah says. "Unconventional, sure. But this is what both Jessica and I wanted for the summer."

"I'm right here," I say. "Would really appreciate for someone to enlighten me since I'm, as I mentioned, right here." I direct my frustration toward Elijah because I could never speak to this angel in that tone.

"Why are you yelling at me?" he asks. He turns to his sister. "I swear, Noona, I will never quite get how you do this, win everyone over so easily. I mean, yes, you are awesome, but that's not fair pulling Jessica onto your side. I kinda like how we've been a team till now," he says, pointing back and forth between us. "Don't jump ship to hers, okay?"

My face blanches. I would never betray Elijah. But his small smirk shows me he's kidding...maybe?

"We're all on the same side here. So you—" she looks knowingly at her brother "—start talking."

"Well, it all started with Yoo-Jin Lee," he says.

"Elijah," his sister says with warning in her tone. "Stop playing games and get to the point."

"No, he's right. You see, I'm also Yoo-Jin Lee," I add.

Hee-Jin looks at me and then at Elijah. "You guys have the same Korean name," she says slowly. I feel like I can actually see the wheels in her head turning.

"Yup, and that caused for quite the confusion at the airport, with the driver, the housekeeper, all the way until our first day of work here at good ol' Haneul Corp," Elijah explains.

"Well, you're the genius who insisted to Dad that you didn't want anyone knowing who you were or have any unfair advantages this summer."

"Like a first-class ticket, a private driver, and a fucking three-story uptown brownstone?" Elijah says.

"You know how Dad is about image," Hee-Jin replies.

"Let me try to explain," I add. "This wasn't supposed to be an issue. Once we figured out how the mistake happened, I was ready to take responsibility for the error."

Hee-Jin shoots a glare at Elijah.

"I was going to take responsibility for my part, too. You know me better than that," he says defensively.

"I also know Dad's tried to teach us to deflect blame elsewhere. I'm not always sure how well you've fought off following his example. I'm hopeful, but, you know. It's hard," Hee-Jin says.

I feel a little bit like an intruder in this room, witnessing this interaction. I'm not part of their family and don't pretend to understand the struggles they've gone through, despite being rich—or maybe because of it.

Silence hangs in the air, which beckons the oversharing beast that lives within me. Fight it, Jessica. Fight!

"The thing is, Elijah and I both wanted different things than what our summers were set up to be," I say.

Welp, here we go.

"I've always dreamed of doing something important but just needed the opportunity to prove that I could. Elijah just needed some time and space to figure out exactly what it is he wants to do with his life. That's not a bad thing. It's just that expectations are piled on his shoulders and he hasn't had a chance to make his own decisions. I mean, my dad doesn't always let me make my own decisions either and that's so frustrating. Like the time when I wanted to go to tennis camp—"

"Jessica?"

Elijah's voice interrupts my momentum. "Yeah?"

"Breathe," he says.

He's not the boss of me. I'm fully capable of figuring out when my body needs air.

But I see it in his eyes. He's pulling me back to the point. When realization hits, I nod at him, taking a deep, steadying breath.

"Anyway, in an odd sense, we—" I point to Elijah and back to myself "—wanted what the other was going to have. So we thought, if it doesn't actually hurt anyone, maybe we could continue on through the summer having switched identities, sort of. It, well, it felt like it could be a win-win for everyone. But maybe we were wrong."

"We weren't wrong," Elijah says. "It doesn't matter to anyone. No one's even paying attention to us. At least, not until we started killing it with the hackathon project. Even my sister has heard about it, apparently. I told you to be good, Jessica. But did you have to be *that* good?" He winks at me and his compliment makes my knees wobble a little bit. I am so freaking easy. Ugh.

"Look, it doesn't matter why you did it and how you've been getting away with it. It doesn't even matter how well you're performing. It's all a lie. And this is not how we do business here at Haneul," Hee-Jin says. Her voice remains gentle, but I detect a sharpness that wasn't there before.

"I can actually hear the eye roll of two hundred plus employees in this building alone," Elijah says. "Dad's entire MO both in work and in life is that the ends justify the means. I'd like to believe he'd be proud of me for thinking this through, but..."

"But instead, if he ever finds out, you'll be banished to some remote countryside cabin and cut off from any and all family money, little brother. That's *if* he doesn't kill you first."

"This conversation is making me uncomfortable," I say under my breath.

Hee-Jin clears her throat and walks over to Elijah, gently tugging his arm. "May I speak to you for a moment out here?"

The two of them step out into the hall and I'm left standing there like the very unwelcome, non-family member, third wheel that I am.

"Look, this whole thing has your fingerprints all over it,

so start talking. What the fuck is going on in your head, Elijah? Explain. Now."

Oops. A third wheel who can apparently still hear everything that's being said.

And wow, even her cursing sounds pretty.

"Well, I know what *you're* thinking, and you're wrong. She's not my type and that's not why we're doing this," Elijah says.

"Oh, I don't know about that. She seems exactly your type—meaning the exact opposite of Dad's type for you."

Why does it sting that Elijah doesn't think I'm his type?

"Elijah, I'm not asking about whatever's going on with you and Jessica. I'm asking you what you think you're doing with this switch game you're playing. And are you kidding me with that stunt you pulled, not showing up to meet your sponsor for Seoul University? You need him to get you registered and ready to start school. I get your desire to rebel, but Elijah, you're pressing your luck. Dad's patience is barely existent on a good day. It would be just like him to make a rash move out of anger and cut you off completely."

"Good, then you can be CEO. Just like you want," Elijah says. He's not as nonchalant as he tries to sound.

"I may want it, but I'll never get it. You know the company would go to our cousin, Seok-Jin, first. And then we'll both be fucked."

"It kinda feels like I'm fucked already," Elijah mutters.

"Well, maybe consider that there are other people involved now. Me, for instance. Mom, too—have you even once thought about how much she's taking on from Dad to protect you? And now Jessica? Elijah, grow up and get in line."

"What if it's not what I want?" Elijah asks. And for the first time, I realize he's just as young as I am. That at this age, how can we possibly know what we want for the rest of our lives?

"Since when did what we want ever matter?" Hee-Jin replies.

The silence between them stretches and I realize I've been holding my breath. And I've been eavesdropping on a very serious and personal conversation...

I walk over to the open door and lean my head out. "I realize this may be a bit overdue for me to share, but, um, I can hear everything you two have been saying."

They both turn to me, the family resemblance striking.

Elijah sighs and looks back to Hee-Jin. "Noona," he says softly, "Jessica is a good person who is smart as fuck and works her ass off. But she would never have gotten this opportunity otherwise. So let's not traumatize her with our family drama. Can you just not say anything that would ruin this? Please?"

"I'm sorry, but it's my responsibility as a company representative to—"

"Save it," he says, raising his voice.

"Elijah." I'm not certain what to say. But I don't want him angry and I don't want him pissing off the one person we need as an ally.

"Noona, why are you even here? Did Dad send you to check on me? And doesn't that piss you off that you're acting as his errand girl instead of doing the important work you're supposed to be doing as COO?"

"I'm here to oversee the execution of Sky High, you little asshole. You know, the biggest thing the company puts on in the States every year? Seriously, do you know anything about the company at all?"

She shakes her head and Elijah doesn't respond. "But if I'm not here to check in on you," she adds, "you might want to be very careful of who might be. I know you both think this is probably some innocent thing you've done and no one is paying attention. But I can't guarantee that's true. And the work you're doing for the hackathon—good stuff by the way, really good stuff—is starting to hit people's radars. There's excitement around it. So one of two things can happen if this thing is a huge success: Jessica gets the credit, which would make Dad take notice, wondering who she is and where she came from. Or two, Elijah gets all the credit, leaving Jessica with only her own hand to pat her on the back. Trust me, I've lived this same scheme a hundred times over through my career."

There's a bitter edge to her tone and even though I've just met her, I hate this for Hee-Jin. I hate that women are still fighting for opportunities and credit and deserved success and upward mobility.

It's not fair.

But she's right.

My face drops just thinking of what the end of summer will bring.

"Hey, I'm sorry, Jessica. I didn't mean to come down so hard," Hee-Jin says, the bitterness gone from her voice. "I'm just tired, jet-lagged. I came here straight from the airport. Hey little brother, can you take me to the brownstone? I'm staying with you."

"Uh…" Elijah stalls.

"Don't give me shit about it. I hear the place is huge. We won't even run into each other, you little brat."

"That's not it. You're welcome to stay with me, if you can find space. You see, I'm, um, staying at the shitty rattrap our benevolent and generous company secured for the ten interns this summer. I invited Jessica to stay at the house," Elijah explains.

"You, living in anything less than a luxe apartment? Huh. Maybe you are growing," Hee-Jin teases. She turns to me. "Well, Jessica, how do you feel about being roommates? You'll barely even know that I'm there."

"Sounds great," I say. And truthfully, it really kinda does. I don't have to be totally alone in that big space anymore. And maybe I'll get to know Hee-Jin better. Maybe she'll even consider mentoring me. And maybe she can tell me some funny stories about Elijah.

Maybe.

chapter seventeen

elijah

We have four days left before the hackathon.

Today I had to go pick up the trophies and the fake, over-sized grand prize check for the winners at the printers. I went from Chinatown to the Financial District, then to Midtown and way up toward Columbia. I'm getting to experience more of New York than I ever thought I would, and the more I see, the more I want to keep exploring. This summer alone won't be enough time, and I'll have to figure out an excuse to come back.

And even though it takes away from my city time, it turns out, I kinda like working hard, making things happen. Believe me, no one is as surprised as I am. I don't know where that fits with my future, but the realization has made it all feel less daunting. I just wish this summer didn't have to end so soon. It's already mid-July and after the hackathon, I'll only have a few weeks left in New York.

There's so much more I want to do. Jessica mentioned wanting to visit the One World Trade building and the memorial. I was down in that area today but didn't have time to stop by. I want to be able to take Jessica there when all of this is done.

She's been working really long hours, and it's like the execs want to pile more and more on her plate so that she fails. It would go against all their tightly held beliefs if a teenager, a girl no less, gets shit done at a higher level than they do themselves. But she has so much grit and determination, I know that she'll be able to handle it. By day, they treat her as their lackey, mostly the notetaker and coffee fetcher for their meetings planning the Sky High Conference. And she's right, if she weren't a girl, if it was me in that role, they never would have dumped that stuff on me.

Hee-Jin has taken Jessica under her wing and tries to protect her from the worst of it. She's been a great influence from what I can tell. Problem is, though Hee-Jin is the boss's daughter and technically the second in command at the company, she still faces a lot of shit, too. Both as a woman and as a young person, since she's only twenty-four herself.

And after Jessica finishes with all that nonsense upstairs, she hustles down to the war room with us to pick up whatever work still needs to get done.

As I get back to the office from running all my errands, I spot her coming off the elevator. There are bags under her eyes and she looks tired. But she smiles when she arrives and greets everyone while checking in.

She really is a dream boss. And even at only eighteen, she demonstrates exactly the kind of leadership we should have at Haneul Corp. The Executive Training Program should be Jessica training *them* on how to do it right, not the other way around.

"How's it going?" Jessica asks me as she checks our progress on the whiteboard. "Thanks for getting all this done today. Wow, you really helped us get caught up." She smiles at me and my heart forgets to beat for a second.

I never knew what my type was. For years, my only frame of reference was the kind of girl my dad thinks I should be with. Well-connected, proper, yamjeonhae with a demureness that signals she's someone who will respect and obey her husband…and of course, rich. It's all so embarrassing and cringey to even think about it this way.

But this summer, I've come to find that my type has nothing to do with class or status or bank account. It's more someone who can be equally strong and soft, who speaks her mind, who cares for others, who has integrity.

No, I'm definitely not describing anyone in particular…

I'm still glowing in the wake of Jessica's compliment when Jason comes over and gently elbows her. "Does that mean we might actually be able to get off work at a reasonable hour?" he asks. "Whattaya say, maybe we should all go out tonight? Not to jinx it, but maybe an early celebration?"

My body tenses like it always does when I watch the easy interaction between them. It's hard seeing something you want but won't have. The fun moments of first getting to know someone…flirting. My first date will likely be with someone of my father's choosing, sitting down at my home's formal dining room, our entire families present, being served a five-course meal and showing off our extravagant wealth. It will be a performance, a show. I'm just glad that I've been able to avoid it so far, but I've seen *The Heirs*. I know how this works.

"I think it's a great idea for us to cut out on time today," Jessica says. "You've all been working so hard, and we're in good shape for the last final days. I wish I could join you all tonight. But I, um, actually have plans." It's ridiculous how my stomach sinks at the thought of her having plans that don't include me. I know it's none of my business. But still.

"You're no fun," Jason teases her. "One day I will get you to come out with us and let loose outside of work."

"It's a deal," Jessica says.

"So, what are you up to tonight?" I ask in an incredibly casual way that makes me seem perfectly normal and not at all like I'm about to burst into flames at any moment.

"Hee-Jin was able to get tickets to *Hamilton*. It's my dream to see that show." Jessica's eyes dance with delight.

My disappointment must show on my face because Jessica looks surprised. "She didn't tell you?"

"No, she didn't. But that's cool. It's really cool of her to do that." It's so entirely not cool. Because my sister should be taking *me* to see *Hamilton*. Rude.

"She said we're all going together, the three of us. She got us all tickets. I thought you knew."

Okay, I'm a selfish dick.

"Really, are you serious?" My voice shoots up an octave. I look around to make sure no one is paying attention to me. As I suspected, everyone's heads are down working. I lower my voice. "I haven't seen her today and," I pull out my phone, "I've been too busy to even check my messages." There's a text from my sister.

Hamilton tonight 7pm. And yes, you have to dress up.

My sister may know I'm dying to see *Hamilton*, but what she doesn't know is that I'd do just about anything to spend some more time with Jessica.

I send a thumbs-up emoji back to her.

The phone suddenly rings and my sister is talking before I can even say hello.

"There's a new outfit waiting for you at the brownstone. You're not wearing those off-the-rack T-shirts tonight," she says.

"Look, I appreciate it, I do. But I'm living with nine other interns and everyone has the same kind of clothes and they're all perfectly fine and happy. Why does it even have to matter?" I ask.

"What does it matter? I'm sorry, but what have you done with my fashionista brother who can't be seen without an oversized logo on his clothing? It's the theater, Elijah. You're presenting yourself out in society. Look, just come by the house to get ready with us and we'll all leave for the show together, okay? I've asked Mrs. Choi to make us something small to eat beforehand and we have a reservation for dinner after."

And with that she hangs up. Not even a goodbye. I look down at my phone and can't help the smile. Hee-Jin has no time for chitchat while she's at work, apparently. I'll have to give her some shit about it tonight.

It's gonna be fun spending time with both Jessica and my sister tonight.

"Elijah?" Jessica calls me over to where she's standing behind Jason, the two of them peering down at his laptop.

"Yeah," I say, walking over to them.

"Jason just told me that the library said they'd waive their fee for the venue rental. Is that true?" Jessica looks up at me, confusion drawing her eyebrows together. When she asks it aloud like that, it sounds outrageous. An in-demand public venue letting us use it for free? Unheard of.

My entire body goes cold and my heart starts pounding. This is where I get caught for paying for the library with my credit card and I get the budget lecture from Jessica again and likely get kicked out of the *Hamilton* invitation tonight, maybe kicked off the hackathon project altogether. I didn't think telling Jason a little untruth as to why we didn't have to request a check for the library would come back to bite me in the ass. But I've already dug the hole with my Black Amex and a lie. Not even a good one at that.

All summer, I've watched Jessica and the other interns come up with ways around obstacles, and trust me, there have been a lot. No one wants to make things easy on people they don't take seriously. But this group has never given up. We've been persistent and solution oriented. At the time, I thought dropping my dad's name, along with putting a mere ten thousand dollars on my credit card, was an easy fix to a problem. I know now that it didn't fix anything. In fact, if the truth comes out, it might make things worse.

"Uh, yeah, well, they felt bad for being such assholes to us that time when we stopped by. So they, um, agreed to let us have the venue for free. So, yeah, uh, I told Jason we wouldn't need to request a check." I kick myself mentally for stumbling over my words.

If Jessica wanted a chance to find me incompetent and dishonest, this would be it. But we just had this conversation at the fabric store. It's why I knew I couldn't tell her then about what I'd done.

And it's why I can't tell her now either.

She stares at me for a second, assessing. I don't blink. I don't swallow. I don't open my mouth.

I'm so busted.

And then a smile forms on her face. "Holy shit. This means we're gonna come way under budget. We might be able to give a cash reward to the second-place team, too," she says, her voice full of excitement.

"That's awesome," Jason says. He reaches over and pats me on the back.

"Yeah, uh, awesome," I say. And honestly, it is. We can give another deserving team a little financial support and no one has to know where it came from. Not Jason. Not Jessica. And not even my dad.

I hate that I was dishonest to do it. But I convince myself that the ends justify the means. I don't regret it one bit. Apparently I'm getting really good at this lying thing...even to myself.

"I'm so sorry. But this can't be helped. We have to figure out the opening keynote tonight. If Bill Gates can't come anymore, we're screwed unless I can conjure up a replacement. Have fun without me. I'm so bummed. Tell Jessica I'm sorry. Also, don't forget that the reservation is for La Masseria at ten o'clock after the show. Have the pork with truffle sauce and tell me how it is. The raves of that dish have made it all the way over to Korea. Gotta run."

My sister hangs up on the other line and I'm staring at myself in the mirror of one of the extra rooms in the brownstone, having not gotten a single word in edgewise. I'm wearing dark Louis Vuitton jeans and a black Tom Ford button-down. They're both tailored to fit me exactly, though I've never had anyone take my measurements for either. Sometimes wealth, and what is attainable with it, is a mystery even to me.

I step into my Celine boots and head downstairs.

Mrs. Choi comes out of the kitchen. "Oh, excuse me, I thought you were Jessica-ssi." She gives me a once-over and narrows her eyes. I don't think she likes that a strange boy has come out of one of the bedrooms. But the fact that she clearly has no idea who I am gives me a sense of relief. I'm quite certain all of our staff have signed some form of NDA, and Mrs. Choi seems to value her job enough not to spill any information even if she found out I was the CEO's kid instead of Jessica. But still, it makes it easier if she's in the dark. "I've prepared a light snack for you both as requested by the lady of the house," she says.

"Thank you so much. That sounds fantastic," I say. She smiles, and it strikes me that I don't see a lot of the people who work for my family smile that often. Also, I don't say thank you that much either. And that sucks. I've come to learn that it feels really good to be appreciated for your work, no matter the task.

Jesus Christ. I am a privileged asshole. Being a kind human

doesn't have to be that hard. Note to self: you've got a lot of thank-yous to make up for. Give them out more generously.

A sound from the second floor of the brownstone makes me look up, and I immediately have to catch my breath. Jessica is walking down the stairs in a fitted red sheath dress. It's sleeveless and simple and perfectly tailored, hugging just the right places. At midthigh, a ruffle circles the hem. It's conservative but sexy. She has on simple gold sandals with a kitten heel, and her hair is pulled back into a ponytail with the ends curled. I've never once in my life looked twice at a neck or a collarbone on anyone before, but now I feel they're fighting to be my favorite body part. I notice every single thing about her. But it's when she catches my eyes and smiles that I can't focus on anything else but that.

I swallow the lump in my throat. I know I should say something, tell her how stunning she looks, but my mind can't seem to form the words.

"Wow, you look hot," Jessica says. Guess she found the words first. "Like, *hot* hot. Like, you're already hot in those off-the-rack T-shirts, but now I think maybe I didn't know the full impact of how hot you could be until I saw you in these very expensive, fits like a glove, looks-like-they-were-made-for-you-and-maybe-they-actually-were clothes which makes it very obvious that *this* is what hot is supposed to look like."

The side of my mouth quirks. Her eyes grow huge and she slaps her hand over her mouth.

"Oh my god," she whispers behind her palm. "I can't believe I just said all of that. Kill me now."

"No, no, I actually recorded it on my phone. You know,

for days when I need to be reminded that I can be *hot* hot. Not just hot," I tease.

"I'm nervous and was so focused on not falling down the stairs in these heels that I forgot to turn on my filter. And I'm now mortified."

"Well, if it helps, I think you look *hot* hot too," I say. Her cheeks pinken a little and if the heat I'm feeling is any indication, mine likely have too.

"Thanks. It's Prada."

I raise my eyebrows, impressed. A couple months ago, Jessica didn't seem to know any designer names. Now she's dropping them like she's worn couture her whole life.

"The shoes are Jimmy Choo and the purse is YSL," she says, rounding out the outfit. And then she breaks into a giggle. "I've always wanted to list off 'who I'm wearing' like on the red carpet of an award show."

So. Fucking. Cute.

"Very nice," I say.

"Well, to be honest, your sister kinda helped me pick out what to wear. She even made me try stuff on over FaceTime while she was at the office. I was so embarrassed, but she would not take no for an answer. She might have been more excited than I was to find my perfect look for tonight."

"Speaking of Hee-Jin, did she tell you that she can't make it out with us tonight?"

Jessica nods. "I'm so bummed she got stuck at the office."

"Yeah, she's a bit of a workaholic."

"She has to be. She works twice as hard as anyone else at Haneul and she still has to fight to be taken seriously," Jessica says. There's a tightness in my chest as I listen to Jessica defend my sister. I'm usually the only voice that speaks up about how Hee-Jin gets screwed over at work.

"You know, I've noticed you've been going through some of that same shit as well," I say.

Jessica looks quickly up to meet my eyes. "You did? I'm not one to whine or complain about things. I just want to focus and do well at my job. But it does suck, I'm not gonna lie. I thought working for a Korean company would be easier. But it's harder than I expected. Maybe this is how it is at all companies, who knows."

"Well, you're killing it. And my sister is always saying how smart you are. Maybe working for a woman-owned company in the future might help."

"Or holding male-run companies accountable for misogyny in the workplace could also help," she counters.

"Touché," I say.

"Okay, enough work talk. We're both looking, um, *hot* hot," she says with a giggle. "So let's go have some fun."

chapter eighteen

elijah

The high of seeing *Hamilton* is like no other. By the time the curtain closes, I'm equal parts inspired and wrecked. My sister had gotten us the most incredible Orchestra Center seats, and both Jessica and I were mesmerized throughout the entire show. I didn't shed any tears like she had. But I was close. The entire night so far has been magical.

I wonder if moving to New York City is an option for my future. I could go to school out here. Hell, I'd even be willing to work part-time at Haneul while taking classes if my dad would agree to the move. There's just something so energizing about the city. I don't feel like I have to have all the answers. I don't feel like I have to pretend to be someone, because here, I can be just anyone. The expectation of who Elijah Ri is expected to be—wealthy chaebol, obedient son, future CEO—doesn't exist here on the streets of New York like it does in Seoul.

"I was thinking it would be really cool to live in New York," Jessica says. "I know it's incredibly expensive and life can be hard here. But there's something about the hustle and bustle that's addictive. I might apply to NYU next year." We're about two blocks away from the restaurant, the streets crowded with people coming out of theaters. I have to lean into Jessica as someone tries to get past me on the busy sidewalk. But I remain close as we continue to walk, my shoulder brushing hers every now and again.

"You're reading my mind," I reply.

"Really? Is that something you'd want to do? Oh my god, it would be so cool if we both ended up here," she says, eyes dancing with excitement.

Without thinking, I place my hand at the small of her back, gently guiding her to the inside of the sidewalk so I can walk closest to the curb and the cars driving by.

She drops her head, tucking the longer bangs that have escaped from her ponytail behind her ear, her mouth forming a small smile.

We reach the restaurant, and just as I open the door for Jessica, my phone rings. It's a restricted number, and I don't know who'd be calling me this late on a Friday night. Without thinking about it, I answer.

"Hello?"

"Elijah."

The voice is cold, stern, emotionless, but heavy.

My blood goes cold.

Fuck. My dad.

"Uh, Appa, I can't talk right now," I start to say.

"How many times do I have to tell you to not say 'uh' at the start of a sentence. It makes you sound uncertain and weak."

I want to scream that I *am* uncertain. I'm uncertain why he's calling me. I'm uncertain why I let him get to me. I'm uncertain about my future and who I am and who I want to be. Uh, uh, uh.

"Sorry, I wasn't paying attention. Listen, Dad…"

"Elijah, I need a word with you about this hackathon you're leading."

All the hairs on the back of my neck stand at full alert. I nod to Jessica to go inside without me. "I'll be right there," I mouth to her. She gives me an uneasy smile, but nods and makes her way to the hostess stand.

"What about it? It's not a big deal. Just a small thing that I'm working on with the interns. Not even something you need to think twice about." I hate downplaying the event and all the planning we've put into it, but I'm desperately hoping he isn't trying to sabotage it in some way. How does he even know about it?

"Listen to me closely, Son."

God I hate it when he refers to me as "Son." It's like he's reduced me to my position in our family tree and all the expectations that come with it, instead of actually addressing *me*, Elijah.

"Make sure you do not put too much time or effort into this hackathon. It's exactly the kind of useless work I do not want you focused on. This is for some middle manager to plan. You are the future CEO of this company. You should not be working with insignificant summer interns. Do you understand me?" His voice has a tinge of warning in it.

Maybe the distance from my dad and his iron fist has made me bolder. Or maybe I've just stopped caring what he thinks enough to rebel. "No, Dad, actually *you* don't understand. Jessica's put a lot of work into this."

"Jessica? Who is Jessica?"

"She's…" I need to change course and quickly. I don't want Jessica on my dad's radar in any way. If he thinks she's behind the hackathon's success, for some reason, he might sabotage her efforts. He has to think I'm the one. And if he got wind at all how I'm starting to feel for her, shit will hit the fan. "… just an intern. She's worked long hours along with the whole intern class doing what I've asked of them. It's gonna be awesome. You'll be really impressed."

"I don't want to be impressed, Elijah. I want you to obey what I'm telling you. Stop wasting your time. Let this Jessica and the rest of the interns feel important for a day. Let them earn their hourly wages. But don't let them become ambitious to do more. The internship program is a charity case, a tax write-off for the company. We do not need it to have attention. We have bigger things to focus on. As of tomorrow, you will not work on this hackathon. I want you to find out how you can help with the Sky High Convention instead."

"But Dad, you can't ask that—"

"Elijah?"

I whirl around and see Jessica standing in the doorway, brows furrowed.

I hold up one finger at her and turn my back so she can't hear.

"Dad, can we talk about this later?" I lower my voice into the phone. Way to sound inconspicuous, Elijah. "I have to go, I'm sorry," I say.

"We do not have to talk later. I've made my wishes clear. Do not disobey me, Elijah. And I'm having you come home to Korea earlier than planned, in a couple weeks. There's a young lady from the Paik family you need to meet."

I clench my fist in rage and want to throw my phone against the brick wall of the restaurant. But instead, I hang up without saying goodbye, dropping my head to my chest. I'm going to pay for that later. No one hangs up on my dad. But I couldn't take it anymore.

I feel the soft touch of a hand on my back and look over my shoulder.

"Is everything okay?" Jessica asks, worry in her voice.

I let out a deep breath, pressing myself a little bit into her touch as if I can gain strength, or at least some perspective, from it.

I don't answer her question, taking her hand instead and pulling her to the side of the building where the streetlights barely reach. I want to hide in the shadows here and pretend that I'm not who I am. Jessica's back is to the brick wall, and I put my arm out and lean in to shield her from anyone walking past on the sidewalk.

"Elijah, tell me what's wrong," she whispers. She places her hand on my chest and I'm certain she feels my heart trying to pound its way free.

I inch closer, slowly, until my forehead touches hers. I shut my eyes, pushing out the sound of my dad's commands. I ignore the anxiety brewing about some girl with the last name Paik. It's just me and Jessica here. My breath evens out and I feel one thousand times calmer.

I open my eyes and pull away just a tiny bit. The way she's looking at me…concerned but infinitely patient. Incredibly kind. I search in her eyes for the person she sees in front of her—a version of myself that even I can like and respect.

I swallow back the swell of emotion, the need. It feels like I've gone my whole life without someone to care about how I'm feeling. And with just one look, Jessica has me desperate for it.

The fingers of the hand that once lay flat on my chest grab the fabric of my shirt and gently pull me toward her. She tilts her head, inviting me to kiss her, and I don't hesitate. I lean in and my mouth meets hers.

So warm. So soft.

"Jessica," I say against her lips. She moves her arms around my neck, running a hand through my hair. Her mouth opens for me and my tongue finds its way. Her entire body is warm and pliant, forming against mine.

I shift, putting all my weight onto my arm supporting me against the brick wall and wrap my other arm around her waist to remove any space between us, lifting her up a fraction to get a better angle, to get even closer. She lets out a tiny gasp, and I can't help it—a moan escapes me in response.

She pulls back a tiny bit for some air. I want to suggest we just forget the need and keep kissing. But the feel of her breath ghosting over my cheek is just as intoxicating.

She looks me square in the eyes, searching for something.

"Talk to me. Who was on the phone? Are you okay? How can I help?" She asks all the right questions to soothe the damage left behind by my dad.

I want to keep kissing her, removing any worry from her pretty face, instead of having to deal with the fact that with one phone call, my father ruined my entire summer.

"It was my dad," I admit, knowing that she'll understand the weight of just those words. "But can we not talk about it right now?" I step away from her but reach out to tuck a strand of loose hair behind her ear. Even though this summer night is warm and humid, Jessica shivers. "Let's go inside. I'm hungry," I say. "Apparently some of the city's best Italian food is waiting for us."

She looks at me for one second longer. I don't know what she reads on my face, but she nods and turns to go, slowing down a step for me to catch up, not leaving my side. She reaches for my hand and interweaves our fingers together as we walk in. I try not to get lost worrying about what it all means. I just want to borrow her warmth and strength in this moment.

And I try to ignore the insistent ticking of the clock counting down to the end of summer, when Jessica won't be by my side any longer.

chapter nineteen

———

jessica

Elijah: Hi

I look down at my phone and burst into a smile. Two letters, one word...everything. My heart picks up speed just seeing his name on my screen.

Jessica: Hi :)

Elijah: Did you have fun?

Jessica: I did!!! I had the best time!

Elijah: I couldn't stop thinking about you all night...

Oh.

My.

God.

He thought about me all night. Despite sitting at my desk in my office with the door closed, letting out a swoony sigh wouldn't be appropriate at my place of work. And yet... I can't hold it in. The breath most definitely releases from my mouth followed by a high-pitched squeal. I spin in a circle in my chair, tapping my feet as I go in a little dance. It's the only way to release the excitement I'm feeling.

Elijah: I can still taste you on my lips

Holy cow. Now what do I say to that? I need Ella's advice immediately. She's the queen of flirting via text. I quickly type out a panicked message.

Jessica: OMG, Ella... Elijah and I made out last night and it was EVERYTHING and now he's texting me saying he can still taste me and I want him to know I'm ALL about doing it again but without sounding too eager or desperate...even though I MOST DEFINITELY am! HELP ME! I need to sound like a sexy kitten. Make it quick. Please and thank you.

I hold my phone to my chest waiting for it to buzz with Ella's response. A smile spreads over my face as I think about whatever it is she's gonna help me say to Elijah to make him ask me out maybe. I don't want to overthink any of this. I just want to enjoy it.

I jump when my phone vibrates with a new message. Dang, Ella is quick!

Elijah: I think you meant to send that last message to Ella. But just want you to know I'm all for the sexy kitten thing

Jessica: *facepalm*

I keep looking at the text exchange with Elijah from this morning, revisiting the feelings of equal parts elation and mortification. I'm still in shock that so much happened in just one night. But maybe that's the magic of *Hamilton*.

The show made me feel...like the world is full of possibilities if I just fight for my place in it. It's given me a new surge of energy for the work we have left on the hackathon. This is my shot.

It also made me believe that Elijah and I could really have something special. And I think Elijah feels it too.

A snapshot of Elijah in those perfectly tailored fitted jeans crosses my mind. I swallow back the urge to let myself drool at the memory. I've never really valued expensive clothing, and besides, I could never afford it either. It all seemed meaningless, spending that kind of money on luxury brands. But now that I've seen the good stuff on Elijah, I know how it can make what is already a pretty perfect body look even better. Personally, I could easily get addicted to how it makes me feel, getting to wear high-end designers myself.

And...then there was that *kiss*. Elijah leaning in toward me against the brick wall. His lips on mine, his tongue doing things...

"Jessica-ssi, we need you in the boardroom," Mr. Song says as he walks by my office door.

I jump up from my seat, knowing my mother would

be mortified if she knew I'd just been caught by an elder while thinking lascivious thoughts about a boy. I nervously straighten my skirt, grab my note pad and pen, and rush to the boardroom. I find myself, yet again, being assigned note-taking duties for the leadership team meeting.

I rotate my hands in circles to stretch out my wrists, preparing to add all the curlicues and long-tails to my letters to provide that "pretty feminine writing." I stop short of dotting my i's with hearts.

If the trade-off for getting to plan and execute on the hackathon is to suffer through the humiliation of stressing over if my note-taking and penmanship pass muster with a group of backward-thinking men on a power trip, so be it.

I'm not throwing away my shot.

I battle intense boredom as each executive goes through their department update. I will never get over how the two women in the room, Ms. Kang and Hee-Jin, are always left to present after all the men have finished and only if there's time remaining. On more than one occasion, I've wanted to ask Hee-Jin how she puts up with the blatant misogyny, the uncomfortable disrespect.

My mom would say, "Don't ask too many questions. More often than not, the answers will come to you without you bringing needless attention to yourself." Sometimes I wonder if her advice throughout my life is just another form of these outdated values.

"We only have a few minutes left, but Ms. Kang, can you tell us anything from Marketing?" one of the male execs says.

Ms. Kang does not even hesitate. Looks like she's well-practiced at not throwing away her shot. "The marketing

plans for the new year will be in everyone's inbox by Friday
and physical copies of the report on your desks by noon that
day. Key points are the hiring of a Social Media Manager to
establish our presence across all platforms. We're behind on
this effort compared to our competitors in the market."

Some of the men around the table begin gathering their
things, and one even has the audacity to stand up as if he's
about to leave. Ms. Kang seems unruffled by the rudeness.
The one tell that she's irritated is her tight grip on her iPad
containing her notes, which is only evident to those who pay
attention...so likely just me. I glance up briefly and see Hee-
Jin's eyes on Ms. Kang's iPad as well. Okay, so not just me.

"And finally," Ms. Kang continues, raising her voice
slightly. "I want to give a quick update on the hackathon and
the incredible work our intern cohort has been doing with
the planning. I've been quite impressed with what they've
managed to accomplish, both in terms of schedule and budget. The event is going to be..."

Mr. Shin from Supply Chain moves toward the door, his
Korean newspaper tucked under his arm, coffee cup in hand.
"Ms. Kang, please only present important things at these
meetings. They're long enough as is. I don't need to hear
about our charity program."

I stiffen at the word. *Charity.* Who do they think these
interns are? Clearly they don't realize this cohort has some
of the brightest young minds working their butts off for this
company. Just because they don't come from money and prestigious families, doesn't mean they're not worthy. In fact...
I open my mouth to say so out loud, but Hee-Jin shoots me

a warning look, lips tight, and the slight shake of her head telling me no. Don't do it.

How is any of this behavior okay?

"I don't know why we listen to Lee Jung-Woo," the man next to me says to the person beside him. I write the name in my notes with an extra flair as I'm feeling particularly sassy right now.

Lee, curlycued *e*'s.

Jung, an extra tail on the *g*.

Woo...

I look closely at the name written by my own hand. It takes me a second to recognize it and connect the dots. That's my dad's name. My head shoots up from my notepad.

"He's always trying to spend company money on needless projects like internships. Do we even know if he's telling the truth about the tax benefits for the company? Sounds like a waste of time and resources, yet again."

"The tax benefits are just an excuse. He wants these programs so that poor kids like he was can get opportunities. How about they just work harder to overcome their lot in life instead of taking handouts?"

I narrow my eyes at the men speaking as my heart races. My dad is a kind, giving soul, but he has never in his life wasted time nor resources. He's way too cheap. But knowing that he's been supporting the internship program all along—and clearly fighting an uphill battle to do so... I swallow back the lump in my throat.

The rest of the table stands, engaged in various side conversations, and walks out as if Ms. Kang hadn't just been in the middle of presenting something important and Mr. Jerk-face hadn't just been talking down about my dad. I'm fuming, a rage burning inside of me that I've never felt before. I want to storm out of this room, to the elevator, and out of the building, as far away from all of this as I can get.

A light touch lands on my shoulder.

"Hey, let's do a girls' night tonight. Pajama party, okay? Sheet masks, cup ramen, cult documentaries. Sound good?"

Hee-Jin's expression is kind, apologetic. I try to read all the words she's not saying, but I still don't quite understand how she puts up with all of this here at work. She's in a position of power, even. Why does she let it be this way?

"Sure, sounds great," I say, though my voice is flat. I can't hide my disappointment, frustration, and now the added concern for my dad. It didn't sound like he was well-liked among these powerful people.

Once the room is empty, I clean up the mess left behind on the table by everyone else, as I always do, and throw my pretty notes that no one reads into the shredder as I leave the room.

When I get back to my office, I pull out my phone and dial my dad. I want to hear his voice. If it's true that he's been the one championing the internship program this whole time, and he's invested in making it succeed, why didn't he ever tell me this? And more importantly, why was he so against me taking part this summer? I wish I could share with him everything I've been doing. I want to show him how important this internship program is and how he should be so proud, not just of me, but of himself, too.

"Jessica, I was going to call you later tonight at our appointed time. Is everything okay?" His voice, despite its usual demanding tone, still brings me comfort. Because whatever happens, I know at the very least, my dad will make it okay in his own way.

"Well, I just found out something interesting," I say.

"Interesting? Like something you're not supposed to know? Are you in some trouble? Go directly to the police department but don't give them any information. I'll call your uncle in New Jersey to come immediately to meet you there…"

"Dad, Dad, wait. I'm not in any trouble, sheesh," I say. "It's just… I was in the executive meeting and they were talking about the internship program and your name came up."

"Jessica—" his voice changes immediately from panicked to pressured "—why were you in the executive meeting?" He asks the question slowly, his words laced with suspicion and some form of accusation. He told me to keep my head down this summer. And that's the farthest from what I've actually been doing.

I scramble for something to say. For a way to explain.

"They, uh, needed someone to take notes. And they wanted someone with feminine writing to do it. And you and I both know I have really nice penmanship. You insisted I pay attention in school even since the earliest days. And I'm so lucky I listened to you because I nailed cursive in elementary school and it's now really coming in handy. You should see the way I write my *j*'s…"

He hasn't said a word, but I can hear the slight whistle of my dad's nose as he breathes heavily. The trouble I'm about to be in…

"Jessica Yoo-Jin Lee," he says.

Oh shit. Not the full name.

"I told you to simply do your work and stay out of the way.

Your performance will do the talking for you. You should not be in these executive meetings. You should not be noticed by anyone. If they find out that I'm your father, it jeopardizes the entire future of the internship program—as well as my own reputation and yours. I've always been against using connections to get ahead and been vocal about privilege creating an unequal playing field. If anyone finds out you're my daughter, they will assume I helped you get the role. People cannot become curious about your background. Do you understand?"

If my dad only realized that having connections is, in fact, the *only* way to get ahead. Things like good grades and hard work only get you so far.

It's an impossible situation and frankly, I'm a little peeved he's asking this of me. Of course I need to stand out. I need to take advantage of every opportunity as if it's my last. Because it very well may be.

So I ignore the niggle in the back of my head, the one wondering why my dad is being so unreasonably protective. Even more so than usual.

If only past me had listened to that small voice in this moment and done just as my father had asked, I would have saved us all a lot of headache and heartache.

If only.

"These are the nicest pajamas I have ever worn in my life. I'm usually an old church youth camp T-shirt and shorts girl when it comes to sleeping. My best friend, Ella, always tells me that if you wear nicer pajamas to bed, you have better dreams."

"You've mentioned Ella a few times. Have you two been friends long?" Hee-Jin asks.

"Yeah, she's been my closest friend since junior high. She's great. She's coming back to New York to visit right after the hackathon. If you have any time, maybe we can all have lunch. She would love to meet you."

Hee-Jin nods politely but doesn't seem enthusiastic about it. I get the sense that meeting new people isn't at the top of her list of favorite things to do. I've never clocked her as a snob, so I wonder if she's secretly quite shy. Kinda like her brother.

Hee-Jin reaches out and touches the fabric of my pajama sleeve. "Oh, yes, these ones are nice," she says, bringing the conversation back to something she seems more comfortable with. Material things. "So soft. I never got used to silk pajamas until recently. It felt too extravagant. Don't get me wrong, I've always had the nicest, highest thread-count cotton pajamas, but silk has been a revelation. Don't you just feel wrapped in luxury when you sleep in them?" She lets out a small laugh. "Oh god, I can't believe I just said that. I must sound like the most annoying rich person, huh? Gross."

I give Hee-Jin a reassuring smile. In this moment, she's so different from the powerful, assured executive. She seems younger, more relaxed.

"One thing I'm learning from getting to know both you and Elijah is that our lives might be different, but we have a lot of the same struggles. Impressing our demanding parents, trying to stand out and being taken seriously. Fighting to do what we want versus what someone else wants for us," I admit.

Hee-Jin examines me carefully, her eyes soft but assessing. "You've really gotten to know him," she says.

"I'm sorry?" I'm not quite sure what she means.

"Elijah. No one ever seems to get to know the real him. People just write him off as spoiled, lazy, incapable. My dad screams at him to stop playing video games all day and step up for the family business. My mom begs him to try harder. No one asks him what he wants. No one tries to see what he's capable of."

"But he's capable of so much. He's super smart. Those games he plays? He actually knows how the back-end code works for them. And I don't think there's a problem that he couldn't come up with a solution for. And he's a natural leader. People just trust him and follow him. And he's so generous, and I'm not talking about money. He's generous with his time and his efforts. He sees someone who needs help and if that person will let him, he'll step in and do whatever he can. Not to be some savior in a situation or to take all the credit. But to truly get someone over the hump of their struggle. I'm not saying he isn't a pain sometimes. And he pretends to hate to work hard but you can tell that he's enjoying it, that he finds some satisfaction in getting stuff done. And…"

It suddenly dawns on me how very quiet it is in the room. Hee-Jin and I planned to watch cult documentaries tonight in the family room. We're both in our pajamas, hair tied back, Shin ramen heated, popcorn in hand. But the television remains off. And here we are, talking about Elijah. And I've gone too far.

"I'm sorry, I didn't mean to act like I know him better than you. I mean, I've only just…"

"Don't apologize for being observant, for having a natural knack for reading people. Don't ask for forgiveness based on someone else's reaction to your knowledge," she says. "Be very stingy with your apologies. We women too often say 'I'm sorry' for things that are entirely not our fault. It's our go-to."

I nod and take mental note, amazed at how Hee-Jin has turned on the company badass persona so quickly. I want to ask her about the executive meeting today, about how she handles being dismissed or underestimated at work. I get the sense that she's been forced to pick and choose her battles.

"And don't ever apologize to me for knowing my brother. I'm so grateful that he has someone who has taken the time and the chance to get to know him. Someone who he trusts enough to show these sides of himself to. Someone who accepts him as he is. He doesn't get that a lot."

I suddenly feel guilty for talking about Elijah while he's not here. But my heart warms that Hee-Jin seems to think I'm someone important to him. It's sad that these people are few and far between. Again, I'm struck at how lonely Elijah's life must be.

Hee-Jin reaches over and squeezes my hand before sitting back into the couch and lifting the remote to turn on the TV. There's a small smile on her face and I'm mesmerized by how much she and Elijah look alike. And how he isn't the only one in the family carrying around a lifetime's worth of pressure on their shoulders.

Maybe time in New York away from Seoul can be good for both of them.

A part of me, a part that seems to be growing stronger by the day, doesn't want this summer to end.

"Okay let me know if you want me to mind my own business but…" I quickly change the subject before these rising emotions put a damper on our night. "I think that young, handsome guy in the gray suit who was sitting next to Mr. Kim at the meeting today is into you. He kept stealing glances at you the entire time, but not like in a creepy way. And when you mentioned that thing about changing forecasts to monthly instead of quarterly, he was really impressed. I mean, this may be totally inappropriate for me to say, but I'd never seen anything like it. It wasn't obvious or anything. But it was like something straight out of a romance novel."

A shy smile spreads across Hee-Jin's face. I've always seen her as so confident and so in control, but she seems disarmed by the comment.

"Thanks, but I can't imagine that's true," she says as a pink blush covers her cheeks. When I think about how lonely Elijah's life must be, I realize that it's probably the same for Hee-Jin. Does she get the chance to have pajama parties or talk about crushes with her friends?

She clears her throat and shutters her expression. "Plus, it wouldn't be appropriate in the workplace," she says.

The sudden change in her disposition throws me off guard and I quickly apologize. "I'm so sorry, I didn't mean to…"

"No, no, I'm sorry. I wasn't trying to shut you down or shame you. It's just that…well… I'm engaged to be married."

My eyes immediately drop to her left hand. No diamond, no ring. Empty.

"It hasn't all been finalized yet. We're planning the engagement party now. His dad owns a very large distribution company, and it was kind of a done deal for us to get married from an early age." She raises her eyes to me slowly. "I know it sounds totally antiquated and backward."

"Do you love him?" I immediately throw my hand over my mouth. I can't believe I just straight-up asked her this. We barely know each other.

"Would you respect me less if I didn't?" she asks.

I swallow a lump in my throat, equal parts sadness and embarrassment. "I don't know if it's any of my business to feel one way or the other about it. Who am I to have an opinion on your life? I promise, I'm not here to judge."

"Thing is, I know it seems old-fashioned, but it's not as weird as it sounds. We met because of our families, but luckily, we like each other. There is definitely an attraction there. But this could've been a lot easier in any other circumstance. There's a lot of pressure on both of us since it's imperative that our companies play nice with each other."

I want to tell her I understand, give her the approval she seems to need from someone, anyone. But I guess, even though Elijah mentioned that stuff like this still happens, it still shocks me. It's especially weird hearing it from a person I respect and look up to as a powerful businesswoman.

A sudden chill hits my spine as my mind plays it all out in my head.

"Wait. Is Elijah matched with someone too?" My voice sounds small and I've forgotten how to breathe.

She doesn't look away, but the silence goes on for too long. I have my answer.

"Oh, yeah, I mean, of course he probably is, not that it's any of my business just like it's none of my business that you're marrying for the company and not for yourself. Not that there's anything wrong with that. And even better if you like each other and you know, love can grow…" My lips keep moving as the voice in my head screams for me to shut up, to run away, to never look back at these people and their world that I don't understand.

I think about the kiss Elijah and I shared the other night. The small touches and secrets kept just between the two of us since our first week here. Being on each other's sides and going through what we have this summer together. I thought… I thought…it doesn't matter what I thought. There's someone else who is supposed to be sharing these things with him for the rest of his life. Not me.

Hee-Jin reaches out and gently squeezes my hand.

"He hasn't even met her yet. It's all just an expectation, a contract of sorts. But there are no emotions attached. And, maybe, it will be different for Elijah than it is for me. Who knows? All I do know is that watching Elijah with you this summer, I've never seen him like this. I've never known anyone to believe in him like you do, which helps him to believe in himself." Her smile is kind but laced with a bit of sadness.

A sadness of my own settles in my chest and I wonder if this will be how I always will feel whenever I think of Elijah in the future—a future I won't be a part of.

"Don't worry about any of that right now," Hee-Jin says as if reading my mind. "Enjoy the summer and let him enjoy it too."

I just nod, grabbing the remote control and turning on the documentary. As I focus my eyes on the screen, I do what I've been all summer, what I've gotten really good at…

Pretending.

chapter twenty

elijah

I don't know how I let Jason talk me into going for a run before work.

But honestly, despite the fact my lungs are burning and my legs feel like jelly and this guy's killer body makes me seem like the scrawny kid in gym class, running up the West Side Highway along the Hudson River is a slice of heaven. If I wasn't gasping for air, I'd probably be smiling right now.

"Hey, let's take a quick break, man. I'm hurting," I wheeze.

Jason nods and slows himself down. He walks over to the nearest greenway off one of the piers and starts stretching. I know he's a good guy, but I don't doubt he loves the looks thrown his way from those passing by. The other night when we were in line at this new noodle restaurant, someone asked if he was a K-pop idol.

I'm used to getting a lot of attention in Korea. Chaebol

families are famous in their own way, and the public wants to know where we eat and shop, the events we attend and who we're with. Here in New York, stripped free of that identity, I'm just like everyone else.

"If we want to make it to work on time, we should probably head back. I need a shower and I traded bathroom times with Roy," I say. I track a seagull sneaking its way closer to a baby holding a half-eaten bagel. The baby's mom is busily chatting away on her phone. But the dog-brother, a French bulldog in a studded harness, has its eyes glued to the bird. This should make for one helluva fight.

"Or we could just keep going this way and shower in the office gym," Jason says. "I've heard it's fully stocked with Laneige body and skincare products. I've been meaning to check it out in there."

I give him a knowing look accompanied by a huff. There's no way we're doing that. We're mere interns. And though no one's told us we can't use the office gym, it's only the hotshots in the company who do so. Men wearing the latest in high-tech workout gear who then change into bespoke handmade suits. I wouldn't be surprised if those assholes kicked us out for trying to breathe the same air as them.

In Korea, I'm one of those assholes.

I shake my head. "I don't know about you, but I'm not that into being treated like dirt and made the fool. I'd much rather wait my turn in our one shared bathroom."

"Sometimes I worry that you're too hung up on status, and more specifically, not having it. You need more confidence, man. You work at Haneul. You have the same employee perks as everyone else. Nobody is looking down on you." He claps me on the back. Nice pep talk.

I hate to be the one to break it to Jason that they are, indeed, looking down on us. I know because I looked down on people who I didn't think "belonged" somewhere in the past.

"Come on. We've both seen how we're basically disregarded there. Have you even made it past the bottom floor of the company?" I ask him.

He shakes his head and shrugs. "Maybe you're right. But if that's the case, it totally sucks. I honestly don't understand how that shit still happens in this day and age. We always use the excuse that Haneul is a Korean company, as if that's a reason to not ever change. To keep these outdated ways of approaching corporate society. Misogyny, classism, racism, harassment...you know that's all considered illegal in the workplace at most companies? At least, it's supposed to be," he says.

"It totally sucks," I reply. "But what I wonder is why anyone stays."

He peers at me as if trying to see straight through to my brain, and I can't figure out his expression. "Look, I know you're pretty private—it's cool that you keep your life outside of work really close to the chest. But, it's obvious you're kinda sheltered in Korea. In the States, we're raised to think that work isn't easy to come by. And a lot of people feel scared to ever be out of work. A bad job is better than no job. And Haneul, despite being awful internally, has a strong reputation in the industry. Or at least it did. If the company doesn't step up and try to advance the work they do though, it'll be a relic in no time flat."

I nod at everything Jason's saying. Because he's right.

Everything I've learned this summer has driven home what I already knew. That the path laid out for me isn't a future I care about. Becoming the CEO of Haneul Corp is not what I want to do. I didn't want it when it was a legacy expectation set on me. And I don't want it even more now that I've seen the shitty company culture. I'm not a corporate messiah. Even if I *wanted* the responsibility, I can't work miracles.

Still, if there's one thing I do want, it's to make sure Jessica gets enough credit for everything she's done this summer to be set up for her future, whether at Haneul or hopefully somewhere even better.

Jessica.

The number of times I've thought about our kiss. How her touch brought me back from the brink of hopelessness and the pit of frustration after talking to my dad. That night was one of the few times I really wished I lived alone in that brownstone. Having nine roommates, including one actual bunk mate, doesn't allow for a guy to be able to take care of his needs while thinking about a certain spunky girl with the softest fucking lips ever.

Jason and I start heading back toward our apartment and the morning air is just crisp enough to cool me down from my thoughts. In a few hours, the July heat will be stifling and the humidity unbearable.

"Hey, so I wanted to ask you something," he says. We're walking side by side, me trying to keep up with Jason's long, confident strides. He's looking straight ahead, avoiding eye contact.

I tense, waiting for it. Because I'm pretty sure I know what he's about to ask, and I don't want to even think about it.

"About Jessica…" he starts.

Fuck, I hate being right.

I stop walking. "What about her?"

Jason's already a few steps ahead before he notices I'm not at his side. He turns to look at me, hesitates, but then back-tracks to where I'm standing. "Well, I know that you two had one of those made-for-TV-movies starts with her giving you her number in the elevator on our first day. And I've noticed you seem to have gotten close. Is there, you know, something going on between you guys?"

I could answer "yes" and let that be the end of it. With one word, I'd be telling my friend to back off. I'd stake my claim, own up to my feelings. I'd rid myself of the jealous beast that emerges every time I see them talking to each other. Jason's a good guy. He'd step down if he thought Jessica and I already had something going.

And we kinda do have *something*, don't we? I mean, our kiss the other night should be proof of that. My tongue slides over my bottom lip as if I can still taste her there.

But a voice of reason, one that sounds suspiciously like my father's, drowns out every other thought. My dad will never accept Jessica. And I can rebel against his wishes in a lot of facets of my life, but this wouldn't just be about me. He can make shit really difficult for the person who I choose to love. And I don't want that for Jessica. I've known this all along. We're in an impossible situation and I have to stop it before anything else happens, before it gets too hard to walk away. Even if I fucking hate the idea of not being with her.

"No," I say, forcing out the word. "Nothing is going on between us." The words feel like knives scraping deeply along my throat. The lie is so very wrong, but this is what has to be my truth.

"Really? Huh, that's surprising. Well, you're definitely closer to her than I am, so...could you do me a favor?"

Shit. I don't think my heart can take asking Jessica out for Jason. "Uh, I think it's better coming straight from you. Girls like when a guy is direct." I hate this, giving advice to my friend about the girl *I* like.

"I don't know. She seems really protective of Ella, which is cool. I just don't want Jessica to hate me for asking her best friend out on a date. I know I don't need Jessica's permission, but she's my friend and I respect her, so I want to make sure she'd be cool with it, you know?" Jason explains.

Ella. Ella?

"Wait, you want to ask Ella out?" I ask.

"Uh, yeah. What did you think I was talking about? Oh, shit. You didn't think I'd be that much of a dick to ask *you* if I could ask out Jessica did you? You *do* know we're friends, right? That sucks, man."

"Sorry. This whole 'having friends' thing is new to me," I admit. "This misunderstanding is more about me than it is about you. And for what it's worth, I think Jessica respects and likes you a lot too. She seemed pretty interested in you and Ella getting to know each other when we were all on the boat."

Jason nods, his easy smile reappearing across his face. Without realizing it, I try to mimic his grin, but *easy* doesn't come naturally to me. I know it doesn't have to be a struggle to just...show feelings. Maybe if I wasn't so emotionally constipated, I could let Jason know I'm glad we're friends. I could tell my dad I don't want to take over the business. I could admit to Jessica that I have feelings for her and it scares the shit out of me.

"Dude, you have a cramp? You look like you're in pain," Jason notes, his smile replaced with a worried frown.

So much for exercising my facial muscles.

"Nah, I'm good." I hide my lie by turning to look out over the water.

Jason stands next to me and joins me taking in the view. "So, no-go with you and Jessica? That's surprising to me. Why, is she not your type?" he asks.

The morning sun glistens on the Hudson River, just a small strip of water separating New York and New Jersey. But the way people talk about it, the divide between the two states couldn't be wider, the lives of those living in each couldn't be more different. It's how things are between me and Jessica.

I take a second to think how much I'm willing to share.

"Truthfully, she's exactly my type. She's smart and funny. She's kinda shy but feisty, too. You know? Like you, I respect her a ton, and I like how she can hold her own with anyone. And she doesn't let me get away with any of my shit," I say. "But at the end of the day, she deserves someone better than me."

What I don't say is that she deserves someone who doesn't have a family that comes with harsh realities and unyielding expectations. And a major dick of a patriarch. My family represents everything that Jessica hates about Haneul Corp. We *are* Haneul Corp.

"That's bullshit. You're a great guy. Don't sell yourself

short," Jason says, nudging my shoulder. If he only knew how much I'm actually worth.

"Maybe not someone *better* than me, but someone who's a better fit than I am. Our lives are just really different," I say.

"I'd have to disagree. Jessica doesn't need someone just like her. She and I, and a lot of the other interns, we all have similar backgrounds. We've been hustling our whole lives to get a leg up on life. We've needed to get the best grades and the best internships just for a *chance* at something better. Now, like I mentioned, I don't know a lot about your life back home. But you've mentioned you've never worked before. And the way you're kind of a fish out of water at the apartment and the office and anytime we go out, I'm guessing all of this is new for you. I kinda feel like Jessica could benefit from someone who isn't trying to prove anything to anyone. Who can just be there to stand by her side and encourage her." He lets what he said hang in the air for a few moments before adding, "Just my two cents."

Shit, I'd pay a lot more than two cents for the truth Jason just spit out. I want to tell him everything. I want to reciprocate this friendship. But I can't reveal who I am, who my father is. I can't risk this secret getting out and putting Jessica in harm's way. I wish honesty was something I could afford to give Jason. I'm just not sure I can offer that to anyone right now. I don't even know if I can give that completely to Jessica.

And she deserves that much, at least.

"Thanks, man. I appreciate that perspective. I just don't know that I'm at the right place to be dating anyone now. And I'd rather not risk fucking it up with someone like Jessica." God, this conversation became bleak. I make another attempt at an easy smile and knock Jason's shoulder with mine. "But good to know you think I'm a catch. You sure you don't have a crush on me? All those nights sleeping in the top bunk knowing I'm right beneath you?"

Jason barks out a laugh. "You know...now that you mention it..."

I give him a light shove and grin—in earnest this time. "I may not be too good for Jessica, but I am definitely too good for you."

I push myself off from the railing and start walking home, knowing my friend's long legs will catch up to me in a couple seconds.

Home. Friend.

I came to New York hoping to get lost for a summer before having to fulfill all the obligations of who and what I'm expected to be. Instead, I'm finding things I never knew I ever needed or wanted.

Home. Friends.

Me.

chapter twenty-one

jessica

It's the big day. The kickoff to the hackathon we've been working so hard for all summer. The entire team left for the library early in the morning to finish last-minute preparations. I'm the last to head out from the office, picking up any stray items. My hands are full with extra boxes of pens, laptop chargers, a couple bags of Sour Patch Kids (to take the edge off), and my clipboard with the run of show top of page.

One of the Haneul SUVs is waiting for me outside the lobby at the curb. I recognize this driver, the one who took me to pick up Ella from the airport. I smile and bow as he takes all the items from my hands and helps me load the trunk. I get into the car and let the air-conditioning cool me down. I'm sweating not just from the heat, but from my nerves.

I need a pep talk, a virtual pat on the back, a fist pump

and a "hwaiting." It's still early out in California, but I dial Ella anyways.

"Hello?" A sleepy voice answers.

"I'm freaking out and I need you to tell me it's all gonna be okay," I say.

"Dear friend, is there any way you can reschedule your crises for later in the days from now on. I haven't even had any coffee yet," she whines.

"I'm so sorry to call so early. I just…"

I hear what sounds like slaps coming through the phone followed by a few gurgles and nose honks, and the unmistakable vibration of lips blowing a raspberry. "Okay, I'm awake and ready. Lay it on me," Ella says.

I have no idea what Ella did to wake up, but I could hug her for making herself available for me. "Um, okay, well first, you know the three-quarter-sleeve cardigan from the McQueen Spring collection in blush? Do you think that's the right choice for me to wear to today's hackathon?" I ask.

"Stylish yet demure. Invites one to be taken seriously, but with a touch of whimsy. Excellent choice," she answers. "And I'm very impressed at your growing appreciation of fashion. You really have changed this summer."

She means no harm, but for some reason I bristle at the comment, feeling defensive. I've had to change to fit the role. But I haven't changed who I am inside. Right?

"Ella? Am I in way over my head? Did I bite off more than I can chew? Am I going to be outed as a total hack, no pun intended?" I word vomit every fear going through my brain at the moment.

"Jessica, listen to me. You've had a taste of the good life

this summer. Fancy clothes, incredible food, *Hamilton* tickets, a slumber party with the company elite, even a kiss from
a chaebol prince. So it may seem like you're living a fairy
tale. But under all the glitz and glam, you're still you. Don't
forget that. You've worked hard, you led an incredible team,
you've all planned for every detail. It's going to be amazing.
It's all gonna work out."

I let Ella's words settle. She's right. It wasn't like I had some
proxy doing the work. That actually was me. And I trust myself. I trust the other interns. I let out a deep breath to com-
bat the nerves.

"Okay. That's exactly what I needed to hear. Thank you.
I love you."

"Go get 'em, tiger," she says. "Now I'm going back to
sleep."

I smile even though she can't see me. "I'll call you later,"
I say.

"I'll be here," she says.

She always is.

I climb up the hundreds of stairs that make the New York
Public Library both majestic and a pain in the ass to navigate.
A trickle of sweat makes its way down my back, paving the
way for the likely torrential downpour of perspiration sure to
follow. The late-July heat mixed with thick humidity is stifling, and the air-conditioning in these old buildings tends
to be unreliable. New York is that odd mix of having a ton
of money to have the nicest things, but an almost stubborn
hold on history and tradition.

This is exactly what the hackathon feels like to me. Haneul

Corp hasn't done anything inventive or new in a long time, despite all the money it has to make something happen. But today, we're gonna change that.

I step into the doorway of the Celeste Bartos Forum, the library's premier event venue, and stop in my tracks, my mouth dropping open in awe. The room is one massive open space with intricate antique lights framing arches all around. The walls are papered in what looks like gold and the highlight of it all, a frosted glass dome that sits above the room letting in a ton of natural light. The room is set up in rows of workstations, our rented tables covered in fabric as tablecloths. Each tabletop is equipped with the necessary electrical accessories: external monitors, power cords, hard drives, and laptops. Each hackathon team is required to use Haneul Corp's machines in order to keep the intellectual property intact.

On both sides of the room, there are snack stations and lounge chairs provided for the participants to take breaks. They'll be here for two full days working on their projects, coming up with the basis for what could be new titles produced by Haneul Corp's gaming division.

Everything is meticulously arranged just as planned. But seeing it all in person after weeks of envisioning it on a whiteboard is something else. I'm amazed. And incredibly proud. We did this. Our team of interns, who no one took seriously, did this.

I feel someone come up next to me. But I don't even have to turn to know who it is. It's his smell—he always smells so good, like walking through the woods right after a rain shower. My entire body is on high alert and the desire, the need to be near him, wills him closer like a magnet.

He doesn't belong to you. He has a whole different future mapped out for him with someone else. The reminder of what Hee-Jin shared with me the other night breaks through the haze of attraction and replaces itself with indignation. He kissed me. And the soft touches all summer on my back, my arm, my shoulder, like his hands can't help themselves. What's *that* about? And worst of all, he believed in me. Made me believe in myself. How was I supposed to not fall for him?

Even if whoever he's being set up with isn't someone Elijah's chosen for himself, it doesn't make it okay for him to neglect telling me, to lead me on.

He comes and stands next to me, looking around the room, taking it all in just like I did.

"Looks good, right?" Elijah says.

"Yeah, it does." I try to keep my voice light and unbothered.

"Is something bothering you?" he asks.

So much for that effort.

I close my eyes, take a deep breath, and try to push out all the feelings swarming around inside me. Elijah technically belongs to someone else. I can't let myself get caught up in a situation like that. Until he figures it out, I have to prevent anything else from happening between the two of us. Even though my heart wants the opposite.

I have no room for romantic drama in my life. I have to focus on why I'm here in the first place. The hackathon. The summer project. My one shot.

I open my eyes. I'm ready.

"I'm just in shock. I can't believe how amazing it looks.

It's not like I didn't think we could pull this off. But oh my god, we're actually gonna pull this off!"

"Honestly, I might have been a bit less confident we'd be able to do it. But everything came together," he says. What's that I hear in his voice? Is it pride? I know Elijah likes to play it off as if he doesn't care, as if he wasn't invested or involved. But the truth is, he was the glue that kept all the pieces together. Every single component of this event ended up funneling through him for final approvals, and he has proven to have a real eye for the detail that all the logistics required. Watching him these last few weeks, I could see the kind of leader he could be for this company.

I want to tell him all of this. I want to sit him down and make him see that he has so much more to offer than he gives himself credit for. I want him to believe that his future is lined with possibility. And what I really want to share with Elijah is how much I've come to care for him.

But I don't say any of it.

The buzz of a crowd grows louder and I turn around to see the participants starting to arrive. Many of them look as awestruck as I'm sure I did when entering the space. They take it all in, this production designed for them to try to create and present an exciting new video game in two days.

"Game time," Elijah says unironically. He winks at me, takes the clipboard from my hand, and approaches the group. "If you are participants in the hackathon, check-in is over here at this registration table. Please get your name badges and table assignments. Grab something to eat and drink. We'll kick off the event in about thirty minutes."

The energy in the air shifts a bit as a group of Very Impor-

tant People enter with their Very Important People postures
and their Very Important People expressions. The judges for
the hackathon. I knew we wouldn't be able to get the time
or attention from any of the executives of the company (other
than Hee-Jin of course), but I'm glad the team was able to
secure some of the managers from both the Engineering and
Development teams. Ms. Kang from Marketing, who assigned
this task to me in the first place—and was the first, other than
maybe Elijah, to believe I could do it—is also here.

"Wow, I'm impressed. This looks great," Hee-Jin says,
walking up with a smile. I recognize this as her work smile,
one that doesn't show too much emotion, but just enough
to convey her message. I take a mental note, as I always do
around her, watching for cues on how to act the part of someone successful, someone to be taken seriously but still admired.

"Thanks, the team worked really hard to pull this off," I
say. I can't quite name the expression on her face. But it's one
I've seen on a face so similar to hers before. Elijah has looked
at me this way sometimes over the past few weeks while working with the interns. Is it disbelief that someone like me could
get stuff done? Concern that this will never work out based
on how I'm leading? Heartburn from the very spicy Shang-
hai noodles we eat almost too often?

Or is it, maybe, respect?

"You've done an incredible job here, Jessica," Hee-Jin says.
"With very little support and barely any resources, you and
the other interns have managed to do something Haneul
hasn't been able to do in years: inject energy and excitement
into something new. I'm really grateful, and, I hope you don't
mind me saying, really proud."

I swallow back the emotion rising in my throat. No one has ever been proud of me before, other than my parents. For a moment, I wish my dad was here to see it all, even though he can never know how significant of a role I had in making this happen.

Hee-Jin looks over her shoulder to the registration table where Elijah is helping Grace and Roy check in the participants. A very different smile stretches over her face this time, unguarded, as if she's forgotten where she is and her role in the company. As if she's just a big sister watching her little brother do something she's never seen before.

And as I catch this moment, I realize that no one believes in him more than her. She's always known how capable he is. And I'm so grateful that he has someone on his side like this.

Elijah glances up just as Hee-Jin turns away, but I'm too slow. I'm still staring, probably with my mouth hanging open. Apparently capable and competent hardworking men are my type. As if I didn't know this all along.

He meets my eyes and gives me a small smile, then cocks his head to the front stage. Right, we're working here, not playing out some Netflix rom-com. He raises one eyebrow, silently asking me if I'm ready.

I hold his gaze for one more second and nod my head.

It's time for me to kick off this hackathon. It's time for all of our hard work to pay off. And it's time to finish everything I've started with these glass slippers and fake identity. I've loved being Lee Yoo-Jin, Executive Trainee at Haneul Corporation. So I'm gonna savor these last moments in this role and whatever happens after, come what may.

I'll always have this summer, this taste of what privilege

and opportunity can provide. And it'll be enough, hopefully, to kick-start my path to earning it for myself one day.

Hee-Jin stands at the front of the room and takes the mic. "Can I have everyone's attention please?" The group of Haneul Corp VIPs, the ones who did nothing for this hackathon but seem prepared to take all the credit for its success, line up just to the side of her.

I turn to Elijah and whisper, "Who do you think will win?"

He shrugs his shoulders. "It should be the pair from Japan. But knowing these engineers and the judges, I think it's going to be the guys from Canada. Both games are good. It's just the guys' game is safer."

I nod. I'm not sure I understand what he saw in either of the two presentations that makes him have an opinion of one over the other. But Elijah's the gamer and I trust his instincts. I just know I personally would love to see the female team from Japan win this, especially considering there just aren't that many women engineers right now in the gaming world.

"I want to thank you all for the time and effort you've put in over the last two days here," Hee-Jin says into the mic. "Thank you, especially, to our Haneul internship cohort for the incredible work you've done planning and executing on this hackathon."

I quell the desire to jump up and down like a cheerleader and I definitely fight the urge to preen like a peacock. Instead, I clap my hands in front of me like a seal, a huge smile taking over my face.

"And now, it is my honor and pleasure to announce that

the winner of the inaugural Haneul Corporation hackathon is… Team OverAppleWatch, Ben Lim and Enoch Song from Canada!"

The room explodes into applause. The participants go around and congratulate the winning team as well as each other.

After handing the large fake check to the winners and taking a bunch of publicity photos, Hee-Jin makes her way over to Elijah and me. "You did it! You all did it. I can't tell you how impressive this whole thing has been. The intern class at Haneul has never done anything of this scale," she says.

I lift my chin, standing a little taller. This time it doesn't feel like I have to fake it. I'm proud of myself. Truly.

"It's all because of our fearless leader," Elijah says, grinning at me. Hee-Jin looks at him like she knows the truth, that it wasn't just me. This was Elijah's idea in the first place, and the entire team came together to make it happen.

Jason comes up to us, handing out glasses of sparkling apple juice to me and Elijah and champagne for Hee-Jin. "I can't believe we pulled it off," he says. "It was amazing!"

"Cheers to a successful first hackathon, and may there be many more in the future, along with more opportunities for each of you to shine in your own ways," Hee-Jin says as we raise our glasses. I'm on top of the world, like nothing could bring me down from this wonderful feeling.

"Jessica?"

I whirl around as soon as I hear the familiar voice.

"Dad? What are you doing here?"

His suit is rumpled and his hair a bit of a mess. He looks to see if anyone heard our greeting, and when it's clear everyone else is in their own celebratory bubbles, he walks up to me. The smile on his face is like the warmest hug I didn't know I needed right now. I go to embrace him but he shakes his head a tiny bit. "Not at work. No one knows you're my daughter. I don't want anyone to accuse you of having an unfair advantage." He reaches out his hand and I stare at it a second before grabbing it and shaking it.

"I came because I wanted to see how this hackathon turned out. I would have arrived yesterday, but the airfare was cheaper if I flew the red-eye out on a Thursday," he explains. Classic Dad. "This is," he looks around the room, taking in the entire event me and the other interns planned, "quite impressive. There has always been incredible potential in what could be achieved with this program. It just never quite lived up to it until this year."

"Yeah, Dad, about that..." I want to ask him why he didn't come clean about how invested he was with the program. And why he didn't want me involved. I understand his position on nepotism and unfair privileges and all that. But he has got to know that if anyone deserves this spot, it's me.

"No, no, we can talk about everything later. I'm just proud that you were able to be a part of this. I do hope you were helpful to whoever was in charge." He searches the room and his eyes settle on Jason and Elijah, both looking busy, both looking important, both looking very male.

In an instant, my joy and sense of accomplishment bursts. I want to scream that I was the one in charge. I did even more than just help out. I led the team that put on this entire thing. But it would ruin everything. He'd know I lied to him all summer. And that look of pride on his face, the one that at the very least says that he knows I was part of a program that he champions in the company, would disappear.

Dad turns to Elijah's sister. "Hee-Jin, I assume you are to credit for this as the executive sponsor? Well done, and thank you for always being an advocate for the internship program."

"Well, Janet Kang in Marketing is the executive sponsor. But really, all the credit should go to Jessi—"

"Mr. Lee? Hello, my name is Elijah. I'm a friend of Jessica's who also worked on the hackathon." Elijah quickly cuts off Hee-Jin before she reveals too much to my dad. He holds out his hand, and my dad looks at it suspiciously before shaking it.

"A friend of Jessica's, you say?" he asks.

Uh-oh.

I step up to intervene before my dad goes into full-on scare-away-any-suitors mode.

But just as I do, a sudden chill fills the air as the buzz and excitement in the room quickly dies down. I look over my shoulder to see what's going on as a group of short, intimidating Korean men in suits enters the room.

"Shit," Hee-Jin says under her breath.

"What the fuck is he doing here?" Elijah adds.

My blood turns cold and I freeze on the spot. Leading the way is a man with a face oddly familiar to me. He walks with a sense of importance, and people step back, bowing, and clearing a path as he makes his way toward us. As he gets closer, I realize where I've seen him before. His is the face of his children.

Lee Jung-Hyun, CEO of Haneul Corp.

And his eyes are on no one else but me.

"Hwe-jangnim." My dad steps in front of me to intercept him, bowing and greeting his boss.

"I should have known you'd be involved in this," Mr. Lee says to my dad.

Their voices are professional, cordial even, but I know all the different ways my dad expresses himself. This, with his jaw clenched, arms held straight to his side, is tense, forced.

"I'm just here to congratulate the internship cohort on a successful hackathon project," my dad replies.

"That's right, wasn't your daughter one of the interns chosen for the program? You were always so against giving anyone an unfair advantage and yet here we are. Seems when it's a personal benefit, you're singing a different tune," Chairman Lee says.

"You and I both know that is not what happened," my dad responds. He turns to me. "Jessica, if you're finished here, I'll take you out to dinner to celebrate your summer."

"She's not going anywhere, not until I've had the chance to introduce myself." All attention is on the CEO, his voice authoritative, leaving no room for discussion. But his focus is lasered directly at me.

He's shorter than both his son and daughter. No hair out of place. No wrinkles in his designer suit. Tie perfectly tied. Just enough cologne to scream richness but not too much to overwhelm.

"When you're not sure if someone likes you or not, Jessica, make sure to lead with a smile. It disarms people," I hear my mother say to me.

I swallow back my fear. I attempt a smile, but I can't stop

my lips from quivering. I try to straighten my back and lift my chin, but I'm paralyzed in this moment.

Because if he knows who I am, and if he wants to meet me specifically, what else does he know?

Or maybe, just maybe, he has no idea at all. He could be interested in meeting the daughter of someone who works for him. I lift my eyes to his, and just as I'm about to bow in greeting, he says...

"So, you must be Jessica Lee. Or should I call you Lee Yoo-Jin?"

chapter twenty-two

elijah

My dad walks right past me without a second glance.

My feet are stuck to the ground and I can't move. What is he doing here? He's never shown any interest in his company's events at this level, and he didn't announce a trip to the US. But it's not a coincidence that he's here at the New York Public Library the same time as the hackathon.

Which means, he must be here for me.

A chill runs down my spine.

My sister regains her composure before I do and rushes up to him. "Annyeounghasaeyo, Chairman Lee," she says as she bows deeply.

He lets out a slight grunt, barely even acknowledging Hee-Jin. He whispers something to a frazzled man trailing closely behind him. Likely one of his many assistants. But his focus is elsewhere, and as I follow his eyes, I see his target.

Jessica.

My father turns slightly, taking her in from head to toe, before plastering his rehearsed smile on his face.

Jessica straightens her back and lifts her chin, doing her best to put on her armor. She smiles but her lips twitch. She's terrified.

"So, you must be Jessica Lee. Or should I call you Lee Yoo-Jin?" he says to her. His voice is oddly warm, a kindness I've rarely heard from him. My brows furrow together and I feel a trickle of sweat drop down my back.

"Yes, sir, I am Jessica Lee," she says confidently. She balls her hands into fists behind her back. When I go to take a step forward to confront him, to shield her from him, she flicks her right hand open in my direction, shooing me away from her. Telling me not to come to her rescue.

I obey her wishes, but my stomach twists into a knot. She doesn't know what he's capable of.

"I am Lee Jung-Hyun, the CEO of Haneul Corporation. I've heard great things about you and what you've been doing this summer in the Executive Training Program." He can't control the tic in his cheek. My dad may be laying the praise on thick, but I know him well enough to see the tension in his face betraying him. "Seems this project of yours has been quite the success."

Jessica nods as her face stretches into a small smile.

Don't fall for it, Jessica.

But there's this tiny part of me, a part that I hate and don't understand, that can't help but hope he'll look at me. Praise me for my hard work this summer, with that rare glimmer of approval in his eyes. Would he even believe me if I told him what I've been up to? I clear my throat to speak…

But my dad shoots a knowing glare in my direction. I'm about to get my ass handed to me, but not now, not in public. Never in public.

"Project of *yours*?" Jessica's father asks, clearly confused. Shit.

"Thank you," Jessica says, looking between her father and mine, "but it's not just my project. The entire intern team worked really hard to make this a success."

"Yes," my father says, "but as the executive trainee, you led the hackathon to its success. You were invaluable, going well beyond what was expected of you." To an ear untrained on the nuances of my father's voice, he may seem to be giving a compliment. But to someone who has heard the inflections when he's unimpressed, disappointed, even furious, all within the same words, I can tell he is not happy. To me, he sounds almost like he's blaming Jessica for something.

He knows what's been going on. Someone's told him or he's figured it out somehow. I look at my sister and although she masks her own freak-out with a shuttered expression, tension radiates off of her. There's no way Hee-Jin told him—she would never betray me like this. But no one else knew Jessica and I switched places, so how could he have found out?

"Come, Jessica, show me around and introduce me to each of the participating teams. Tell me what this hackathon has managed to do for Haneul Corp," he says, walking away with his hands clasped behind his back. Hee-Jin falls quickly joins him a step behind and Jessica does as well.

"Jessica..." I call out weakly.

"Jessica..." her father calls out at the same time.

Jessica doesn't stop for either of us. We're left staring after her, helpless.

"You said your name was Elijah? And you're a friend of Jessica's?" her dad asks me.

"Yes, um, I'm one of the interns who worked with her on this project," I answer.

"Elijah, I'm a bit confused as to what is going on here, and Jessica doesn't seem to be available to clarify for me right now." His jaw is tight, his words clipped. I don't know if he's angrier at Jessica walking away from him, or the fact that she did so with my father.

This is not good.

Jessica and I have not discussed how we would handle it if we ever did actually get caught. We didn't get our stories straight about how we might come clean about the choices we made for this summer.

"Sir, I don't know if I'm the right person to give you those answers. I'm sorry. But I do know that Jessica has been working incredibly hard, taking advantage of any and every opportunity to succeed. And she's done so in the hope of making you very proud. I have no doubt this will make it possible for her to get letters of recommendation she needs so she can actually apply for scholarships next year," I say.

"I'm sorry. Did you say she needed letters of recommendation? So she could apply *next* year? Meaning she didn't apply for any scholarships *this* year?" he asks.

Fuck.

Fuck, fuck, fuck. I forgot she hadn't told him that. This is bad. But honestly, this isn't my top priority right now. She's in my dad's cross hairs. I need to rescue her or something. If I don't step up and take the hit, Jessica will be the one in the line of fire.

"Actually, I think I'm mistaken. That's not what I meant. In any case, will you excuse me? I need to, um, settle things with the other interns." I bow and turn and get myself the hell out of the waters I just muddied with Jessica's dad.

Once I'm a safe distance away, I watch as my dad dotes over Jessica in a way I've never seen him do before, leading her around the room. My sister even seems totally taken aback by it. I wait for my opening, and finally the group of Haneul executives circle around to greet my father, leaving Jessica to congratulate the winning hackathon team.

I gently grab her by the arm. "Hey, can I talk to you for a sec?"

She looks up and me, eyes questioning, but nods and follows as I pull her off to the side.

"What did my dad say to you? Are you okay? Is he pissed? How did he find out?" I can't stop the questions from pouring out of me.

"He didn't ask me about any of that stuff. He just kept congratulating me and telling me how impressed he is with the work I've done." Her smile lights up her face and her posture is straight, chin raised. But this isn't the armor she puts on when she's pretending. It's real this time. "He's taking me and the other executives to dinner."

"What? Why?"

"To celebrate. And guess where we're going? Nobu. Can you believe it? I finally get to try that five-hundred-dollar dinner." Her grin widens, but I feel sick to my stomach. Nobu is where my dad goes when he's in shark mode. And a month ago, she would have refused to eat at a place that costs that much money.

"I'm coming with you," I say.

"Oh, um, okay. But can you just make sure that's fine with your dad? I, uh, don't know who's all invited to this thing. Sorry."

Hee-Jin comes up to the two of us. "Jessica, we're leaving. You can ride with me to the restaurant." She looks over at me, slightly frazzled. "Elijah, it's a work dinner, just Dad's exec team," she says.

I open my mouth to protest, to insist I come along.

"Elijah, don't worry, I'll do my best to protect her," Hee-Jin says.

But I am worried. There's so much that Jessica doesn't know, that I don't have time to warn her about. Like the fact that my dad requires everyone to wear black or dark blue to not distract from the meal, and Jessica has on a yellow blouse. Or that he doesn't allow anyone to have ice in their drinks for whatever fucked-up reason. Or that the seat to his right is the place of honor. But if you're next to him on his left, you're on his shit list and he'll turn his back to you the entire night to make a public fool of you. God, I hope she isn't seated to his left.

But most of all, I have to make sure she remembers that he's not a good person, to please please please don't fall for his act. I want to say to her, *Don't let him wine and dine you and change your mind about me. Trust me. Believe in me.*

"I'll call you later," Jessica says. "I promise." She grabs my hand and squeezes. But before I can squeeze back, she's let it go.

And all I can do is watch her walk away.

chapter twenty-two

—

elijah

Hey, can we talk? I text Jessica again.

I haven't seen or spoken to her since yesterday's surprise appearance by my dad at the Hackathon. I haven't seen or spoken to my dad either. None of this bodes well.

My screen remains blank.

"So is this a good time for me to point out the obvious, that something doesn't seem right in the land of Haneul Corp?" Jason asks.

We're back at our tiny intern apartment. Despite the weak window A/C units that do nothing to lessen the stifling heat and humidity, the usually-empty fridge and diet alarmingly lacking in fruits and vegetables, the lumpy beds, and the complete lack of privacy, somehow, through the course of this summer, this place has come to be a safe space.

But in this moment, the walls feel like they're pushing in on me.

I don't have it in me to explain everything to Jason right now. So I shrug my shoulders and go back to staring at my phone, willing for a message to appear.

"Maybe you want to get something off your chest? Free yourself from the burden of a secret? You know, like why the CEO of the company shows up and hey, come to think of it, you kinda look a lot like him." Jason keeps pushing.

I look up slowly and meet his eyes. There's no accusation there. Just curiosity.

"There's so much that needs to be shared with everyone, I know. It's just, I gotta get ahold of Jessica first. And I swear, I'll tell you all about it later." I can't divulge anything without talking to Jessica—I don't want to make assumptions for her. But I'm tired of living the lie. I don't hate the life it has allowed me to have this summer, but it sucks deceiving my friends, the people who have come to trust me and like me for who I am, not who my family is.

Jason nods. "It's Saturday morning. She's likely not at the office. Maybe she slept in after the hackathon? Or she could be sightseeing. Doesn't she live by Central Park?"

The park.

"Yeah, good thinking. Hey, let's catch up later. You're right, there's a lot I need to come clean about. But for now, I gotta go," I say.

I rush out the door, leaving Jason and my lies behind.

"I thought I might find you here," I say. Jessica is wearing denim shorts and a white V-neck T-shirt, her hair tied back in a messy ponytail. She reminds me of the girl I ran into at the airport our first day here.

She looks up at me, eyebrows raised. "Wow, I thought this stuff only happens in the movies. You found me at a random bench in Central Park?" She narrows her eyes at me, realizing the odds of this happening are quite small, actually.

"Not random. You told me about how this is Ella's favorite spot in the park," I remind her. "I promised I'd come here with you." I take the seat next to her on the bench. "And I could lie and say I got lucky with timing. But I actually went by the brownstone first. Mrs. Choi said you were going for a walk." Jessica's smile is warm, but not the kind that usually lights up her entire face. She's bracing herself for the conversation we're about to have. I lean forward and grab the end of the bench seat on either side of my legs, holding on.

She nods, lowering her gaze. "I'm sorry I haven't answered your messages. I was busy with…"

"…with my dad?"

She still can't meet my eyes. She's looking just off to the right of me at something, at nothing. "How could I say 'no' when the CEO of Haneul invites me to dinner to celebrate?"

"Well, we have to figure out how we're going to come clean to our dads about this summer. Obviously my dad knows already. But yours is looking for answers."

"Why does it have to be a big deal?" Jessica asks. "Your dad knows, yes. But he hasn't even brought up the fact that I'm in your position and you're in mine. I don't think it bothers him," she says. I see the thoughts running through her head. Is she trying to convince me or herself of this?

Problem is, I know my dad, and I'm just waiting for shit to hit the fan.

"It bothers him. Trust me. He does not like being played the fool. And he may not take it out on you. I hope he doesn't. But I'm counting the minutes until it's time for him to take it out on me," I say. "It's probably why he's kissing your ass. He knows it makes me uncomfortable."

"Or maybe he's just impressed with the work I've done?"

I roll my eyes.

Wrong move.

She glares at me, her jaw set. She straightens her posture and lifts her chin like she does every time she's faced confrontation. I know this battle stance. In fact, it's one of the things I find so attractive about Jessica. These moments when her grit and determination outweigh any uncertainty.

But her face wears an expression I don't think I've ever seen from her despite the months we've spent together. There's fire in her narrowed eyes, mouth tightened to a thin line.

She's pissed.

At me.

"Are you saying I don't deserve to be recognized for my hard work? This is exactly why I spent all those late nights at the office and worked so hard all summer. Your father introduced me to someone at dinner who said he'd write me a letter of recommendation immediately, and he's even gonna call his friend—the provost of UC San Diego—to set up an introduction."

There's a twinge of desperation in her voice. She needs to believe that all of this is real, that my father really would do this for her out of the kindness of his heart.

But what she doesn't understand is that he doesn't have a heart.

She sighs deeply, tilting her head back toward the sky before facing me again. "Look, I know you and your dad have issues and don't agree on much. It's just that, well, I'm really grateful for everything he's done for me in such a short time. This will change the course of my life," she quickly tries to explain.

No, I can't let her buy into this. I won't.

"He doesn't mean it. He's using you..." I say.

"So what?" Her words catch me off guard. *So what?* Jessica tightens her lips and breathes out of her nose, nostrils flaring like a bull ready to attack.

"...to get back at me," I clarify.

"And you used me to get back at him."

Her words cut like a knife. "What are you talking about?"

"You used me to get exactly what you wanted this summer, Elijah. You suggested I take this role so you wouldn't have to do anything."

"Are you serious? You of all people know I've worked my ass off this summer." Has she forgotten how I took care of all the shit that no one wanted to do, the shit that no one gives credit for or notices? I did that. Fucking logistics. And I loved it.

And I loved that she noticed. She appreciated my work.

"I didn't mean it like that," she backpedals.

But she can't take it back. It's out there. Now it's my turn.

"And what? You didn't get exactly what you wanted from this deal? You're gonna receive that precious letter of recommendation. And it's probably gonna be handed to you from the fucking CEO himself. Congratulations. You've sold your soul to Haneul Corporation. Have a happy life. We've seen how that's turned out for everyone, including your dad."

Jessica jumps to her feet and stares down at me, pointing a finger in my face. "Don't you dare bring my dad into this," she says.

"You can't just pick and choose who's dragged through this, Jessica. Have you even talked to him since yesterday? Or have you been too busy hanging out with my dad?"

Her eyes widen and she opens her mouth to deny that she's basically forgotten her dad is even in town. But she can't seem to find the words. She knows there's no excuse that she could say to me.

"Jessica, your dad fought for this internship program even though he knew the execs wouldn't give a shit about it. And at the end of the summer, after all you've gone through at this crappy company, you're siding with Haneul over your own dad?" I ask. *Over me?*

She lets out a long breath, drops her shoulders, and looks away from me. "I'm not siding with anyone. If anything, I'm choosing myself, and I shouldn't have to feel guilty about that," she says. The anger isn't in her voice anymore. She sounds tired, resigned.

"Elijah, we've had this conversation multiple times before. You and I," she says, then hesitates, "we're, we're not alike."

I can't take it. I stand up, and her eyes raise to look at me.

"You mean our *lives* are not alike," I say. Because if this summer proved anything to me, it's that I can fit in with other people. I don't have to hide away in some ivory castle. I can work, make friends...fall in love...just like everyone else. Just like Jessica. But the words stay locked away. I don't say any of it.

She shakes her head and takes a step back, putting space between us. I don't like this move one bit. "No, I mean, *we* are not alike," she responds, gesturing between the two of us. "We don't think the same way. We don't approach things the same way. You've never had to live your life accountable for anything. You know, you can mess up or don't do your best and someone's gonna cover for you no matter what. Meanwhile, I can do the best job I possibly can and someone's still gonna find fault."

It feels like Jessica is blaming me for all of this. Like I'm the reason the world favors the rich and privileged.

I can feel heat rising in my bones, my temper flaring. "You can't be mad at me for the families we were born into. I can't change the fact that I'm a chaebol," I say.

She turns her back to me and looks straight ahead in the distance. The juxtaposition of Central Park and the city skyline so close by is supposed to make this specific spot magical. Instead, it feels like we've just been scammed by a false sense of beauty, when the lies and demands of the city are just minutes away.

"Elijah, remember what you told me from the start? Rich people use other people to get what they want. Last time I checked, you're the one handing over hundred-dollar bills to security guards, bribing fabric store managers…" she glances over her shoulder back at me, "…paying the New York Library on your personal credit card and lying about it."

He knows. And he told her. My dad told her. And she's using information he gave her against me. What exactly is she accusing me of? Using money that I have to pay for things we needed? What's the harm in that? It's not a fucking sin to be rich.

"You didn't seem to have a problem enjoying the *Hamilton* tickets and all those designer clothes and that huge brownstone. Do you think those things are free? Money gets you things you need, the things you want. Don't get angry at me for spending my family's money for the library when you've been loving all the other shit this same money has given you this summer," I say before I can stop myself.

"Fuck you."

I freeze.

Jessica never swears.

And hearing it come out of her mouth, it sounds sharp like razors, slicing through her outer shell. Two words betray how hurt she is. And I feel it deep in my core.

I tell my feet to move, to go stand beside her. I want to hold her and apologize and ask if we can try to figure this all out together. But I'm stuck to my spot, the feeling of betrayal growing roots within me. She sided with my dad over me, didn't she?

"Jessica, what are we fighting about? Is this about the job? Our bank accounts? Or is it about us and our feelings and—"

"—and some girl waiting back home for you?" she asks.

My jaw falls open at her words. "Wait...what? What are you talking about?"

Her entire face drops, along with her shoulders. As if the weight of some secret, bigger than the one we've been keeping together all summer, has settled on her. As if she's finally built up the nerve to ask me a question she's been keeping from me.

"Is there someone you're going to be set up with in Korea? A daughter of someone important for Haneul Corp?"

I scan my brain for what she might mean by this, what she might have heard. And it hits me, the conversation with my dad over the phone, the night Jessica and I went to *Hamilton*. The daughter of the Paik family...but that's all just my dad spewing nonsense, making plans for my life I have no intention of following through with.

"No, no. Are you kidding me? Do you think I'd agree to be set up with some random person because it's good for the company I don't give two shits about? And you think I'd be here in New York falling for you if that were true? Seriously?"

Jessica searches my eyes for some truth I'm not telling her. Or for some proof of a lie.

"You're falling for me?" she asks quietly.

"I am." I said it. I meant it.

But she doesn't return the words. Instead, she stitches her eyebrows together and swallows. She sits down on the park bench, her hands gripping the slats like mine were at the start of this conversation. Her feet don't reach the ground and she swings them back and forth, watching them as they move to an unheard rhythm.

There's something about this that is so utterly charming, I just want to wrap her in my arms and kiss her. I want to take her far away from here, from my dad, from our mistakes and make it right for her, for us.

I sit down next to her, but not too close to scare her away.

How quickly things have changed. All summer, our bodies felt drawn to each other, like we couldn't get close enough.

"Do you remember when we first met up at the coffee shop?" Her voice is so quiet, I can barely hear her. She's talking down at her feet, not at me. None of this feels like a good sign. "The day when we first figured out the mistake, and then you made the suggestion that we switch lives for the summer?"

"Of course I do. Best first date of my life," I say. I force a smile to overcome the sudden awkwardness between us.

She closes her eyes as if pained to open them and see the truth. "You told me I should take this opportunity. You knew I needed to have something, anything, given to me to make my road ahead easier. You talked me into this by presenting a path I would never have been offered before. And I took it. Because you were right." Jessica opens her eyes and turns to look straight into mine. "I'll never have a chance like this again, Elijah. I need your dad's help."

I know my father. I know how he operates. He's a negotiator. He's a shark, waiting to devour his prey. He isn't doing any of this out of the goodness of his heart or because he's impressed with a lowly intern. Even one as remarkable as Jessica. "The introduction to the 'right' people, the letter of recommendation…what did my dad ask of you in return?"

It's like the world stops in the seconds before she answers.

"He told me to go home now and that he'll contact me in a few weeks, after Sky High. He said he needs time to set some things up for me, to take care of what I need. There's no use for me to stay here in New York while I wait anyway…"

"He's kicking you out? Of the company? Of New York?"

She shakes her head. "No, it's not like that."

That's when it hits me what my dad is planning. It's as if my father's own hands are reaching into my chest and taking hold of my heart, strangling it. He'd do anything to keep me from being happy on my own terms. "No, he's kicking you out of my life."

"Elijah, it's not like that either. He actually, um, didn't mention you at all."

"Jessica. C'mon." I throw my hands up in the air. "What in everything that I've told you about my dad makes you think he'd give anyone something for nothing in return?"

"I'm certain, Elijah. He didn't ask me for anything."

"For now. But he will," I say without doubt.

"Why can't you just believe this is something your dad wants to do? Why can't you acknowledge that the work we did this summer could be enough to impress the CEO of the company?"

"I can't believe how naïve you're being. You only agreed to this plan in the first place because you needed it. But now it seems like you want it," I say. "Enough to believe whatever my dad promises you...at whatever cost."

"Honestly? I don't know what I want. But what about you? You wanted time to figure out who you are. And now that you've figured it out, what are you gonna do about it? You talk a lot of talk, but are you actually gonna leave the security of your life? Are you gonna tell your dad that you don't want to be set up with this girl? That you don't want to be CEO of Haneul Corp? That you don't want everything he wants from you?"

"It's not as easy as just saying it, Jessica."

"But it won't ever be easy if you *don't* say it, Elijah."

We're at a standstill.

"I leave tomorrow," she says, a finality in her tone. Well, at least one of us has the guts to take what they want. I just didn't believe she'd toss me aside so easily to get it.

I've got to find out exactly what my dad is up to. Rip off the Band-Aid and get it over with. Accept whatever punishment he wants to give me as long as it's not one he doles out on Jessica too.

"I have to go," I say, quickly getting up from my seat. I have to leave now or I never will. "Jessica, go and talk to your dad. See what he thinks about all of this," I say.

"And what are you going to do?"

"I'm also going to go talk to my dad. He and I have got some unfinished business."

chapter twenty-three

jessica

I knock on the door marked two-fourteen at the Courtyard Marriott in Times Square. The room is right next to the elevator, and I can hear the chatter of people below through the elevator shaft along with the ding at each floor as it arrives. I wonder if my dad requested this much less desirable room location for a discount.

There are stains on the carpet in the hallway and some scratches on the door near the peephole. The lighting is slightly yellowed and I notice a tiny corner of the wallpaper starting to pull away from the wall. All in all, the place is well used, but clean and serviceable. Before this summer, I would have thought we splurged on a hotel like this.

But apparently things like room location and minor signs of wear and tear are different to me now. These details make me judge the person associated with them. As if a summer pretending to be the one percent has made me actually think like them.

I'm nervous. My palms are sweating and my heart's trying to pound its way free from my chest. I don't think it's that I'm afraid my dad is mad at me.

It's more that I'm afraid he's disappointed in me.

The door clicks open. My father looks tired. There are dark circles under his eyes.

He reaches for me and pulls me into a hug. It's awkward. I'm stiff. Our family doesn't really show outward signs of affection. But it only takes me a second before I let go and melt into him. I circle my arms around him and place my head to his chest. His heartbeat is strong and steady.

"I'm glad you're here, Dad," I say as we pull apart. "There's so much I want to tell you."

"Come inside honey," he says. I only then realize that we're still in the doorway. I follow him inside and stand awkwardly in the middle of the room, not sure where to sit.

My dad opens the mini fridge next to a chest of drawers with fake wood paneling, and I get a strong whiff of something pungent. Kimchi or some kind of Korean food. I have no doubt he filled this tiny refrigerator to the brim in order to save money by not going out to eat. When I think of the huge kitchen and pantry overstuffed in the brownstone, and the lavish dinner Mr. Lee took me to last night, guilt overwhelms me.

Dad pulls out a red can of Coke and pops it open, passing it to me. He only ever drinks water or tea, so he must have bought it specifically for me when I got here...eventually. I can't believe I kept him waiting an entire day while I schmoozed with the CEO of his company.

Keep it together, Jessica, I say to myself, blinking away the tears that are forming. I take a sip of the soda, the cold bubbles burning just a little bit as I swallow them down. Before this summer, I used to need a Coke a day—preferably full-fat—to survive, but in this moment, I'm realizing I haven't had one in months. There are fancy flavored sparkling drinks and natural sodas stocked in the refrigerator of the brownstone. It took a lot of getting used to at first, but eventually, like wearing designer clothes and having a prestigious young leadership role in a huge company, it became a part of my everyday life. I came to like those things. At least that's what I told myself.

Something about this Coke feels so ordinary. So...me.

There's a comfort in remembering that my dad knows me this well. The real me. Unlike anyone here in New York—not Elijah, maybe not even myself anymore. It's a huge relief that my dad is here, that I don't have to wear a mask, that I can let go and be completely in his care...

"Jessica Yoo-Jin Lee..."

Oh shoot. He's pulled out the full name again. I'm in for it.

"You are grounded until you turn thirty years old. And, and...you'll start working at your Aunt Eunice's car wash/dry cleaners full-time, including weekends, until you start school."

"Dad!" He hasn't even heard my full confession. "You can't do that. You don't even know if this punishment suits the crime. And anyways, Suds and Steamers is closed on Sundays."

He narrows his eyes at me, probably wondering if he can talk my Aunt Eunice into staying open on Sundays.

"I messed up, Dad," I say, finally breaking the silence. My voice comes out sounding like a little kid's.

He places both hands on his hips and lets out a deep, tired sigh. "Sit down, Jessica, and start from the beginning."

I make myself comfortable on the crisp white bed, crossing my legs and tucking both my feet under them. I clasp my hands, look down at my thumbs, and begin the story of how Elijah and I swapped places for the summer. How I found myself in the favor of the CEO of Haneul Corporation.

I'm not sure if anything's salvageable from the choices I've made this summer. I want to be proud of the hackathon, leading the team, and even the offer that Mr. Lee has given me to help with my future. But something about it all, as I lay it out before my dad, feels dirty. It was achieved by dishonesty and deception.

When I'm done and finally look up at him, his eyes are closed but his breath is steady. I know he was listening by the way he's nodding his head.

I wait for him to chastise me. I wait for him to tell me he's angry and disappointed. I wait for him to extend my grounding until I'm fifty years old.

What I don't expect is the tear that trickles down his cheek. I track its movement until it hangs from his chin and finally lets go, dropping to the ground.

"Dad, are you crying?" My throat is so thick with emotion I fear I might choke on it. I've never once in my entire life seen my dad cry.

He quickly wipes his eyes with the heel of his palm. He

looks down at his hand and stares at the wetness, as if he too is surprised to find tears there. "I'm so sorry Jessica. I'm sorry that I couldn't provide the opportunities that you deserve. You worked as hard as you could to produce the best grades, and yet you had to worry about your financial situation. About letters of recommendation and scholarships. You had to accept a choice lesser than what you're capable of by going to junior college. And because you believe that the world is unfair, you took an opportunity to live a lie this summer in order to open up some doors for yourself. And all of this is on me. It's my fault."

"It's not your fault," I insist. "It's my fault. It's the ridiculous higher education system's fault. But we can't change that. I'm not even mad that I had to take a summer internship. In fact, it turned out to be a great experience. Dad, we managed to put on the first ever hackathon at one of the largest tech companies in the world." If I focus on all the good, maybe it'll lesson the guilt that I had to lie my way to do it.

He drops his head to his chest. "Jessica, Haneul Corp may be shiny on the outside, but inside, it's broken, its way of doing business backward." He reaches out and grabs both my hands in his, raising his eyes to meet mine. "So much of who we become as adults is influenced by the work we do and where we do it. My hope for you is to get this experience at places that value people and take pride in honest work. Companies that don't just give lip service to diversity and inclusion, but respect everyone regardless of gender identity, age, economic background. I want your world to be expanded by the work that you do, not limited. And because Haneul is not that kind of company, you made a dishonest choice to get what you thought you needed. I was resistant for you to come work here, Jessica, not because I didn't think you could. But because I wanted so much better for you."

I swallow back the shame rising in my throat. I don't know what to say. Tears push their way to the corners of my eyes, threatening to fall. I'd always believed my dad was trying to control my choices. And come to find, he was trying to direct me to better ones.

My dad stands up and walks to the window, looking out at the bright lights of Times Square shining twenty-four hours a day. I wonder if he's mentally tabulating the electricity costs.

"What's done is done," he says. The softness of his voice gone, replaced now with the all-business tone I'm so used to from him. "I'll meet with Chairman Lee and discuss appropriate next steps. I'll accept whatever disciplinary action he decides for me."

"For you? No, Dad, everything I did this summer, good and bad, was my choice and I have to live with whatever the consequences," I say, struggling to convey a strength I don't feel. "But honestly, I don't think anyone's gonna make a big deal about this. I know that sounds like wishful thinking. But these people, the ones in charge, they have bigger problems to deal with than some drama in their internship program, right?"

"The people you're talking about care very much about how they're perceived. If they think you've made a fool of them, it could end badly. I've tried to champion this internship program for years. But it's been a struggle to get any support behind it."

"Yeah, but that's the thing, Dad. This year was different.

We made an impact." I muster all the hope I can into my voice so he can see how proud I am of what we've accomplished despite the obstacles.

"That's exactly what I'm worried about," he says.

I drop my head into my hands. The only thing these adults care about is perception, not the truth. How can a company run like this?

"Chairman Lee has offered to put in a good word for me, and he's arranged to have someone write a letter of recommendation for a scholarship or something. He wants to help me in some way," I say.

"No," my father says without hesitation. "Absolutely not. You will not accept anything from that man. He cannot be trusted, Jessica." My dad reaches out to grab my hand, squeezing comfortingly. His eyes are sad but resolute. It dawns on me how similar his words are to Elijah's warning about his father.

I want to rebel. I want to tell my dad he's overreacting. I want to scream that Chairman Lee has something to give and it's *nothing* in the grand scheme of things for him to do so. So why wouldn't I accept whatever he offers?

I may have deceived my father this summer, but I've never directly disobeyed anything he's told me to do. Well, he did tell me to stay out of trouble and I guess I blew that one. But still.

It's frustrating that he and Elijah are both so stubborn that they can't just let it go. I get it, Chairman Lee is not a good guy. But that doesn't mean he's got some sinister plan up his sleeve just by jump-starting my future. I know my father despises Haneul Corp, but honestly, isn't every huge company out there just one and the same? I'm here. I've put in the work. Why can't I benefit from it all?

"We'll find another way," my dad goes on. "You'll walk away from this summer with a hard lesson learned and nothing more. We'll figure out the rest as a family."

"I still don't understand why we can't just accept his help," I say in one last-ditch effort to convince my dad.

"Some things are not worth the cost," he replies, "and I'm not just talking about dollars."

chapter twenty-four

---

elijah

I dial my sister's number.

"Where is he?"

"Elijah, trust me when I say you do not want to see Dad right now. He's furious with you, and Mom is doing everything she can to keep him from cutting you off this instant."

"Mom's here?" She never travels with my dad for work. If she's here, it's because she's really worried about me. Mom has always been the only one who can calm my dad down when he's on a tirade—and she's only successful maybe half the time. "Where are they, Hee-Jin?"

"We're all at The Plaza," she says with a sigh.

They're only a few blocks away so I break out into a run. Despite the unbearable humidity and the sidewalks filled with huge crowds of people visiting the area around Central Park, I make it there quickly.

The Plaza Hotel looks like a castle in the middle of New York City, tall columns with chiseled statues bookending the entrance. I rush through the massive front doors, looking around the grand lobby—past priceless artwork hung on walls, leather and velvet sofas more like museum pieces than places to comfortably sit, and hotel guests dressed in what they've determined in their minds as their "New York best" but entirely impractical—realizing that nothing about this opulence attracts me.

I find the elevators and follow a bellman with a luggage cart stacked with at least ten pieces of Globe-Trotter trunks, suitcases, and garment bags. He looks up at me and scans from head to toe, probably wondering what I'm doing here in my generic T-shirt, my average jeans, my everyday Nikes. I don't give a shit what he thinks of me.

"Penthouse, please," I say to him, as he's standing in front of all the buttons to the floors of the hotel.

He narrows his eyes, hesitant to comply.

I reach over and press the *P* button myself and then lean against the back wall of the elevator, close my eyes, and try to catch my breath, preparing myself to have it out with my dad.

The bellman gets off on the ninth floor and I don't bother to even look at him. If he's so suspicious about me, call security for all I care. A part of me wants to call out to him and say that my father would never have us stay in any room that wasn't the top floor, while his guests with their overpriced luggage are only here on the ninth.

But I stop myself. Because that would be something a spoiled asshole would say. I actually don't care about being recognized as someone rich enough, someone deemed worthy to ride in an elevator to the upper floors of The Plaza. I'm so over how people judge others and their value, their right to be somewhere, by how they show off their money. I'm so over how *I* used to be before this summer.

So I wait till the doors close again and ignore the lighted number announcing where I'm going. I just ride all the way until the bell dings and when the elevator doors slide open, I get out to face my doom.

My father's back is to me as he looks out the window toward the expansive view of Central Park. His phone is held up to his ear and I hear him yelling at someone in Korean about flight times.

My mom sits on the oversized white sofa in the living area of the penthouse suite. A memory of Jessica freaking out over me sitting in the white sofa in the brownstone threatens to bring a smile to my face, but I hold it back. Mom's legs are crossed at the ankle, her hands clasped in her lap. Her eyes lowered a perfect forty-five degrees. A glass of white wine sits off to her right on the black marble side table. I watch as a drop of condensation makes its way down toward the stem. For some reason, the one thing I think about is how distressed my mother must be if she forgot to put a coaster under her glass.

My sister sits in one of the gold armchairs at the dining table just off the living area. I glance over at her and she gives me a small smile. It strikes me as odd that she's not sitting next to my mother. I wonder how much Dad's already taken out on her about this whole fiasco.

"I'm sorry," I mouth to her. She shakes her head and waves

her hand slightly as if to tell me not to worry. I let out a deep, even breath.

"You thought I wouldn't find out?" I jump as my dad's strong voice cuts through the tense air, startling me. There is no warmth in his tone. He doesn't speak to me as a father to a son, but more like an employee he has no time for and is annoyed he has to deal with.

"I was going to tell you…" I try to explain.

"Don't lie to me, Son. If you wanted to keep this a secret, then you shouldn't have thrown our name around carelessly. Using connections to secure the library for your little hackathon, but thinking it wouldn't get back to me. Do you truly believe the world is this easy?"

Shit. That didn't even cross my mind. I'm an idiot.

"I… I was just trying to help," I say.

"You're a foolish child, Elijah. When will you grow up? I've worked hard to give you every opportunity in your life and you treat it all like it's nothing to you."

"You've worked hard?" My voice echoes in the pristine hotel room. I can't believe the lies he tells himself. "This whole company was *given* to you, Dad. Just because you are your father's son. What have you done to earn this? You've inherited it all and ruled with an iron fist. And your plan is to pass this company and the legacy down to me without giving me a choice? Well news flash, I don't want to follow in your footsteps into this life. I don't want everything to be handed to me on a silver platter. I want to figure stuff out on my own."

"And what have you figured out during this summer of rebellion?" He steps closer toward me. His face stone, no tells, except for the slight squint of his eyes. Disapproval. Disgust.

"I've figured out that I shouldn't have to be told what my entire life will be at only nineteen years old," I say.

His eyes burn with fury, but I'm not afraid. If I don't fight now, I'll be stuck with a future not of my choosing. It feels like the most pivotal moment I've ever faced.

"You are a stain on this family name with your laziness, your deception, your inability to step into your role and your responsibilities, your refusal to obey. You've humiliated yourself and have made every attempt to humiliate me."

"And that's what matters most, right Dad? That you save face so no one knows the truth—that you're just a tyrannical leader of a failing company."

Before I can decipher the movement, my father's hand is raised, ready to strike me. But I don't flinch nor do I cower. Instead, in that brief moment, I lift my chin in defiance. He can hit me all he wants. The pain will be momentary. What I have to say is worth standing up for.

I hear Hee-Jin's scream come from my right just as I brace myself for impact.

"That's enough!"

My mother stands and places herself between us, facing my dad, grabbing his wrist before he strikes. Her voice angry, commanding—unlike I've ever heard it.

"What are you doing?" she asks accusingly. "This is your son. Is this company, are these riches, more important than your own child, your flesh and blood?"

He says nothing. And in that too long moment of silence,

in that flare of his nostrils, he says it all. I close my eyes slowly and drop my head.

"Dangshin, I will deal with my son as I see fit," he says to her.

"He's *our* son, and I will not let you raise a hand to him," she bites back.

For a moment I'm afraid he's going to turn the full force of his wrath from me to my mom. But instead, he pulls himself free from her grip and lowers his hand, looking over her shoulder directly at me. "I don't know what you think is going to happen next for you. You've all but thrown away any chance of getting into Seoul University, and it will cost us an incredible amount of money to rectify that. You've lost the confidence of the executive team at Haneul and there will need to be some major internal PR to change that. Your reckless behavior and foolish escapade this summer will end up costing me a pretty penny. So I'm telling you this now: from this moment forward, you need to get in line, Lee Yoo-Jin. And let me remind you that it would be in your best interest not to cross me."

"Father, I am well aware that you have never once had my best interest in mind."

His nostrils flare again.

"Don't worry, Dad. Despite the fact that the thing I hate most in this world is giving you what you want, I'll do it. I will go back to Korea with you and Mom. I'll enter Seoul University. And I'll fall in line however you see fit in the company."

He narrows his eyes at me and cocks his head to the side, trying to figure out my angle. My mom turns to me and reaches for my arm but I shake it off. I don't mean to hurt her feelings, but she can't talk me out of this. If there's one thing Lee Jung-Hyuk has taught me, it's the art of negotiation.

"But, Father, I have one condition. You will pull every string necessary to get Jessica into the school of her choice, *and* you will pay for her tuition." I stare him down. "And you will not require her to come back and work for Haneul at any point. Sign the check and walk away. Don't ever even think of her again. Only then will I do what you expect of me."

A small smirk crosses my dad's face. "Son, this is truly where you are in over your head. I have no interest in Jessica Lee, and I will gladly never give her another moment's consideration. Don't you worry."

It's then that I realize I've been swimming with the great white shark. I thought I'd given him what he wanted so he could give me what I needed, but I played right into his hands.

When all is said and done, I'm quite certain I will have been the one to lose it all.

chapter twenty-five

jessica

"Forget college scholarships, you need to write your memoir and sell it for seven figures. This entire thing is gold. Get that Netflix money, girl."

I'm packing up my clothes, taking my original outfits from the bottom drawers of my—well, Elijah's family's walk-in closet and putting them into my old suitcase.

When I told Ella the CliffsNotes version of what happened post hackathon, how all the poop hit the fan, she jumped on a plane and came to hold my hand. That's what best friends—with emergency credit cards and rich grandmothers who don't pay attention—do apparently. I'm so grateful. Because I don't know that I could walk away from New York, from Elijah, alone.

Elijah and I haven't spoken since our big fight in Central Park two days ago. I want to reach out to him, but I don't know what I'd say. And I'm still hurt by his words, and even more so, the look in his eyes that I was a completely different person, someone he didn't know at all.

Ella reaches for one of the cardigans folded in a top drawer. "Holy shit, this Givenchy cashmere is so freaking soft." She pulls it out and holds it up against herself as she looks in the full-length mirror. "Are you sure you don't want to take anything home with you? Did they say you couldn't?"

I shrug. "They didn't really tell me much, to be honest. But I don't think it's right. Anyways, these never really were my clothes. I just borrowed them. Just like I was borrowing this identity. So don't get that sweater dirty, okay? I can't imagine what the dry-cleaning bill would be."

"You could call your Aunt Eunice and ask her," Ella suggests with a sly smile.

"I don't think Suds and Steamers has ever handled anything that nice," I say.

"They won't miss one little sweater." Ella's eyes are pleading, her mouth in a pout. "There are a lot of clothes here. Just this one piece, please," she whines.

I laugh. She really is too adorable. But I don't want to get on anyone's bad side...well, anyone *else's* bad side, that is. What I don't need is to be arrested for stealing.

"When will you ever wear a cashmere sweater living in Orange County?" I ask.

"It's not about *needing* it. It's about *wanting* it. So soft," she says, rubbing it against her cheek.

"And therein lies the exact mindset of the filthy rich," I say. The truth stings. Maybe I would have considered it an inconsequential thing before, taking home just one piece from this entirely new wardrobe. But after hearing Elijah call me out on enjoying this all a little too much, well, I don't want to look too closely at whether that is true or not.

"You should take the clothes with you and sell them like the con artist dude on that Netflix documentary," Ella suggests. "Didn't he live off the money for a while?"

"Wait, wasn't it his girlfriend who ended up stealing his clothes and selling them to pay back the money he took from her?"

"Whatever, either way, who's gonna wear this stuff? It's probably just going to charity," Ella says. She really is taking this much harder than I am.

"I don't even know if they're that generous, this family." The words leave a sour taste in my mouth. I shouldn't talk down about the entire family. I know that both Elijah and Hee-Jin are incredibly generous. Like the first dinner I had with Elijah, when he ordered so much food at that old Italian restaurant because he wanted to share with me. And Hee-Jin got us those *Hamilton* tickets. That was the night Elijah kissed me.

The vise grip these memories have on my heart makes it hard to breathe. I know now how decidedly different our lives are. It's clear why Elijah and I could never work. In society's eyes, he's not just out of my league—we're not even playing the same sport.

I swallow back the disappointment and sadness. I can't drown in my feelings about the unfairness of it all. I have to look ahead and figure out what to do next. I wonder if I'll ever get to stop worrying about the future and just enjoy the present.

If there's one thing I won't let myself regret from this summer, it's the fun I had with Elijah in each moment. I don't want to imagine what tomorrow looks like when I'm back home and won't see him at the office or having the chance to explore parts of the city together.

I want to talk to him, to settle things so we can move forward, whatever that looks like. I don't think I'll get the chance though. And if I did, would he even want to see me?

"Hey, you okay?" Ella walks over beside me and wraps an arm around my shoulders.

"Yeah, just thinking of everything I need to do before we leave. My dad is gonna be here in a few hours to take us to The Met and then to the airport. I have to finish packing."

Ella gives me a small squeeze. "Are you gonna try and talk to Elijah before we go?" Hearing Ella say his name out loud makes me miss him even more. I hate not knowing what's happening between him and his dad. I hope he's all right.

"I doubt I'll have time," I say, the words coming out of my mouth like I'm choking.

Ella turns me around so I'm facing her, her hands firmly on my shoulders as she peers into my eyes. I know she's looking to see how fragile I am, so I muster a smile. I may not be okay in this moment, but I will be. I have to be.

She nods wordlessly and carefully folds the overpriced but oh-so-pretty cardigan, putting it back in the drawer where she found it.

"You don't need this stuff anyway. I like you just fine no matter what you wear. Even that ratty three-seasons-old shirt from Urban Outfitters," she teases, tugging at my sleeve.

"Four seasons old, actually," I laugh. "It was on clearance, too."

We continue packing in comfortable silence until Ella asks, "What are you gonna do when you get home?"

"Stick with the original plan: go to junior college, get a job, save up some money, transfer as soon as I'm able." Truth be told, it all sounds a little miserable now. Before the summer, I'd accepted this fate for myself. But it's hard going back after having had this opportunity, knowing what's possible and what I'm capable of.

Ella looks at me and nods. "I love a girl with a plan."

I smile at her. "Hey, let's hurry up so we have time to get a dollar slice before my dad comes."

"Yes! And here's an idea: let's get our hands super greasy, come back here, and touch the white sofa," she says cackling.

"No way, they'll probably make me pay for the cleaning," I say.

The chime of the doorbell rings through the entire house.

Mrs. Choi isn't here and Hee-Jin has been gone all weekend. I want to believe it's because the Sky High Convention is next week and she's at the office working on last-minute details. But I also can't help but feel like she's avoiding me.

When I agreed with my dad that I wouldn't accept any help from Chairman Lee, it just made the most sense for me to leave the internship a couple weeks early. I wasn't sure this was the right move, but Dad assured me that I should head back to California. That way, I could stay out of sight and hopefully, out of mind, to the powers that be. It all sounded ominous. But Dad said he'd take care of everything, including last-minute flights back to Cerritos. That's how I know how serious he is about this. He wants me home, far away from Haneul Corporation.

My one regret is not getting to experience the Sky High Convention. I'll have to imagine the winners of the hackathon being announced and their game title being shared with the thousands of attendees. If it's still happening, at least. I'm sure Elijah and Jason and the other interns will be there to see it.

I was forced to leave all my work in limbo. But from the very beginning, I knew I would be the one to lose everything if this plan imploded. And I did. I've lost the respect of everyone who works at Haneul. I lied my way into a role that wasn't mine. I lied to everyone I got to know this summer.

And that's on me.

I open the door and standing there is Sunny Cho, my assistant.

"Hi, Jessica." Her smile is polite but not warm. Uncomfortable. "I brought your personal items from the office. You didn't have much, just some favorite pens and a few other things."

"Thank you," I say as I grab the small, almost-empty bag of my personal effects. I always thought to bring more stuff, a picture of my family or one of my dog. But I knew any sign of my life could be looked into and my real identity discovered. So I never did. "I appreciate you coming by."

I expect her to leave, but she remains in the doorway, looking awkward.

"Do you want to come in for a drink or a snack or something?" I ask.

Her face twists to an even more uncomfortable expression. Shoot, this isn't my house, and what's in that kitchen isn't mine to offer.

"I actually need to get going. But is your father here?"

"My father? No, he'll be here a little later to pick me up and take me to the airport," I explain.

"Oh, okay, so he will be here later? That's good then. I, uh, have these letters here from Human Resources. One is for you and the other is for your father."

My skin goes cold and my heart stops. I know what a letter from Human Resources means, especially one personally delivered. *Thank you for your service. Your job with us has been terminated* is my guess.

I take the letters from Sunny and bow for some reason.

She awkwardly bows back and stiffly turns to walk away.

"Hey Sunny," I call out. She looks at me over her shoulder, paused halfway down the stoop. "Thank you for everything this summer. I'm sorry I lied to you. I hope I didn't put you in a difficult position—which is silly because of course I probably did, for you, for everyone."

"Honestly, Jessica? It was a pleasure working for you. I know you're gonna make it big somewhere, someday. I'm rooting for you." And with that, she smiles and goes on her way.

I close the door.

"Who was it?" Ella asks.

"It was my assistant—my former assistant," I correct myself.

"I can't believe you had an assistant," Ella says.

"Yeah, me neither. I mean, it's not like I was supposed to have one."

"She probably had a better summer working for you than

she would've for Elijah or anyone else. And I see you worrying, but she won't be in trouble. She didn't know the truth."

I want to believe Ella's words. I hope that's the case.

"What's that?" she asks, pointing to the envelopes with the Haneul Corporation logo on the front.

"Letters from Human Resources," I say. "One for me, one for my dad."

Ella's eyes grow huge. She's definitely thinking what I'm thinking.

"Well, open it. Might as well get it over with," she says.

I tear open the seal. I've never been fired from a job before, and this is going to severely stain my perfect record. Well, this and the fact that I deceived an entire company this summer.

But before I can read the contents, the loud chime of the doorbell rings again.

"Did you forget something?" I ask as I open the door, expecting to see Sunny.

"I don't think so," my dad says as he walks past me and into the brownstone. He whistles aloud as he takes in the foyer. "I don't know what I expected his homes to look like, but this is ten times more lavish and impressive."

I can tell he's trying to calculate costs in his head. I'll tell him what I've learned from my Zillow search later.

"Are you all packed up ready to go take in the majesty that is the Metropolitan Museum of Art?"

For being as practical and cheap as my dad is, he loves a good museum. Especially one as huge and stocked as The Met.

"Jessica has a letter from Human Resources," Ella confesses. That rat.

"What?" My dad turns to me in surprise. "What does it say?"

"There's one for you too," I say, handing over the envelope with his name on it. "I haven't read mine yet."

I look at Ella with her round curious eyes. I look at my dad with his squinted concerned ones. And then I look down at the letter.

Dear Miss Jessica Lee,

We are happy to inform you that you have received a full scholarship from Haneul Corporation for your education at the higher learning institution of your choice.

   Please contact me at the Human Resources department for all the details.

Sincerely,

John Im

Human Resources Manager

I read the words one more time, my eyes quickly rescanning the page to make sure I'm understanding correctly.

I raise my head slowly. "A full scholarship," I whisper. "Not just connections or a letter of recommendation. A full scholarship. To the university of my choosing."

"An offer you can't refuse," Ella says.

I turn at my father, waiting for him to shake his head and say not to accept anything offered to me from Haneul Corp.

But he's looking down, eyes skimming the other letter, the one addressed to him.

If they're offering me a full scholarship, then maybe they're offering my dad a raise, or a promotion, or some kind of award for the successful internship program this year. My heart leaps with hope.

"Dad? What does your letter say?" I can hardly contain my excitement. I feel like jumping up and down with him in celebration.

His eyes finally meet mine.

"It says my employment with Haneul Corporation has been terminated." There is no emotion in his voice. None reflected on his face. He either expected it or is in complete shock. Either way, *I'm* in complete shock. How could they do this to him? I'm speechless, frozen on the spot.

"Shit, what the fuck, that sucks," Ella says, clearly not speechless.

"Wait, that's not fair. They can't do that. It's a mistake. Dad, you didn't do anything wrong."

My brain goes into overdrive over what to do next. I can only think of one thing, one person to call. I grab my phone from my pocket and dial Elijah. He has to do something about this. He has to talk to his dad. He has to help us figure out a way to fix it.

A voice I only recognize from commercials and movies comes on the line.

The number you have reached is no longer in service.

chapter twenty-six

elijah

A crisp morning in September...

"Mom, I'm fine. You can stay in the car."

"I'm not falling for that again," she says, referring to that day months ago when she dropped me off at the airport before my first flight to New York. It feels like a lifetime ago. If I had known then that for two months, I'd be living a different identity all while falling for someone unlike anyone I've ever known, only to lose everything in the end, I don't know that I would have gotten on that plane.

Who am I kidding? I would do it all over again, just to recapture those moments I had with Jessica. I haven't seen or talked to her since our argument a month ago in Central Park. The sting in my heart still catches me off guard sometimes when I think about her. My whole life changed this summer in New York and she had so much to do with that. It's changed even more since I've been back in Korea. I hope one day I'll be able to tell her all about it.

I hold the door open as my mom slides out of the back seat, followed by my sister. "I'll call you when we're ready," Mom says to the driver, who takes the car to be parked in Incheon Airport's garage.

"You sure you have everything you need?" Hee-Jin asks. She looks down at my luggage quizzically, as if wondering how I can fit my entire life into just two suitcases.

"I'm moving to Los Angeles. It's warm there. I don't need much," I say.

"If there's something you've forgotten, just let your uncle know and he'll take care of it," my mom says. "My brother is thrilled you'll be close by. He seems to think it'll give me more reasons to come visit him and your grandfather. And you know what? He's right." She smiles at me and runs her hand through my hair. "You should have gotten a trim before you left."

"I think I'm gonna grow it out. See how that feels," I say.

She presses her lips together and nods. The last two months since we've come back to Korea have thrown our lives as we've known them upside down. It's all taken some getting used to for my mom, especially letting me make my own choices for my future. When I told her I wanted to move to the States, she struggled with it. She isn't trying to control my choices or anything, but she worries about me.

I haven't talked to my father since I returned to Korea, since the disastrous ending to my summer in New York. After that fraught conversation at The Plaza, we left immediately. I didn't even get to say goodbye to any of my friends.

I never got to see Jessica again.

But my dad made a promise, and Hee-Jin made sure it was followed through with by Human Resources without his meddling. Jessica got a full scholarship to whatever school she wants to go to. I can be okay knowing that the entire summer wasn't a waste for her. At least she got the happy ending. It took me an additional month to fight for mine. But here I am.

I wish there could have been a happy ending that included the two of us together.

"I think you'd look good with longer hair," Hee-Jin says. She looks younger, more relaxed with no makeup on and her hair in a neat braid.

"Good luck with everything. Hopefully by the time I graduate, you can hire me to be an engineer for your new company or something," I say. I can see the worry bloom across her face at my words. Breaking away from the massive tech corporation that has been our family's legacy for generations is no small feat. But there's no denying the fire in her eyes when she talks about her new start-up venture.

"I'd love to have you on staff one day, when you're ready. I have no clue where we'll be in a few years, but I'm confident and hopeful. Even though I had to sign a non-compete when I left Haneul, limiting what kinds of games we can produce, I think there's a lot of opportunity for specialization and disruption." She pauses, laughing to herself. "I'll spare you the TED talk, though."

"I don't mind at all," I say, and I mean it. "You deserve

this, and if anyone can make this happen, it's you. You inspire me, Noona."

Hee-Jin's eyes fill with tears. "You're the brave one, Elijah. I'm so proud of you." Her voice breaks and she grabs me for a hug before stepping aside.

My mom holds my face in her hands before wrapping her arms around me tight. "Call me when you land," she whispers into my ear. "And Elijah? Be happy. Every single day, make choices to make yourself happy."

And this time, those words don't scare me at all.

"Elijah, over here!"

My eyes track the voice among all the other noises in the busy pickup zones at LAX. It's a full-circle moment, I realize. LAX bookending the summer that started off like a dream but then turned into a nightmare in New York. And now I'm back in the States.

But I couldn't bring myself to return to the East Coast. New York has lost its charm for me.

I finally spot my tall, ridiculously handsome friend standing, waiting by his Toyota Camry. To think I tried pretty much all summer to hate him and it never happened. Instead, Jason's managed to become one of the closest friends I've ever had.

"What's up, man?" I say once I reach the car, grabbing his hand and pulling him in for a hug. "Thanks for picking me up."

"No problem. Get in. Let's get some food before going home."

Home.

When I was able to secure a spot for the fall quarter at

UCLA—definitely using family connections and money with such short notice, but I swear to myself this will be the last time—the first person I contacted was Jason.

The first person I wanted to call was Jessica. But with the way everything ended between us, there's no way she'll want to see me. Maybe one day in the future, now that I'm closer to where she lives, we can meet up and clear the air. Hell, it's possible I'll even tell her how she makes me feel. How she's one of the reasons I had the guts to stand up to my dad and take control of my life. How she inspires and motivates me. How I think about her all the time and wish there had been a way for us to be together.

In any case, Jason let me know that his apartment was short one roommate, so it was a no-brainer. We've already lived together in the closest quarters, and we wouldn't even have to share a bunk bed this time. I get my own room and everything—and it's not far from campus either. A dream.

"How was your flight? Are you too exhausted if I take us to a really good banh mi place that's a little out of the way?"

"Banh mi?"

"Vietnamese sandwiches. To die for. Really."

"Sounds good. I'm down for anything," I say.

Thankfully the freeway traffic isn't as bad as some of the horror stories I've heard about California. My eyes get a little heavy and I close them for just a minute.

Someone nudges my arm and I wake up, startled, uncertain where I am, the sun beating on my face through the window. Thank goodness I remembered to reapply sunscreen.

Will I still be able to afford my Korean sunscreen on my new budget?

"Wake up, sleepyhead, we're here," Jason says.

I shake the fogginess from my head and take in our surroundings. We're parked in a nondescript shopping center. There are some small restaurants and eateries and stores, but for the most part, it's not busy. I see the "Best Banh Mi" café at the other side of the lot.

"Dude, why did you park so far away?" I ask.

"What, are my chauffeuring skills not up to your standards, Mr. Lee?" After I came clean to Jason about who my family is, he hasn't stopped giving me shit for it. But it feels good not having to keep anything from him anymore. "Don't want anyone dinging my doors," he says by way of explanation.

We get out of the car and I notice there are plenty of dings in his doors. There are also very few cars in this lot. But I shrug because stretching my legs for a few more steps sounds like heaven after a twelve-hour flight—in coach.

We walk past a small hardware store, a 99 Ranch Market, a boba tea café. Things are not as flashy as they are in Seoul or New York. But I like it.

I look into the window of a cute ice cream shop. The name on the door says, "Scoops de Loop."

Wait a second.

Scoops de Loop. Where have I heard that before? Is there a location in Korea, in Gangnam or Hongdae?

"Hey, let's grab some ice cream before we get the sandwiches," Jason suggests. He doesn't wait for me to answer and opens the door, holding it for me. I stare at him in confusion, and he pushes me into the small ice cream shop.

"Welcome to Scoops de-Loop, where we scoop to your heart's content…"

The voice immediately registers and my heartbeat picks up before I even see her. She's standing behind the counter in a striped apron, a paper hat that looks like an origami project gone wrong, and a large name tag. And her eyes are wide with shock, staring right at me.

Jessica.

My mouth is completely dry and I try to swallow, but apparently my heart has decided to lodge itself in my throat. I take in every bit of her. There are no designer clothes for her to hide behind. Just the fierce, loyal, smart, driven, beautiful girl of every one of my dreams since summer.

I feel another shove from behind me and I stumble a step closer, never taking my eyes off of her.

"What are you doing here?" Jessica asks.

"I, I…"

"Elijah has moved to Los Angeles and we were craving banh mi sandwiches but wanted ice cream as an appetizer," Jason says, coming to my rescue.

I whirl around to him. "You knew she worked here. You planned this," I say to him.

"Dude, talk to *her* not me," Jason says, grabbing my shoulders and spinning me back to face Jessica.

Thing is, I don't know what to say. I've run it through my mind a million times, what I'd tell her if I ever saw her again. But nothing felt right.

I'm sorry.

I miss you.

I love you.

"I'm sorry I loved missing you," I say.

She furrows her eyebrows, confused. "What?"

"I mean, shit, what I wanted to say is I'm sorry. And that I've missed you. And I love—"

"You guys gonna order?" the customer behind us asks, clearly irritated. "If not, can I get a double scoop of pistachio and strawberry in a waffle cone for me and a salted caramel single in a cup for my daughter?" He steps up to the counter and Jessica shakes herself out of shock.

"Yes, of course," she says as she begins to scoop their order.

"You love her?" Jason asks me, definitely not with his inside voice.

I give him a *shut-up-you-asshole* look and try my hardest not to flee the building.

The customer finally leaves with his ice creams in hand and I'm back to having a full-blown heart attack as I face the girl I can't stop thinking about.

"What are you doing here?" she says. She quickly looks to Jason before he can butt in. "I don't want your answer, I want his."

Jason holds his hands up in surrender. "Okay, okay. I'll wait outside," he says. He sends an exaggerated wink at me as he leaves.

"Elijah, answer the question. What are you doing here?"

"I'm, uh, starting at UCLA in a couple weeks. Engineering, if you can believe it. I think I may want to program games myself one day." It feels good to say. For once in my life, I'm excited about something pertaining to my future plans.

She nods slowly, not taking her eyes off of me.

"How about you? Did you decide which school to go to? You know, um, with the scholarship?"

Her eyebrows shoot up. "Oh, so you do know about that, huh?"

"Yeah, well, it was kinda part of the deal with my dad. I said I'd go back to Korea with him if he gave you the scholarship and then left you alone. I was worried he'd try to screw you over, but Hee-Jin said the scholarship was approved without a hitch."

"Without a hitch," she says. There's no emotion in her voice. I feel like I'm missing something.

"So...did you decide where to go?"

"I'm taking classes at the local junior college. And I'm working part-time at an interior design firm as well as here at the ice cream shop."

"You work two jobs and go to school?" I ask.

Her nostrils flare and if looks could kill, I'd be dead on the ground. "Well, that scholarship may have been approved without a hitch, but it definitely didn't come without a cost."

"What? I don't know what you're talking about. I went back to Korea so that my dad would leave you alone. That was our deal. I mean, we eventually had a huge blow-out and my mom moved me and my sister into an apartment on the other side of town. I don't speak to my dad anymore. But my mom has been amazing and really has supported me."

Jessica lets out what sounds like a sigh of relief. When she speaks again, her tone is warmer, kind. "I'm so glad, Elijah. I was really worried, but I'm happy it all worked out. I mean, I'm sorry about your relationship with your dad, but I'm glad you're finally able to do what you want with your life."

She puts on a smile, but there's a sadness in her eyes.

"Jessica, what aren't you telling me?"

She straightens her back and lifts her chin. "The day I got the letter about the scholarship, my dad was fired from Haneul Corp."

"What?"

"Yeah. They said he had been told many times not to overfund the internship program, but he kept finding ways to support it. And that was grounds enough for termination."

I can't believe I didn't see this coming. Why did I think I could go up against my father and win? Why did Jessica's dad have to pay the price?

"But Elijah? It turned out for the best. He has a job at a smaller company now and he really likes it. We had to sell our house and move into a condo, but it's close to his work and to my school. Everything is...different. But it's good. And I'm learning a lot at this interior design company. I haven't declared a major yet, but I think this is what I want to do. Put all those hours watching HGTV to good use. And the owner of the design firm already said she'd gladly provide a recommendation letter if I need one down the road."

"That's amazing, Jessica. I love this for you." *I love you.* I want to say it, but I know I have no right to after what my family did to hers. And I disappeared, fled to the other side of the world while she was left to pick up the pieces.

"Thanks, Elijah. I'm really happy for you too," she says. "I didn't realize what you went through to secure that scholarship for me. But I didn't end up accepting any of the money. It didn't seem right."

I nod, thinking about how much trouble and heartache money has caused us.

"I've missed you," Jessica says.

I let out a deep breath because the words feel like a healing balm I didn't know I needed.

"God, I've missed you so fucking much, Jessica."

She smiles and shakes her head. "Some things never change."

"Shit, sorry. I mean, shoot." I laugh. It feels so good to be teased by her again.

The bells on the door jingle and Jason peeks his head in.

"Jessica, what time do you get off? Come meet us for banh mis next door when you're done. I'm calling Ella to come down too," Jason says.

I turn to look at her and she meets my gaze. I look at her with all the love and hope I can.

Everything seemed to be against us this past summer, and for a time, I thought I'd never get to reconnect with Jessica again. I don't want to even consider that now. We're here. And maybe it's fate, or a thread that binds us through a common name, or just goddamn luck. But I'm not fucking this up. I'm not letting anything get between us now.

I let out a breath, raise my eyebrow, and ask her a question not just about tonight's dinner, but about every moment from now onward. "Whattaya say, Jessica? You in?"

A slow smile spreads across her face as if she knows exactly what I'm asking. "Heck yeah, Elijah. I'm in."

epilogue

---

jessica

One Year Later

"Okay, what time are your mom and sister flying in?" I ask.

Elijah jumps in front of me to catch an errant Frisbee that was flying directly toward my face. I swear, this campus gets more and more rowdy before a holiday. Everyone feels so free to be reckless.

Reckless. Maybe that's what made me think it was a good idea to get all our families together for Thanksgiving. My parents, Elijah's mother and sister, Ella and her grandmother, and Jason and his sister (his parents are on a cruise to Alaska).

And the kids are doing the cooking.

I'm regretting my choices for the tenth time in the last ten minutes as I stress over the grocery list.

Elijah sends the Frisbee back toward its rightful owner.

"Thanks," I say.

He throws an arm around my shoulder and pulls me close as we walk through the quad. He's mastered being able to place a kiss on my head without missing a step.

I transferred to UCLA my sophomore year. And Eljiah is here thriving in the Engineering program. The classes are tough, but he's the hardest-working person I know. My design classes are challenging too, but they feel like an investment in my future career, and that's totally worth it.

"They get in around 11:00 a.m. tomorrow. My mom and I are gonna make mandu for the appetizers. And Hee-Jin wanted to do sweet potatoes Korean style."

"Awesome. That leaves the salad and mashed potatoes for Ella and the desserts for Jason. Turkey, stuffing, and kimchi are on me."

"Is it too much? I can help with whatever you need. I *am* great at logistics." He looks down at me and winks.

I pull us to a stop, guiding his hands around my waist, rocking on to my tippy toes, inviting a kiss.

He bends down a little and meets my lips. We're both smiling as we start the kiss. But when he pulls my body to his and our hips meet, I feel how much he's enjoying this and it immediately makes me hungry for more. I open up my mouth and invite his tongue in to taste, to explore.

For all the ways that Elijah can be tender with me physically, when he's turned on, his kisses turn ravenous.

I'm obsessed with them.

I push myself a little closer till there's no space left between us. He groans. "Jessica," he warns, "we're in public. In the middle of the quad. In broad daylight."

He's right. "Okay, fine," I say, adding an extra pout to my voice so he knows I'd rather *not* stop, but I will. "But you started it."

His mouth pulls at the corner into a wicked smile.

I fight to stay steady on my feet.

I pull back, putting a safe distance between us but wrap my hand into his as we continue to walk down the path. It's early and I'm starving. We're heading to our favorite deli shop, famous for their loaded pastrami sandwiches, just off campus in Westwood Village, trying to beat the lunch crowd. This place reminds us both of the little coffee shop where we first met up in New York. Where we made the choice to intertwine our lives together in a harebrained scheme called The Name Drop.

"Whose turn is it to pay?" I ask.

"Yours," he says. "So I may add an extra pickle and a second bag of chips and a large Coke to my order." He squeezes my hand and picks up his pace, pulling ahead of me by a couple steps, dragging me behind.

It gives me just the perfect view of his cute butt in his worn jeans. He bought this pair from the Gap during our summer in New York. In fact, I think his threadbare T-shirt was also from that time. So much has changed. Gone are his designer clothes and internal calculator of worthiness. Gone also is the massive chip on my shoulder and my need to prove myself in every situation.

"Come on slowpoke, I'm hungry," he says, looking over his shoulder. "Wait, are you checking out my ass right now? Is that why you're walking so slow?"

I laugh. "Busted."

"Pick it up. You know if we get there past twelve, it'll be packed," he says.

We love this place. We go there all the time. They know us. They like us. They'll save a table for us.

"Well, then we'll just have to do what we always do," I say. "Pull the name drop."

He stops and peers down into my eyes, blocking the sun so I don't have to squint as I look back up at him.

We both smile and say at the same time... "Lee Yoo-Jin, party of two."

★ ★ ★ ★ ★

acknowledgments

I am so grateful for the opportunity to write books. It isn't easy. This doesn't come naturally to me. It's hard work and a huge mental battle. I'm not studied in craft. I'm not well-read in the classics. I'm not the most determined, nor the hardest worker. I'm a bit of a loner.

But I'm stubborn as hell.

Storytelling, writing, the business of publishing…it has required me to try, to fight, to push. Push past those things that are my limitations, go outside my comfort zone, to hurt a little and to heal a little. And I refuse to fail.

So, I'm practicing craft. I'm reading all kinds of books to be immersed in stories. I'm trying to overcome my own laziness and my penchant for procrastination, my doubts, and my internal battles with imposter syndrome. And I'm leaning into those who are here to help me and those who have so kindly stood by my side through this journey.

Because I want to keep telling stories. I will stubbornly keep writing books.

Thank you to EVERYONE who read and supported my first book, *Seoulmates*. Your time, your reviews, your posts, your word of mouth are how I was able to go through this process all over again with my new novel, *The Name Drop*.

To Bess Braswell, I'm incredibly grateful for your continuous support and belief in me. Publishing with Inkyard truly has been the best experience.

To my editor, Claire Stetzer, for most of the life of this book, it was just you and me with these words. Thank you for your patience, your keen eye, your belief in the story, for "getting" me, for making this a book to be proud of.

To my agent, Taylor Haggerty... I'm told there's no such thing as a "dream agent," but I'll have to disagree with that statement. We should all have chances in our lives to know we are in the BEST hands. You are those best hands for me. Thank you so much. I know it's awkward that I'm so obsessed with you. *shrug* :)

To my team at Inkyard/Harlequin/Harper: Brittany Mitchell, Justine Sha, Laura Gianino, Gigi Lau, Alexandra Niit... and everyone who has been instrumental in making my books REAL and getting them into the hands of readers... I am eternally grateful.

Michelle Kwon, illustrator extraordinaire, you're my kindred spirit. Thank you for taking my random ideas and putting form to them, creating such beautiful bases for these book covers.

I am INCREDIBLY lucky to have a community of writer friends who SHOW UP and have proved time and again that they've got my back.

Lauren Billings and Christina Hobbs...not just my writing life, but life as a whole, has more joy with you both in it. My besties, my sisters, my ride-or-dies. You are the cause of my euphoria. LOVE YOU!

To the Kimchingoos—my friends, my family...thank you for always being there with encouragement and understanding...and laughs, so many laughs. Love you, Jessica Kim, Graci Kim, Grace Shim, and Sarah Suk.

Thank you to my dear, dear pals who came out to celebrate my debut with me. I sometimes get lost in my head and go to that bad place where I wonder, "Does anyone like me?" But you all came and wrapped your arms around me and never let me feel alone. Elise Bryant, Annette Christie, Alexis Daria, Auriane Desombre, Kristin Dwyer, Adalyn Grace, Adriana Herrera, Kaitlyn Hill (and Stephen), Marisa Kanter, Naz Kutub, Brian D. Kennedy, Stephan Lee, Axie Oh, Erin Bay, Lauren Hennessy, Priscilla Oliveras, Louisa Onome, Suzanne Park, Benson Shum, Sasha Peyton Smith (and Charles), Sarah Younger, Rachel Lynn Solomon (and Ivan), Gloria Chao, Mazey Eddings, Kat Cho, Rebecca Kuss, Courtney Kae, Carlyn Greenwald, Julie Tieu, Marisa Urgo, Rochelle Hassan, Erik J. Brown, Serena Kaylor, Jenna Voris...thank you for your friendships, for belly-busting laughs, for meals and drinks together, for partying with and supporting me.

My best advice to all writers—form those group chats and cherish them for the long haul! To my group chat besties: The Slackers, The Coven, The Naggy Shrews, Wonwoo's Crop Top, BTSVTXT... I am eternally grateful. Friendships, safe spaces... I love you all.

To Cari...thanks for everything, always. For the best talks

about Korea, about food, about traveling, about books. I'm so happy you're in my life!

To Jason, Adrian, and Ben...grateful you've always been there for me.

To my family... Umma, Sunny, Wayne, Caleb, Chrissy, Bear, Buttercup, Karou...plus Ann, Julianna, Vicky, Greg, Miles, Peter, Rachel, Katherine, Alex, Bill, Mike, Allison, and Genie especially...thanks for the support and love.

I'll never not thank BTS for what they've unlocked in my life and in my creative process. I wasn't sure I'd reach the finish line with this book. But the song "Run BTS" became my battle cry. Kim Namjoon told me I was beautiful and encouraged me to run. The dedication for this book is to him and from him to you all. Borahae.

Thank you to Seventeen for some of the best memories during the "Be the Sun" tour. I was overwhelmed by life and the process and you taught me how to find the FUN in it all. You helped me to fight for my joy and I'm truly changed because of it. Diamond life forever.

To the readers—I'll be honest... I started writing for ME...a challenge to myself to prove that I could. But I've come to realize, it's all for YOU. The writing, the editing, the marketing, the signings and conversations. You, dear readers, are who make it worth it. Who give it purpose and bring the feelings of accomplishment and value. THANK YOU for letting me tell these stories and share them with you.

I'm CERTAIN I have forgotten people that matter. And for that, I'm so sorry. But just know that I'm well aware I could not have done this alone, without you. And I definitely would not have had as much fun. LOVE TO YOU ALL.